Dream Parlor

Dream Parlor

by

Christopher Andrews

Dream Parlor

ISBN number: Softcover 0-9713553-0-4

This book was printed in the United States of America.

A Fine Line Publishing Co. book
http://www.Fine-LinePC.com
for extra copies please contact by email
books@fine-linepc.com
or send by regular mail to
Fine Line Publishing Co.
Copies Dept.
P.O. Box 502
Vinton, Va 24179

CONTENTS

Thanks to Jonathan Lawrence and our whole team from the "Dream Parlor" feature-film, and – as always – to my parents. But most of all, this one's for Yvonne.

>>IN THE 21st CENTURY, THE UNITED STATES OF AMERICA AND UNIFIED EUROPE, IN AN UNPRECEDENTED MOVE TO ESTABLISH A GLOBAL *UNIFIED NATIONS,* UNVEILED THEIR PLAN TO RECALL ALL U.S. AND EURO CURRENCY OVER A TWO-YEAR PERIOD. CONCURRENTLY, ALL CITIZENS WERE TO RECEIVE COMPUTER IDENTIFICATION CHIPS, CALLED *IDCs.* THE CHIPS, DEVELOPED USING A REVOLUTIONARY NEW CYBERNETIC INTERFACE GELATIN, WERE TO BE SAFELY AND PAINLESSLY IMPLANTED IN THE BACK OF EACH CITIZEN'S RIGHT HAND. THEY CONTAINED ALL PERTINENT INFORMATION, SUCH AS FULL IDENTIFICATION, MEDICAL HISTORY, AND FINANCIAL STATUS, TO MAKE EVERYDAY CHORES—BANKING, HEALTH CARE, SHOPPING—MORE CONVENIENT. DUE TO THEIR *SMART FUNCTION,* THE IDCs COULD BE TRACED VIA CELLULAR SATELLITE LINKS, MAKING ILLEGAL ACTIVITIES, SUCH AS DRUG TRAFFICKING, VIRTUALLY IMPOSSIBLE. THE U.S. AND UNIFIED EUROPE

PROUDLY PREDICTED THAT IF EVERYTHING PROCEEDED ACCORDING TO PLAN, THE IDCs WOULD LEAD TO A ONE-WORLD ECONOMY WITHIN FIVE YEARS. GLOBAL PEACE AND A NEW WORLD ORDER WERE JUST AROUND THE CORNER . . .

The steel birds of prey circled above. Young Elijah Barrett looked up at the hovering Police Organizer craft, but he could barely make it out from his short viewpoint amidst the rolling waves of the human sea around him.

His father's voice somehow drifted down to him over the chaos. Led by his anxious mother—and she *was* anxious, whether she wanted him to know it or not—Eli pushed forward toward his father. Mencer Barrett, slender, tall, *proud,* called out to the gathering before him from the back of an old flatbed truck, acknowledging the line of Police Organizers around him only when it served to further his points. *The Constitution guarantees us the Right to public assembly,* his father cried, *so why did I need a permit to be here tonight? Why are there men with* guns *all around us?!* Eli didn't understand everything that his father was yelling about, but he knew that it was very *important.*

Eli watched as a government man in a business suit climbed up onto the back of the truck beside his father. The man shook his finger in Mencer's face, shaming or warning him it seemed, but his father simply did what he did so well—he turned the situation to his *advantage.* He seized the man's accusing hand and twisted it, exposing to the crowd the new IDC chip that everyone had been talking about at school—before Eli was removed from the public system in favor of *home education . . .*

("What do ya mean, your dad's not gonna let you get one? Everyone's *gonna get one, you dork!"*

"Nuh-uh! My dad says it's a trick, and the government is tryin—"

"I heard about your *dad, Eli. My uncle says he's a trouble-maker."*

"My mom said he's a freak!*"*

"That's not true! My dad's a great man!*"*

"Oh, really? Then how come he's not gonna let you get an IDC? Haven't you heard about all the great stuff you can do when you scan your chip?")

. . . Mencer indicated the clear-and-black chip on the suited man's hand. *Is* this *what you want?!* he demanded. *Is this what you want for yourselves, for your* children?!

No! The bluster of the crowd grew more indignant, more *hostile.* Eli looked around nervously, his heart quickening in his chest and butterflies fluttering in his stomach. He wished his mother would pull him free of this!

The IDC isn't about your convenience! his father insisted. *It's about* power . . .

The government man pulled his arm free and shoved Mencer aside. A surge pulsed through the crowd, and for a frightful moment Eli lost sight of his father.

Now listen to me, the suited man ordered.

Then everything *really* went crazy. As the suited man leaned forward, trying to stare his authority into the masses, a spectator burst forth from the rest of the crowd. Before the Police Organizers could react, he leaped onto the side of the truck, wielding a knife which he thrust at the startled government man. Eli and his mother broke into the front of the crowd just in time to see the Organizers grab the man with the knife and hurl him to the pavement.

Eli gaped in shock and confusion. His mother was yelling, his father was yelling, *everyone* was yelling as the Organizers beat the man with their clubs. The man wasn't even holding the knife anymore—he was just trying to protect himself.

Mencer jumped over the side of the truck. He tried to reach the beaten man, but one of the Organizers turned on *him* and pushed him back into the side of the truck. Eli's mother tried to go to him, but then more men in suits grabbed *her*.

Eli panicked. He swung at the men holding his mother, hitting them with all the strength his eight-year-old body could muster, but they wouldn't let go.

His father finally shoved his way past the Organizer, but the policeman spun around, lashing out with his club. He caught Mencer across the side of his left knee, bringing the larger-than-life man to the ground.

Before the horrible sight could even sink in, Eli was lifted right off his feet and carried forward as the protestors reacted to the assault, converging on the Organizers and suited men. The heat of human bodies and human *rage* threatened to smother Eli. Legs, knees, feet, and flailing arms pounded him from every angle, and for the first time in his few years, Eli experienced *fearing for his life*.

Finally, the swell of protestors ebbed just enough to allow Eli his path. Mencer knelt before him, clutching at his broken joint and drawing breath through clenched teeth. Eli had never before seen his father so vulnerable, so *mortal.*

Sensing his son's presence, Mencer lifted his head. Eli reached out with a numb, caring hand and touched his father's face, feeling the heat and sweat so foreign to his gentle visage. In spite of the turmoil around them, Mencer met Eli's gaze and actually smiled at his little boy.

Around Mencer's neck, a small, wooden cross had dangled into view. Eli reached out and touched the reassuring symbol.

It was over now. This would all stop soon and everything would be all right. They would go home and—

A Police Organizer parted the crowd like a shark. His arm was

Around Mencer's (Richard Hench) neck, a small, wooden cross had dangled into view. Eli (Andrew Martin) reached out and touched the reassuring symbol.

a blur of violence as his club cracked against the back of Mencer's skull. His father's head jerked unnaturally to the side, snapping the cord from around his neck, and Elijah Barrett found himself standing alone, the wooden cross dangling from his clenched fist.

Like the passing of a torch . . .

Murdering Elijah Barrett's father, and letting Eli live to remember it, was the biggest mistake the System ever made—as if Goliath had given *the stone to David. Deep inside, everyone knew we could not win that day, but few realized just what it was we stood to lose. It was more than a simple endeavor for power—it was a quest to control our minds . . .*

. . . and deplete our souls *. . .*

CRUCIFY!

The glaring spotlights swept over the studio audience as they jumped and cheered for the hovering digital cameras. The electric eyes sailed through the sound stage, finally coming to rest on the beefy, chrome-plated letter -X- riveted to a concrete overhead girder. A side curtain parted, and the cheesy Host stepped out to bask in his typically warm reception. He parted his arms over his head as if in mass embrace of his beloved fans, then turned his toothy grimace to the cameras.

"Welcome back to the Execution Channel!" the Host called into his old-style microphone, and the audience erupted into another round of cheers and applause. The Host milked the response within a centimeter of its death before continuing, "Our first example on 'Death Row Tonight' is Citizen One-One-Eight-One-One, surnamed Elijah Barrett, *son of the sociopathic* Mencer Barrett. *Eli's convictions include* tampering *with government records,* embezzling *food rations for Non-Citizens, and* propagating *spiritual awareness. Before the break, we asked* you*—our voyeur participants, as well as the Citizens here in the studio—how One-One-Eight-One-One should be deleted from the system . . . and* The Verdict Says?!"

Citizen 11811, surnamed Elijah Barrett
(Christopher Andrews).

The cameras whip-panned around to focus on the studio audience as they shouted out in mob-like passion, "Crucify! Crucify! Crucify!*"*

The cheesy Host mugged for the cameras once more as he called back, "Yoouu asked for it! . . . Yoouu got it*!"*

He parted his arms in the air again as he stepped aside. The backdrop beneath the chrome -X- *broke away, revealing an old, rugged cross, gaily trimmed with blinking Broadway-style lights. Two muscle-bound men, stripped to the waist and oiled to highlight every ripple of their physiques, lowered the massive cross flat onto the stage floor.*

From the wings, the bruised, bloody, and badly beaten twenty-eight-year-old Eli Barrett staggered out, led by three vixens clad in slutesque executioner leathers, their bodies of such sexually-provocative proportions, they flagrantly slapped Mother Nature in the face. The audience went berserk.

The muscle men seized the helpless Eli, throwing him backwards onto the cross. Before he could react—and it was very uncertain whether or not he even had the strength to do so—two of the vixens held him down while the third handed huge spikes to the men, who positioned each of the stinging points firmly against Eli's palms.

The audience cacophony reached a fevered pitch as the muscle men raised mallets high into the air and brought them down with full force—then the heavy, deafened sound of metal on metal silenced even the studio mob. Every vein in Eli's body swelled as the steel shanks pierced his hands, embedding deeper into the wood of the cross with each blow. The audience was morbid and still.

When Eli was finally secured to the dense timber at his hands and feet, the unaffected vixens posed and gestured as the muscle men ceremoniously raised the cross into the air, finally dropping its base hard into a hole in the center of the stage floor. Eli's shoulders were wrenched from their sockets as the cross locked into an upright stance . . .

* * *

Eli's blue—and bloodshot—eyes popped open. His own staccato breathing rasped loudly in his ears, topped only by the throbbing of his pulse. A moment later, his panic declined just enough for him to grasp the concept that his crucifixion had been a nightmare.

But it could *have been real,* a little voice reminded him.

Throwing the thin sheet aside, Confirmed Citizen 11811, Elijah Barrett, bolted from his cot to the undersized mirror over his utility sink. Trembling, he twisted the controls until a stream of water finally sputtered and spit from the faucet, then bent and splashed it onto his face. Rational thoughts were steadily working their way to the forefront of his mind, but he still could not resist the urge to examine himself for any signs of injury. He inspected his slender body, then checked his hands—and he wasn't really surprised when he found them unmarked . . .

Well . . . almost *unmarked . . .*

Turning his right hand over, Eli regarded his IDC. It was about 2 x 4 centimeters, with its interface housing dark to signify his status as a Citizen.

Just like the Suits that night . . . just like the Organizers.

His mother had no choice, of course. Openings for Citizenship were disappearing at a frightful rate, and what good would it do to honor her husband's memory if it landed herself and their son on the streets as Non-Citizens?

As an adult, Eli could appreciate her predicament—and tried not to imagine what personal sacrifices she might have subjected herself to in order to insure they passed her Vocational Screening and his Aptitude Test. As a child, however, he saw the world in fewer shades of gray, and he'd been bitter towards her for making him "betray" his father and take the chip. He felt especially *guilty* for that bitterness after his mother . . .

Well, at least *Nora* had been there for him.

Eli at last settled down to meet his own gaze in the mirror. His sand-colored hair, cut short for efficiency, was darkened slightly by sweat, and the tap water dripped over a face that, in spite of the passing of many hard years, had maintained some semblance of youth and innocence. If two decades of living and working in the System hadn't erased that countenance from his face, then a simple nightmare stood little chance of doing so.

But, if nothing else, he thought wryly, *it's inspired me for my next assignment.*

Glancing at his watch, Eli decided that he wouldn't be getting any more sleep tonight. Taking three steps to the opposite wall of his living unit, he took his brush and paste from their shelf. Back at the sink, he began brushing his teeth.

THEY ALWAYS DO

Nora flicked her tongue over her front teeth. She was beyond noticing the fuzzy texture of built-up plaque, but the coppery taste of blood got her attention. An experimental finger demonstrated that the same teeth were just the slightest bit loose as well. She rolled her shoulders, but the ache in her joints worsened *rather than receded.*

How ironic that a person who'd never spent even an hour at sea could be showing signs of scurvy . . .

She made a mental note to dig especially deep in the local trash bins for any fruit she could find, no matter how nasty*—even an apple with a worm would provide her much-needed Vitamin C.*

The problem, of course, was quite academic—Nora Puente simply was not yet skilled at life as a homeless vagrant.

Oh, pardon me, that's *"Non-Citizen"* according to the latest political lingo.

While she'd never been rich, she hadn't been the most impoverished kid on her block, either. She'd been halfway toward becoming a Registered Nurse when the world turned upside-down—in fact, if she hadn't been so involved *in her studies, she might have paid more attention when they announced the new government's Vocational Screening . . . and how critical it was* not *to miss your scheduled testing date! She wasn't used to not being allowed to hold a job or own property . . . or stop by the local supermarket for something as simple and necessary as a tooth brush, loaf of bread, or bottle of multi-vitamins.*

Nora straightened her back, which brought another piercing throb. She shook her head and, in spite of the pain, grinned.

When Doctor Corbit promised how real this would be, *she thought in sheer wonder,* he wasn't kidding . . .

Then the boy and his mother appeared . . . and all other considerations left Nora's mind.

There they were, just like before . . . two new Citizens, their opaque IDCs in such critical contrast to Nora's clear. They emerged from the early morning fog, the adult in the lead but somehow not really guiding the boy. The mother stared straight ahead, not seeing anything beyond her own tortured thoughts, and the boy occasionally sneaked glances down at the small wooden cross hanging from his neck—there had been talk of banning all religious icons, and Nora was surprised that the mother allowed the boy to wear his so openly.

Nora watched them approach, and she felt both excited and apprehensive, a guilty pleasure that she strove to accept and ignore.

Just like Doctor Corbit said . . .

As the pair passed her, Nora rose to her feet. This was cheating a bit—she hadn't actually followed them quite so closely the first time—but she wanted to be near when it *happened.*

Although the mother remained oblivious, the boy noticed her, and he slowed to stare at this strange NC who trailed after them. The woman continued at her same pace, and her hand slipped from her child's.

"I know you," she whispered, not truly aware that she was speaking aloud. It was all so real . . . *"I know you."*

The boy merely stared, his back to his mother at the crucial moment.

Turn around now, *Nora urged silently.* Turn around and see . . .

The boy did turn, and his breath caught when he spotted his mother collapsed to the ground. He rushed to her, and Nora's lips quivered and eyes moistened in pity as she watched him shake her, urging her to awaken. He looked around frantically and appeared to see something further down the alley—perhaps a passing Citizen, perhaps the ghost of his own denial. The boy rose and moved away . . .

. . . and Nora went to work.

She knelt over the woman, pushing her onto her back. Placing her hands the proper distance up the sternum, Nora dove into CPR.

The boy heard the pumping movements and turned to watch her. Nora cleared an air passage, gave a few puffs of the Breath of Life, then returned to pumping her chest as the boy walked numbly back toward them.

Nora quickly realized that it was hopeless—the woman's lips were already blue. For a massive coronary, CPR was rarely enough—without a defibrillator, there was no chance.

Slowly, Nora stopped. She hesitated to meet the boy's eyes—indeed, she would spend the next years fearing that the boy secretly blamed her for failing—but she forced herself to look up. Any moment now, the boy would fall into her arms, crying and trembling, his heart breaking beyond all hope. And Nora would be there for him, holding him tight, and promising that . . .

Something was wrong.

The boy wasn't crying. He was staring at her blankly, his eyes cold and dry.

On the ground beside her, the woman's body vanished in a breeze of morning fog, but Nora was beyond noticing.

What's happening?! Corbit said—!

Then, the words she had dreaded hearing for the last twenty years:

"You let her die," Eli spat, his eyes suddenly no longer cold but fiercely hot, "I hate *you!" Turning sharply, Eli marched away.*

"Wait!" Nora cried, her heart thundering in her chest. "Don't leave! I tried *to save her . . . "*

This was all wrong! Everything was coming apart! When that husky Organizer turned her over to Corbit, she'd been more confused *than afraid, but the famous doctor had explained that he simply needed her help*—her *help—and that in return, he would give her something few Non-Citizens dared to think about anymore.*

He would give her her dreams.

Corbit wanted nothing more of her than that she dream, and keep on dreaming as long as she liked, as long as she could, *until . . . what? He had never been clear about that, but it had been evident that he expected* something *to eventually happen.*

But this *. . . Please, God, don't let* this *be what he wanted! This was no dream—this was her greatest nightmare, her most secret* guilt, *displayed right before her mind's cringing eye!*

"This isn't right!" she cried to the heavens, praying the man outside might hear. "This isn't the way it happened!"

She turned back to the sight of the retreating boy. He blamed her. He hated *her! All these years, hadn't she always known how he secretly despised her?* Hadn't she?!

"Elijah, you were there!" she pleaded. "I tried *to save her! Remember, Elijah, remember?!"*

Eli stopped, turned, and glared at her with unadulterated bitterness *and* loathing *. . .*

. . . and Nora's soul *died.*

She had failed. She'd failed Eli, failed in the only true task ever meant for her. She was the lowest of the low, unworthy of drawing another breath. She deserved to be struck down by God himself, smitten and burned out of existence . . .

. . . and then, she was.

* * *

"Come on, Nora . . . "

The haggard Hispanic woman screamed on the dreamslab, twisting back and forth, her right hand almost-but-not-quite pulling free from the interface gel. Her hair was matted, her face dripping heavily with perspiration—sweat of heat, sweat of *pain*. Her eyes darted back and forth beneath closed lids in rapid eye movement.

Doctor James Edward Corbit gripped the edge of his work

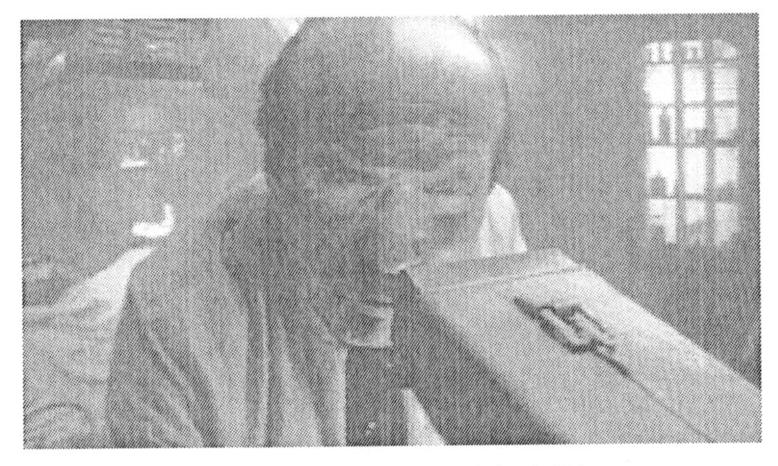

Dr. James Corbit (Harold Cannon) divided his gaze between his subject and the monitor scope that displayed her brain-wave patterns.

station, his anxiety having nothing at all to do with Nora's personal danger. The surly man divided his gaze between Nora herself and the monitor scope that displayed her brain-wave patterns.

In the background, the computer's synthesized voice rattled off various attempts to stabilize the subject—all of which were *failing.* "*Warning: Regressive bio-feedback in progress. Endorphin increase: No effect. Alpha-wave suppressant: No effect . . .*"

"Listen to me, Nora, you can do this!" Corbit continued, insistent. "You can beat this thing!"

Nora screamed again at the top of her lungs. Corbit grunted—his REM-emitters gave him only vague insight into the specific content of his subjects' dreams, but it looked like the mainframe's defense this time was to consume her in *flames*!

"Keep fighting!" he urged. "Come on, Nora, come on!"

Her convulsions grew worse, and she began to hyperventilate between bellows of agony. She cried out in her native Spanish, her words slurring together.

Then the smell hit him—the pungent reek of burning flesh.

Corbit glanced over his shoulder at her smoldering form. He'd seen physical manifestations in response to the mainframe's torment before—indeed, the *Powers That Be* were pushing him for increased psychosomatic reactions every day—but he'd never witnessed anything this *extreme*. Her blood must be literally boiling, raising her body temperature to seemingly *impossible* levels. Heat blisters erupted all over her body, like paint peeling from overheated metal, and blood trickled from her eyes, nose, and ears.

The computer voice raised in volume, spouting warnings of the subject's rapid decline, "*Warning: Lethal psychosomatic reaction—subject will* not *survive . . .* " As if Corbit couldn't figure that out for *himself*!

Corbit rushed to her side, biting back the nausea prompted by the close proximity. He leaned over her scalding face, switching to Spanish in false empathy and raging for her to fight, to *win*!

The woman writhed violently one last time, her IDC hand finally wrenching free of the interface gel as she choked her last breath. The IDC itself had practically melted right into her skin. Smoke rose from her charred flesh.

"*Total synaptic hemorrhage*," the computer stated with objective finality. "*Link to mainframe severed. Session terminated.*"

Corbit glared blankly down at the dead woman. Some long lost part of him wondered if he should *feel* something for her, some instinctive human emotion in response to the pain and suffering he had caused her. He considered his own IDC, wondering what it would feel like to have it cooked right out of his body. He knew how ingrained into the nervous system the IDCs really were. Who else in this God-forsaken hell-hole had explored its potential further than the man who invented the *Dream Parlor*?

But he felt nothing for her, beyond what she represented for him personally: Another damned *failure*.

"Private Entry, March Twenty-First: The subject, Nora Puente, appeared stable, at first . . . they always do . . . "

Slowly, begrudgingly, Corbit stepped back and shut down the dreamslab's primary generator.

"Shortly after the assigned dreamscan slipped into free fall, the subject experienced regressive bio-feedback, triggered by some bitter-sweet memory tainted with suppressed guilt. I increased the pleasure stimulation to her fantasy early in the process, but this had little or no bearing on her will to stay *in her selected dream."*

Corbit methodically pulled the extra material of the blue-green bed sheet up and over, covering Nora's corpse and cutting the stench just a bit.

The same damn thing every time. They start off fine, entertaining themselves with whatever petty joyrides their limited imaginations could conjure, then *wham!*—the mainframe reacts, and their dreams ricochet off into *hell.* What was the catalyst?

Taking a moment, he removed the top of the skull sitting to one side of his work station. He selected a candy at random and popped it into his mouth.

"Guilt," he speculated idly as he munched away, "it's gotta be *guilt.*"

"What I need is a strong subject to get anywhere—if I can break the unbreakable, I'll be ready to move forward with my research. However, finding a Citizen whose mind has not been totally molested by the System is like finding a virgin whore."

Sighing, Corbit pushed away from the table and proceeded to dispose of Nora's remains in the usual fashion . . .

DO YOUR WORKLOAD

The *Data Processing Center*: A tall, imposing, primary computer core, with octopus-like tentacles of data conduits splayed out in all directions. Cold, featureless walls, a ceiling that rose into eternity, or so it seemed. Poor air circulation, temperature pitched low for optimum efficiency—for the *core*, of course, not the *humans* at work. Almost crowded, yet the conversation kept to an absolute minimum . . .

A fairly typical job environment for working-class Confirmed Citizens.

The numb, slack-faced Citizens, their glassy-eyed stares shifting only occasionally with the barest hint of head movement, sat at work stations poised in a circle around the core. Each station consisted of a spherical, glowing red retina scope lit from within. The Citizens' right arms rested upon angled slopes, their hands encased within organic interface gel. The gelatin interacted with their IDCs, the cybernetic fibers working against the similar nodes in the housing tube of each chip. The muscles and tendons of their hands flexed and contracted at different intervals as the Citizens inputted various commands, while their free left hands manipulated glossy, white trackballs protruding from the table top.

At one of the confined work stations on the far side of the octagonal room, a single, masculine right hand was *not* in its gel, but instead using a stubby, chewed-on pencil to create the likeness of an ethereal woman, the outline of her blank face nothing more than delicate markings. The owner of the artistic hand leaned forward to examine the fruits of his labor and, in doing so, stretched to the point where a small wooden cross pulled from the confines of his collar, dangling the keepsake into view.

Glancing around the room, more from habit than out of any real fear that the surrounding zombies would notice, Eli covered his father's cross and stuffed it back into his shirt. Deciding it would be less conspicuous if he retied the cord later, he tugged his heavy peacoat more snugly around him and returned his attention to the sketch.

Beside Eli, his station partner, Jacob Moore, pulled his hand from the interface gel. He stretched the kinks out of his neck and rubbed his tired eyes, then threw a worried glance at his artistic co-worker. A moment later, Eli felt the disapproving stare.

"Do your workload," Jacob chided in a hushed whisper.

Eli shrugged at his nervous friend. "I'm finished," he whispered back.

Jacob shifted uncomfortably, then scolded, "Don't rock the boat." He returned his hand to his interface gel, red light refracting off his glasses as his computer reactivated.

Eli almost resumed his drawing when he felt another pair of eyes. He looked to the next station to his right, where another friend—Dana Levy—frowned at him. If *she* heard their exchange, then they had been talking too loud. The last thing he needed was a lecture from Ruth, their department head, on the finer points of station efficiency—she was about as warm as the DPC itself.

Dana shook her head, then followed Jacob's lead back into cyber-limbo.

When they were both once again engrossed in their duties, Eli glanced around the still, silent workplace and decided that it was indeed time to return his attention to another job at hand.

Let's see, where did I dream . . . oh, yes, "Death Row Tonight" . . .

From his right sleeve, Eli produced a thin wire with a narrow, electrode tip. He deftly ran the wire underneath his palm, then up through his fingers, snapping the end into the interface housing of his IDC. He then placed his arm upon its rest and slid his hand into the gel.

Responding to Eli's call, the computer eye brightened. Fingers of red light stretched out for him like a spider spinning a web. As the scope reacted with the nerve endings of his retinas, Eli perceived a flash of white . . .

Within the private, electro-static world of cyber-limbo, floating through swirls of data and information that his mind subjectively interpreted as concrete imagines it could work with, Eli "floated" in the crowded vacuum, face-to-face with a facsimile of *himself.*

>DATA ENTRY REQUEST: Eli thought at his doppleganger. >ACCESS CURRENT RUNNING FILES WITHIN EXECUTION CHANNEL DATABASE.

>>*ACCESSING*, the Computer-Eli responded.

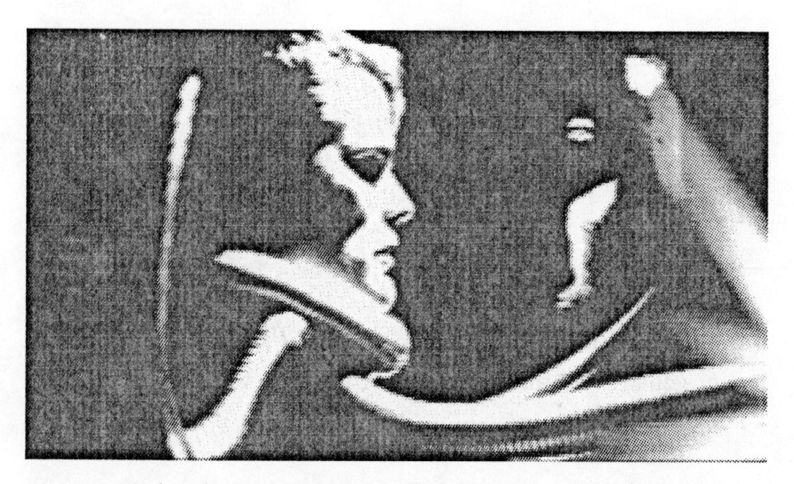

Within the private, electro-static world of cyber-limbo, Eli "floated" face-to-face with a facsimile of *himself.*

The Execution Channel, a sadly popular television program, publicly executed political prisoners, or any other brand of trouble-makers, in a variety of creative ways before a live studio audience. The broadcasting network supported a state-of-the-art security system that its designers claimed would revolutionize cyber-limbo.

Eli had cracked it on his fourth attempt.

>>*RUNNING FILE*: the Computer-Eli reported. >>*NON-CITIZENS TO BE TERMINATED AND DELETED FROM SYSTEM—NOW TRANSFERRING CURRENT LISTS FOR EXECUTION CHANNEL . . . DOCUMENT COMPLETE. ENTER ADDITIONAL IDC NUMBERS.*

>RECEIVE UPLOADS NOW.

Eli's left hand released the track ball and moved up his right sleeve, following the trail of the wire. Hidden from sight, he pressed something that *clicked.*

>>>*WARNING:* the other Eli suddenly stated with increased volume and lowered pitch. >>>*VIRUS INTRODUCED INTO SYSTEM—EMINENT DATA LOSS. CREATING BACKUP FILE—*

>*NO*, Eli ordered. >DO *NOT* CREATE BACKUP FILE.

The Computer-Eli fell silent. The image flickered for a brief moment, then announced, >>*DATA HAS BEEN LOST, FILE SYSTEM DAMAGED. DO YOU WISH TO CONTINUE?*

Eli withdrew his hand from the gel. He took a moment to shake off the mild disorientation of cyber-limbo, then unplugged the wire from his IDC.

He was returning the wire to the confines of his sleeve when the alarm buzzed loudly, announcing the end of the work day as it echoed obnoxiously through the room. Eli cringed for a moment—someday, Jacob's paranoid prophecies might come true, and he would hear his number called over that same speaker—then collected his pencil and drawing of the faceless woman.

Jacob bumped into him as he passed—probably on purpose if he was going into one of his pouty moods—and Eli rose to follow.

EVERYONE'S SORRY ABOUT SOMETHIN'

"Productive Citizens are the Strength of our Union . . . "

With a high-pitched rumble, the subtrain sailed along its magnetic track.

"Nonproductive Citizens are a Detriment to themselves, and to Society . . . "

Inside, the rare mélange of Citizens and Non-Citizens sat in various states of oblivion.

"Non-Citizens are Productive when they Keep their Place . . . "

The subtrain car was a bit on the cool side, and most onboard braced themselves against the chill. Eli, on the other hand, having spent the day in the refrigerated DPC, had his work coat off—it lay across his lap, serving as a backboard while he continued work on his latest illustration.

"Productive Citizens are the Strength of our Union . . . "

Eli had long ago learned to tune out the droning rhetoric. The Organizer hologram at each end of the train peered back and forth, spewing its oratory as it stared down at the subtrain's occupants.

Rumor had it that it was also an observation device, and—never having been able to confirm or disprove this speculation—Eli treated it as such.

Luckily, the System had yet to lower an outright ban on *drawing*.

Stroking a final line across the hair, Eli shifted the pencil to the blank face—and hesitated. Instead, the pencil moved to a familiar position between his teeth.

He looked down at the faceless woman and gently ran his fingertips across the featureless expanse. What would he draw there? What had he *ever* drawn there?

The familiar ache rose, but, as always, he pushed it down. What right did he have to yearn for anyone? Did *he* really want to do to someone else what his *father* had inadvertently done to his mother? If he ever got caught, that's *exactly* what would happen—he would *widow* the one he loved.

And who could *that* be anyway?

He again considered the drawing. He knew whom the general shape resembled—at least, he knew where his inspiration had come from. For the past month or so, he'd occasionally glimpsed a gorgeous woman, a Citizen, on the subtrain. He'd never seen her before, which in itself was a bit unusual—the System wasn't exactly supportive of *career changes*, so most Citizens took the same trains to and from the same jobs around the same time every day for years on end.

Eli had thought about approaching her, but what would he say? Even if there weren't so many reasons *not* to associate with the stranger . . . he wasn't exactly *experienced* at that sort of thing.

The status lights over the subtrain doors switched from green to red, and the car lurched to a halt. Eli gathered his paper and coat as the Citizens and Non-Citizens—avoiding eye-contact with one another—moved to the exits. Eli slipped into the stream of bodies and climbed the steps, glancing over his shoulder briefly—

There she was again!

She'd moved in and sat across from where he had been moments earlier. And she was alone, as usual.

Eli stepped back down to the lower steps so that he could better see her—he stretched his neck until he had a clear line of sight around the ambling people between them. She glanced in his direction, made eye-contact, and smiled.

Man, she was *beautiful.* Her face was delicate and soft, her petite body trim and *healthy*—something rare even to Citizens these days. Light, shoulder-length hair and large blue eyes, full lips. . .

Eli wanted to go back and talk to her, he really did. But . . .

"Productive Citizens are the Strength of our Union . . . "

Slowly, the woman realized that he was still gaping at her, and she looked his way again—no smile this time, just discomfort. He was just staring at her like an *idiot*!

"Hey, slim, you're blockin' the exit."

Eli looked down. An older, Middle-Eastern man waited impatiently to get off the subtrain.

"S-Sorry," Eli stammered as he moved forward . . . and away from the woman.

"Everyone's sorry about somethin'," the old man grumbled.

"Non-Productive Citizens are a Detriment to themselves, and to Society . . . "

The doors lowered, and the subtrain pulled away.

TECHNICAL DIFFICULTY

Ah, home sweet home.

Down the long, narrow corridor, dimly lit by overhead, nervously-twinkling flourescents, the floor was crowded with unwashed, unkempt Non-Citizens seeking shelter and rest in the warmest, driest place they could find. An occasional cough triggered a chain-reaction of other sickly bodily sounds that took a depressingly long time to fade away.

Citizens and *Non-Citizens.* The new way of life. Either you were skilled or you were not, either you were educated or you were not . . . either you worked for the System, or you did not. The System didn't go *out of its way* to "delete" all of the Non-Citizens; they merely endorsed the largest display of human *apathy* in the history of the world. As long as they were content to stay out of the Citizens' way, to survive off the scraps and left-overs, and to answer to any Citizen's beck-and-call, the System was content to *ignore* them. Of course, if they ever caused any trouble, there were always Organizers . . .

. . . and the Execution Channel.

Near the center of the hall, Eli carefully made his way over the heaps of bodies with routine precision. Overhead pipes, exposed for all to see, clanged and chugged. The only window at one end of the corridor had broken long ago and in turn had been boarded up by one of the tenants—no landlord to call and nag in these times.

Eli approached his own door and pressed his IDC against the scanlock. A small light on the box shifted to green, and Eli pushed the door open.

Entering his sparse, dingy-gray hallow, his presence triggered the room's sensors, and illumination pulsated to life. He hung his work coat on its peg, then moved to his cot and touched the main control panel. The projection system whirled to life, and the huge, wall-sized screen opposite his bed lit up. He scanned through a hundred channels in a matter of moments, occasionally picking up on a brief eyeful of sex, violence, or propaganda. The television wouldn't stay on the station where you last left it—the Big Boys *wanted* you to have to zoom past all of their waste until you found something you could stomach . . . or *research*.

He finally stopped on channel 438—the Execution Channel. The familiar -X- logo appeared over its valley of flames, and the Host's voice continued its loop:

"Welcome to the Execution Channel! We apologize for the delay in our featured programming. Due to technical difficulty, the examples scheduled for this evening's 'Death Row Tonight' have been canceled. 'Death Row Tonight' will return tomorrow at its regularly scheduled time. Stay tuned for our basement snuff films, coming right up . . . "

A smile slowly crept over Eli's face as he reached up into his right sleeve and unstrapped from his forearm his *scrambler*—a small, deliberately-nondescript device that fit easily into his palm. The scrambler was the result of the two totally opposed schools of training: The System's, and his father's. In another time and place, Eli could've patented it and made a fortune—in the here and now, the System would have loved to know about the little device that was Eli's chief hacking tool.

The Execution Channel's Voice-Over took a break, and a commercial came on in place of the chrome -X-.

"*Welcome to the* Dream Parlor," a woman's accented voice intoned from the speakers. "*You are now entering a world of* pure imagination—*a realm of* lucid dreams . . . "

Moving across the room to the basin, Eli knelt and tucked the scrambler into a slot hidden underneath, then rose to face the mirror. Turning the flow handle, he listened to the sound of depressurized water straining the pipes until it finally decided to spit out. He took several handfuls and splashed his face, much as he had after his nightmare that morning.

". . . *live for your dreams* here, *at the original* Dream Parlor—or, *experience the* rest *of your life at one of our convenient world-wide outlets . . .* "

Lifting his head, he caught his reflection in the mirror. For a long moment, he studied it with the same scrutiny he afforded his drawings.

"Don't rock the boat," he told his reflection. He meant to mock Jacob's nervous warning, but it didn't come out quite as he intended. When had Jacob become so chiding anyway? Granted, he was correct in how dangerous Eli's activities were, but hadn't Jacob been *supportive* of those same risks not so long ago? Or had Eli *always* been this alone and merely *pretended* he had more allies? He wasn't sure anymore.

". . . *here at the* Dream Parlor, *you can be* everything *you want. . . go* any*where, do* any*thing* . . . "

Eli glanced over his shoulder. A computer-generated hand swirled against a beautiful, clouded sky, finally halting with its opaque Citizen's IDC showcased.

". . . *no questions asked*," the woman concluded. A beat later, a smarmy male voice added the fine print as the image was obscured behind screen-filling words that matched the final send off, "*For* Confirmed Citizens *only*."

Eli straightened up and toweled his face dry. *Seems like they're playing that commercial all the time these days.*

As he pulled the towel aside, he found the image had changed from the *Dream Parlor* commercial to one of an appetizing meal.

The new graphics matching the announcer's words asked, "*What are you hungry for when you don't know what you're hungry for? Mmm, doesn't that look good?*"

Eli's stomach grumbled in response.

PLACES YOU DON'T BELONG

A distinctly *un*appetizing spoonful of protein mush plopped onto Eli's plate. He passed on the next dish—a weak excuse for dessert—and contented himself with the mush, apple, and bread roll he had already collected.

"Productive Citizens are the Strength of our Union . . . " the indoctrination droned throughout the Food Park, but Eli no more heard it now than he had on the subtrain.

Moving to the credit collection station, he extended his right hand to the Food Park attendant.

"Hey," Eli said casually as the man scanned his IDC.

The attendant glanced nervously up at him, then diverted his eyes back down to the control panel as though he hadn't heard him.

Not yet thinking anything of it, Eli continued, "How're you doing?"

The older man's tension only increased, his large eyes darting back and forth as sweat actually began to form on his brow. He still refused to acknowledge Eli's greeting as he instead looked impatiently to the next Citizen in line.

Confused, Eli turned away and headed out toward the condiments stand. He was distracted by the odd exchange just enough that he didn't notice when his father's cross, never retied over the day, finally worked itself loose and fell to the ground.

The attendant nearly gasped as he peered down at the fallen icon. A heartbeat later, his gaze rose to follow its owner as he crossed the large cafeteria . . .

Eli collected some utensils and a napkin, then headed over to the tables arranged before a stylized sculpture of an Organizer's face. "Dana," he greeted as he approached their usual seats. "Jacob."

"Hey, Eli," Dana answered as she scooted over. Jacob said nothing.

Eli sat beside her just as the attendant, clutching a napkin in his hand, stepped up beside them.

"You dropped this," the man muttered as he set the bundle before Eli.

Nonplused, Eli stared at the wadded napkin. Reaching out, he unfolded it just enough to view its contents.

Oh my God!

On the outside, Eli froze for a moment—he didn't trust himself to do anything else. Then, mechanically, deliberately, he closed his hand around the napkin and forced himself to say, "Thank you."

The attendant grunted and hastened back to his work place.

"What'd you drop?" Dana asked curiously.

Before Eli could lie to her, Jacob reached over and snatched the napkin from his hand. "What is it?" he teased, thinking perhaps it was something merely personal and embarrassing. Eli started to yank it back but swiftly realized that he wasn't getting out of this, at least not with Jacob.

Jacob was grinning until he opened the bundle, then his face dropped sharply as he caught sight of the cross. His expression shifted to anger, and perhaps even *nausea*, as he glanced at Eli, then back toward the attendant. When he absorbed exactly what had just transpired, he slammed the cross and its make-shift sheath down on the table. Bolting to his feet, he turned and stormed away without a word, heading straight for the adjoining bar.

Eli rose and took a few steps after him before hesitating. As he turned back around, he saw Dana reaching out to inspect the napkin herself. Not ready to have *both* friends mad at him, he covered it before she could touch it.

Dana stared up at Eli as he wavered undecidedly between following Jacob or staying. When he made a definite lean in the direction of the bar, she chided, "Just let him go." She, too, had seen Jacob like this before and apparently figured, *whatever* was in the napkin, it was best to leave him alone until he cooled off.

Eli, on the other hand, shook his head—this conversation had been coming for some time, and maybe it was better to just get it over with. "I have to talk to him."

Heading toward the bar, he stuffed the napkin and cross into his pocket. Dana chuckled to herself as she returned to her dinner . . .

Strobing lights and flourescent wheels airbrushed the walls, tables, and ceiling of the heavily-shadowed room. On a raised platform, a Non-Citizen women danced seductively to the mood music playing over the speakers—here, at least, the Organizer's chant did not drone, although an Organizer *was* present off to one side. The dancer swayed and rocked, her clear chip occasionally catching the light. Aside from the music, the bar was eerily quiet—the conversations flowed in hushed voices as Citizens made underdeveloped attempts to interact with their peers while at the same time avoiding undue attention at all costs.

Jacob scanned his chip as the bartender poured a beer into his waiting mug. He snatched the cup the moment it was ready, heading to one of the tables just as Eli rounded the corner in pursuit. Choosing a seat near the dancing NC, Jacob plopped down and removed his glasses to rub his eyes. Eli stood over him, waiting, his arms spread in friendly surrender. When Jacob spotted him, he muttered, "If the Organizers catch you with that, you're gonna end up *on the Execution Channel.*"

Jacob (Kevin Moore) rolled his eyes. "I am *sick*," he spat, "of hearing about The Great Mencer Barrett and his little uprising, so give it a rest."

"Relax, all right," Eli said as he sat across from him. He offered what he hoped was a disarming smile. "It's something I got from my father. It's a memory, it's a token."

Jacob rolled his eyes. "I am *sick*," he spat, "of hearing about The Great Mencer Barrett and his little uprising, so give it a rest."

Eli's smile dropped—this was a sensitive area, and Jacob *knew* it. "Jacob, *I* am not my father," he said, then added with earnest regret, "*Believe me*, I'm not."

"But you've got his blood in you, Eli," Jacob continued. "That's where you get your rough edges from."

Eli sat back, pulling away from his friend physically and emotionally. "I'm an efficient Citizen—no one can argue that."

"Yeah, you get your workload done, but then you poke around places you *don't belong*."

Suddenly, Eli wasn't so eager to have this conversation after all. He glared at Jacob for a moment, then rose to his feet.

With unexpected fierceness, Jacob leaped up as well and placed a blocking hand on Eli's chest. "*Sit down*."

Eli squared off, and for a moment his father's strength *was* clear in his eyes. Jacob pulled his hand away, then glanced around. A few Citizens were watching—as was the Organizer at the counter. Instead of forcing the issue, Jacob slipped back into his seat and gestured for Eli to do the same. After a moment, Eli complied, but his apologetic demeanor was gone.

His tone lower and attitude softer, Jacob pushed on. "Why do you keep taking these chances? You *know* we're under a microscope."

"The scrambler is *working*, Jacob," Eli asserted firmly, "and people are getting to *live* a little bit longer. No one knows where it's coming from—no one's even *said* anything."

"*Yet*," Jacob hissed. "Can't you just live a *normal life*?"

"What," Eli taunted, "to be left alone and live in peace? To just find someone and settle down into a *safe little bubble*?"

On that note, Jacob refused to look chastened. His expression read, *Of* course, *don't you?*

Eli considered that briefly before admitting, "Okay, yeah, sure, I want that, but I want that for *everyone*." He pressed on, his anger growing as he spoke. "And if working in that freezing *pit*, and altering certain records is what it *takes*, then *that* is what I have to *do*!" He paused, trying to cool off before continuing, but the steam was releasing now, and he stabbed on, "And since when did *you* become such a poster-child Citizen? You used to *agree* that things needed to change." He shook his head in disgust, looking over at the dancer without seeing her.

"Yeah, well, things *have* changed," Jacob returned. "Call me pragmatic, but what your father wanted you to do *can't be done*. How did he expect you to change the *whole world*?"

For that, Eli had no quick answer. Faltering, he offered, "One life at a time."

" 'One life at a time,' " Jacob mocked with disdain. "*Spare* me, *please*." Then, easier and more heartfelt, he urged, "All I'm asking, Eli, is blend in a little. You deal with your creative juices at the *Dream Parlor*, but *not* in public, and *not* at *work*."

You deal with your creative juices at the Dream Parlor . . . What did the *Dream Parlor* have to do with anything?

"Why do you guys go there so much?"

Thrown by the change of subject, Jacob asked, "Where?"

"The *Dream Parlor.* You, Dana, *everyone* at work . . . you go there all the time."

Befuddled, Jacob answered, "Of *course* we do. Who *doesn't*?" Fed up, he shoved his drink aside, snatched his glasses, and marched away from the table and his crazy friend.

A waitress wandered by and collected the abandoned mug. Alone and in silence, Eli sat and considered Jacob's response.

DO YOU HAVE ANY PLACE TO GO?

"Nonproductive Citizens are a Detriment to themselves, and to Society . . . "

As the subtrain rumbled along back toward his living complex, Eli sat in typical silence and contemplated his argument with Jacob . . . or, more specifically, the *end* of it.

You go there all the time.

Of course *we do. Who* doesn't?

Something about this whole *Dream Parlor* thing had been nagging at Eli for some time now. It wasn't anything specific, nothing he could put his finger on. Just a general *gut feeling*.

"Of *course* we do," Jacob had said. "Who *doesn't*?" As if it were the most natural thing in the world, as if Eli were bizarre for even asking about it.

Eli hadn't been exaggerating when he indicated that *everyone* at the DPC attended the *Parlor*. And now that he really sat and thought about it . . . well, he wasn't exactly a *social butterfly*, but he couldn't think of a single Citizen he knew who hadn't mentioned going to the *Parlor* at one time or another.

On the surface, the *Dream Parlor* seemed harmless enough. Eli had never really paid much attention to the verbiage on television, but, if he understood correctly, they *created lucid dreams.* Although Eli had an aversion to the mysterious notion of tampering with brain waves, it was primarily the government's endorsement of the *Parlor* that made him dubious. Call it well-founded prejudice, but his rule-of-thumb was that if the System liked it, then it was probably *no good.*

But what if there's more *to it than I first thought?*

Slowly, Eli lifted his gaze from the floor of the subtrain. Glancing across the way, he spotted a man rubbing his forehead in angst. A second later, social habit lowered his eyes to the man's IDC—Citizen.

Eli turned his head to the left. Another man sat nervously chewing his fingernails, his eyes vacant and despairing—another Citizen.

And to the left of *that* man sat another Citizen, and Eli was willing to bet—

He looked up from the dark IDC and realized that this latest subject wasn't just a Citizen, he was an *Organizer* . . .

. . . and he was looking right back at Eli.

With practiced stoicism, Eli dropped his eyes back to the floor, as though he'd simply been daydreaming and hadn't really seen the rough-looking official at all.

After a few seconds, the Organizer decided that there was nothing of interest and looked away as well.

Slowly, cautiously, Eli returned to reviewing the other occupants of the subtrain. Although the jolt with the Organizer had thrown his thought-process for a loop, he felt he'd been *on* to something, a correlation between the coveted, well-provided position of Confirmed Citizenship and . . .

As Eli looked to the rear of the car, an infant cried, and he lost his train of thought once more.

Sitting center on the very back seat, a tattered woman cradled her baby. An overhead light spilled its hue onto the mother's dark hair and shoulders. In spite of her impoverished grunge, the woman seemed content in her moment of human bonding.

Mesmerized, Eli's eyes lowered to the woman's right hand, which she was using to steady the infant's head.

Her IDC was clear—a Non-Citizen.

In the back of Eli's mind—the part still trying to follow the trail of his original observations—he noted that here, in this train car full of chilly despair, the *only* person who seemed remotely content within her moment was an *NC*, the supposedly *dejected* of society.

"Non-Citizens are Productive when they Keep their Place . . . "

Eli glanced up at her again.

Oh, no. No, Eli, this isn't a good idea. There's an Organizer *sitting two meters from her! This is* not *a good idea!*

Taking a breath, Eli rose to his feet. Steadying himself with the hand post, he slowly made his way past the Organizer, who watched him curiously, toward the NC woman.

I know what I'm doing, he told himself. *I've had to do this in public before.*

Never in front of an Organizer, *you* moron*!*

The street woman's blue-green eyes flickered nervously up at Eli as he lowered himself into the seat next to her. Almost imperceptively, she pulled away from him—the best she could manage without *appearing* to pull away. Then her gaze dropped back down to her baby as though she hadn't noticed him . . . just like *Eli* had done with the Organizer. Under other circumstances, he might have smiled at that.

Instead, he merely sat in silence for a moment. Then, "What's your name?"

The woman stiffened, but answered cautiously, "Two-Four-Six-Zero—"

"If I wanted your *number*," Eli interrupted as he looked at her directly, "I'd ask for your *number*."

The woman swallowed and corrected, "E-Elizabeth Hudson."

Satisfied, Eli returned to staring straight ahead. "Elizabeth," he commented idly, "good. And your baby?"

"H-her name is Hannah."

Eli allowed himself a half-smile. "That's a beautiful name."

Pleasantly surprised at this kind observation, Elizabeth actually turned and looked at *him*. "Yes," she agreed, touched, "it is." She smiled.

The subtrain began to slow. Eli glanced over at the status light. It hadn't yet turned red, but it wouldn't be much longer now. "We're coming to my stop," he told her, his voice colder again. "When you get off the train, do you have any place to go?"

Harshly reminded of whom she was talking to, the woman's smile fell away. Averting her eyes once more, she drew a choked breath and said, "Sir, as a Non-Citizen, I'm required to do whatever you ask . . . "

"Good."

"But my *child*—!" she pleaded.

"Come with me," he cut her off, his tone a little more forceful. The subtrain door swung open and he stood. Helpless, Elizabeth followed suit.

Then, as Eli made his way up the stairs, the Organizer *also* stood and reached out, grabbing Eli by the shoulder.

Willing his poker face not to falter, Eli glanced down at the hand, then into the man's eyes—*submissively*, of course.

The Organizer glanced back at Elizabeth, then winked at Eli and grinned. "Don't *catch* anything," he warned.

Eli merely looked to his feet. The Organizer released his hold, and Eli led Elizabeth out of the subtrain. The Organizer stared after her a bit, considered calling her back for himself—she wasn't bad looking for an NC—but then changed his mind . . .

As the subtrain pulled away, Eli glanced around. Satisfied that no one was watching for the moment, he spun on his heel and lowered his face to Elizabeth's level. She cowered, probably expecting a violent kiss or worse, but she didn't back away.

"Don't talk to me," he whispered urgently, "keep your head down, don't even *look* at me until we get to my complex."

He continued on his way as though he'd never stopped—Elizabeth obediently followed.

THAT KIND OF OFFER

Eli ushered the Non-Citizen and her baby down the creaking stairs to the basement level of his living unit, then headed for the steel track door leading into the storage bunker. It was dark, out of the way . . .

. . . and, most importantly, *private.*

Reaching inside an old conduit port, Eli felt around for a brief moment before finding the old-style maintenance key. He slid it into its gate, twisted against the rusted tumblers, then returned it to its hiding place. Elizabeth shuffled out of his way as he hefted the weighty door open.

Once the entrance was clear, Eli headed straight through to the back of the shadowy room. Elizabeth reluctantly followed him in, looking around as she went. The old bunker was mostly barren now, with only a few crates scattered about. Shafts of light spilled through dirty windows near the top of one wall. Elizabeth glanced into that light . . . then sighed inwardly. More resolved than panicked, she kissed her baby lovingly on the forehead and laid her gently upon one of the crates. She then methodically pulled her top off her shoulders.

In the meantime, Eli was still fussing around in the back alcove—with what, Elizabeth could not see from her vantage point. "I found this place, a few years back," he was saying. "I don't think anyone even remembers it's still down here. It's not much, but it serves its purpose. It's out of the way, and we've never been *interrupted.* If you want, I can give you an extra blanket, try to make you more *comfortable . . .*"

Too world-weary to bother cringing, Elizabeth moved to expose her breasts. At that moment, Eli glanced up, and his face dropped.

Stupid! he cursed himself. *Thoughtless, stupid* idiot! "No!" he called out as he rushed to her side. "No, no, Elizabeth, Elizabeth, no," he rambled. As he reached her, she stole a confused glance at his face before dropping her eyes back down. She didn't understand.

How could *she, you cruel* bastard*? Is she supposed to be* psychic*?!*

"Elizabeth, it's—it's *not* that kind of offer, okay? I—I didn't want the Organizer to catch on—!"

Just then, a parade of noises echoed into the storage room from the stairwell. A burly vagrant—a long-haired, thin-bearded man of about forty, wearing a derby and carrying an old, one-eyed Pug dog—appeared in the entrance . . . and then a small troop of Non-Citizens marched into the room.

Eli offered an embarrassed smile as he said to Elizabeth, "*This* is what I was trying to tell you about." He waved to and greeted a few of the homeless people as they continued to pile into the room. They spread out and found different crates to sit on, or curled up on the floor—none of them took any notice of the dazed Elizabeth, who pulled her top back into place.

One of the last NCs, a cute waif girl, walked between them saying, "Hi, Mister Eli."

"Hey, Sara," Eli returned.

Elizabeth stared at the Citizen before her in wonder.

The burly man—having passed the dog to one of the older NC children—ambled across to them, looked Elizabeth over, then shook his head as he pulled Eli aside. "You've *really* got to work on your approach."

Derby (Kevin Crowther) looked Elizabeth (Judy Dash) over, then shook his head and pulled Eli aside.

"Give me a break." Eli pulled away from the large man, but he was smiling the whole time. "I met her *in public*—what was I *supposed* to do?"

"Uh-huh."

"Oh, shut up," Eli said as he jokingly thumped the man on the chest and turned away, heading for the back alcove.

Elizabeth marveled at the tête-à-tête—a *Non*-Citizen giving a *Citizen* a hard time about *anything*?! As impossible as it seemed, there was clearly a *bond* between them!

She had no idea how right she was . . .

*

Eli had known "Derby" for years, almost as long as he had known Nora. Their meeting had been at a critical point in Eli's life.

Eli was in cyber-tech school at the time. His parents had been dead for nearly six years, and he'd been more cut off from Nora than ever before. Puberty sometimes made it difficult to remember his father's lessons, as it suddenly seemed much more important to fit in and make friends. He was still a few years away from meeting Jacob, and he was struggling to make it through the loneliest time of his life.

And something else was changing for him—he was starting to really notice girls. It was this particular frontier, in fact, that led him to Derby for the first time.

Some of Eli's classmates—he could no longer recall their names—of the same age and budding interests sympathized with Eli's new curiosity and decided to "help him out."

"Meet us at the main gate one hour after curfew," they told him.

"Why?" he asked.

"Just be there," they insisted with knowing grins.

Eli met the three boys as instructed. Any one of them knew enough about the IDCs to override the security lock and escape into the city proper, but Eli let one of the others do the honors that night. He was both excited and nervous about the evening's mysterious outing, and he was more than happy to follow the others' lead.

At first, the quartet of underage boys merely took pleasure in flaunting authority and running around after-hours. Their illicit journey eventually carried them into the older parts of town. In another age, the run-down terrain might have instilled fear in the young boys' hearts, but no longer—they were Citizens, and the only "street people" anymore were Non-Citizens. And NCs knew to keep their place.

Unfortunately, that catch-phrase had a whole different meaning to Eli's companions.

As they cut through an alleyway, the other boys confused Eli when they suddenly slowed down and shifted from ignoring the NCs to inspecting them. He tried to ask one of them what they were up to, but he was shushed for his efforts. Eli grew more and more restless until finally—and unfortunately—the boys found what they were looking for.

"You," the oldest boy commanded, "come with us."

The NC whom he addressed, a not-unattractive woman in her early twenties, looked up at them in sleepy confusion.

"Hey, do you see this?" the boy barked, holding his right hand so that his dark Citizen's chip was visible. He then used the same hand to slap her, hard. "I told you to come with us. Do you want me to call an Organizer?"

The NC struggled to her feet. She towered over the young boys, and Eli knew that if it weren't for her social status, she probably could have resisted them with some success.

Eli's schoolmates led him and the NC further into the alley. Once they reached its dead end, they sent the remaining NCs away and ordered their victim to strip.

"Um, guys . . . ?" Eli stammered even as his eyes widened in awe of the fully-developed female exposing herself for him.

"I get her first," one of the others argued.

"No way. You had the last *one first, remember?"*

"That doesn't count! She didn't even have teeth*!"*

"Shut up," the oldest boy again took charge. "You really *want to be fair?* Eli *should get her first. He's never even* done it *before!"*

"That true, Barrett?"

Eli nodded numbly, his jaw slackened—the NC now stood completely naked, one hand shamefully resting in front of her privates down there, *the other hand and arm trying to hide her breasts. The other boys laughed at Eli's tied tongue.*

"Come on, man," they urged. "Kiss her! Touch her! Use her*!"*

As guilty as it made him feel, Eli was *tempted. After all, she was an* NC. *And it wasn't as if they were* raping *her or anything—she was just standing there, not putting up any kind of a fight.*

Would it really be that *wrong?*

Of course it would—and Eli knew it.

They urged him on. He refused. They blew him off, jeering at him as a lost cause and a faggot, and moved in themselves.

And he tried to stop them.

Strictly speaking, it wasn't the smartest move he could have made. Maybe he'd inherited his father's spiritual strength and maybe he hadn't, but Mencer had never placed a great emphasis on fighting skills. *The three boys made short work of Eli, and he might not have even* survived *the incident if it hadn't been for Derby.*

Two of them were holding Eli on either side while the oldest boy pommeled him. Eli's vision was starting to blur, so he didn't notice the large man moving in with impressive stealth. The oldest boy cried out when his arm suddenly wrenched back out of its socket. The other boys released their hold on Eli, who dropped to one knee.

"Hey!" one of them whined, his voice trembling. "You—you— . . . you can't do *that! You're an* NC*!"*

"Really?" the derby-wearing giant replied with a crooked grin. He looked down at his clear chip as though seeing it for the first time. "I hadn't noticed."

Eli coughed, gaping at the burly vagrant. The oldest boy whimpered and sobbed, clutching at his swelling joint. "I-I-I'm gonna tell the Organizers!" he wailed.

The man didn't so much as blink. "You're on the wrong side of town, kid. I'd quit while you're ahead." One of the others took a sideways step, but the man froze him with a look. "Don't even think about it."

He didn't have to elaborate—they stood their ground.

Reaching out, the NC helped Eli stand. "You okay?"

Eli nodded.

*"That was pretty brave of you, takin' up for a Non-Citizen like that." The man chuckled. "*Stupid, *but brave. What's your name?"*

"One-One-Eight—"

"Your name, *kid."*

". . . Eli."

" 'Eli,' huh? You can call me Derby. *Why're you here with these punks anyway?"*

"I . . . I wanted to make friends."

Derby laughed harder at that. " 'Friends,' huh? You've really *got to work on your approach . . . "*

The incident really could *have led to quite a bit of trouble—*Execution Channel *trouble—for Derby, but the boys never reported it. Maybe they were humbled and cowed by the experience, learning a new respect for the neglected half of society. Or maybe it was the fact that Eli threatened to drain their IDCs of all their credits if they* didn't *keep their silence.*

One could never be certain . . .

*

Elizabeth Hudson, holding Hannah close to her breast, knew *none* of this, of course, as she watched the adult Eli playfully thump the older Derby on the chest and move back into the rear alcove of the storage bunker. She merely looked on in amazement as the Citizen began passing out blankets, starting with two mulatto children.

Eli motioned to the waif girl—*Sara* he had called her—and asked her to take over as he stepped back out into the main room once more. Derby caught his eye and met him halfway.

"Where's Nora?"

"I don't know," Derby replied, as though it was a subject he'd intended to breach on his own. "I haven't seen her all week."

Eli sighed. "The food?"

Derby grunted at that. "Late, as usual."

Eli rolled his eyes and marched out to the main entrance.

Food? The food?

Elizabeth's breath quickened. This couldn't really be happening, could it? A Citizen providing shelter and blankets and . . . *food*? She *had* to know!

Following him, she asked tentatively, "Eli . . . ?"

But she didn't get any further. Eli held up a hand to cut her off as a new set of footsteps sounded from the stairs. A few seconds later, a man appeared, a medium-sized cardboard box in his hands. Eli stepped out to meet the newcomer.

"You ready?" the Food Park attendant demanded, as though *he* had been kept waiting. Eli shook his head in annoyance but said nothing as he reached out to take the man's burden.

The attendant pulled the box away. "*Credits first.*" He extended the debit scanner, a portable version of the one he used in the Food Park. "And hurry up. I . . . I don't feel too good."

Eli considered the sweat running down the man's face and dampening his shirt. "Again?"

"*Still,*" was the his only answer.

Letting the subject drop, Eli linked his IDC to the scanner as Derby joined them. The device began siphoning his credits.

"Got careless at the Food Park today."

Eli knew the man was referring to the cross. He switched the scanner from his IDC to the attendant's, reversing the process and *adding* the credits as per their usual agreement. Hoping to downplay the incident—especially in front of Derby—Eli merely responded, "Uh, yeah. Sorry about that. Thanks again."

The credit transaction completed, Eli returned the man's scanner, and he in turn passed the box to Derby. Stuffing the device back into his belt, the attendant turned toward the stairs.

"See you again next week?" Eli asked.

The man glanced at him . . . then left without answering.

Eli and Derby exchanged a weary look. They'd both noted their food contact's growing distress over the last few months, and had discussed their mutual concern that his reliability was waning. Then Eli felt even worse when he stepped over and made his first real inspection of the box's contents.

"Is it just me," Derby mused as they took in the bread rolls, apples, oranges . . . all told, about *half* as much as the attendant usually provided, "or is he gettin' *skimpy* on us?"

Eli wanted to shout, to swear, to chase after the man and *demand* to know what the hell he thought he was doing . . . but instead he bit back his frustration as best he could and said, "It's better than nothing. Pass it out."

Elizabeth let Eli pass her without a word. Her questions forgotten, her undivided attention fixated on the box of food in Derby's arms.

She didn't have to wait long. Derby reached into the box, fished out an apple, and extended it to her. She seized it, and sank her teeth in for several hearty bites in a single breath.

A few minutes later, Eli made his way to Sara and another girl, both of whom were sitting on a crate and reading an oversized book. He bent and held a piece of fruit and bread out to each of them. "Thank you," they echoed as they dove in with vigor similar to Elizabeth's.

As they chewed their food, Eli casually picked up the book they'd been sharing. He recognized it immediately as *Windsong*, a popular children's piece from his parents' days—his mother had read it to him more than once, although he'd forgotten the details over the years. He remembered three intertwined stories in three different time periods—medieval times, a Western, a prehistoric era—but he no longer recalled *how* they connected to one another. But he hadn't seen this, or any *other* children's books, in a very long time.

Sara, sensing his surprise, mumbled around her mouthful, "My Guardian Angel gave it to me," as if that explained everything.

" 'Guardian Angel?' " he echoed, but the girl had returned her attention to the meal at hand.

"Don't you believe in Guardian Angels?"

Eli looked over his shoulder to the new voice, and answered Elizabeth with a shrug. "Yeah, sure, I guess. I just didn't know they gave out children's books." He returned *Windsong* to its owner and stood.

"Only food and shelter?" Elizabeth challenged—with her eyes lowered. Eli stared at her for a moment, then accepted her point with a grin, so Elizabeth pressed on. "I can't believe there aren't *more people* here. Surely the other NCs—"

"Well, yeah, word gets around," Eli acknowledged, "more than I'd *like*, actually. But most of them are too afraid."

"Afraid?" Elizabeth marveled as apple juice ran down her chin.

He nodded. "This whole set-up would be *conveniently* considered a 'public assembly' . . . not to mention the fact that they'd want to know where all the fresh food came from. That apple feels good in your stomach right now, but if we were *caught* tonight, *I'd* lose my Citizenship, and *you'd* be barred from the next Vocational Screening."

Elizabeth accepted the last part. Most Non-Citizens were starving, yes, but they also *hoped* to one day achieve the status of "Confirmed Citizen"—after all, the System needed to keep its workforce strong, and it couldn't very well wait for young Citizens to grow up to replace retired, removed, or *deleted* adults. After all, productive Citizens were the strength of their union, and NCs were productive when they kept their place, yes? Getting a mouthful of bread wouldn't be worth the risk for many of them.

But all this merely explained why many NCs would stay away, in the fear of missing out on what they *might* have—it said nothing of the man who truly had so much to *lose.*

"If this is so dangerous," she began, and Eli immediately grew uncomfortable, "how come you—?"

Eli waved it away as though it were nothing. "It's . . . because I made a promise to someone," he said as he moved away from her. "It's no big deal."

" '*No big deal*?' " Elizabeth repeated incredulously. "Look at everything that you're *doing* here—"

Eli turned back to her, and there was heat in his eyes—not *fire*, but definitely heat. "It's *no—big—deal* . . . all *right*?"

Elizabeth cowered, dropping her gaze and holding her baby closer, the rest of the apple momentarily forgotten. Eli realized immediately what he had done, the buttons he had unintentionally pushed, and guilt washed over him . . . which only frustrated him *more*. He swallowed the apology that sought to escape his lips and bolted for the main door.

He didn't make it. At the threshold, Derby—who had witnessed the entire exchange—seized him by the shoulders.

"Hold up there," he chided. Eli gritted his teeth, but allowed Derby to maintain his hold as the grip slowly turned into a pacifying massage. A bit of the tension slipped away under his friend's warm tone. "*Eeaaasy*, big fella . . . that's the *ghosts* talkin' . . . juuust let it go."

Eli sighed, and suddenly felt the need to explain himself, his outburst. "It's just that people expect *so much*. You know what I should do is just stop *nursing* everyone and let them learn how to take care of *themselves* for a change."

Derby wasn't buying any of it. "What about *Nora*?"

At that harsh reality-check, Eli shrugged the man's hands away and shot him a look that would have withered any other NC in the room. "What *about* her?" He held Derby's unwavering gaze for a moment longer, then stomped out of the room.

Timidly, cautiously, Elizabeth—who had listened to *Derby's* conversation with Eli, just as the burly man had listened to *hers*—walked up to join her fellow NC as he stared after the Citizen. Derby noticed her and offered his warm grin.

"Sorry he went off on you like that," he told her gently. "He gets testy when he's forced to look in the mirror." He shrugged. "That's just Eli."

Elizabeth nodded, even though she didn't really understand what Derby meant, and asked, "Who's Nora?"

Derby's mood sobered a bit. "Someone he cares a whole lot about." Then, almost as an afterthought, he added, "She tried to save his mom's life."

"Did she raise him?"

"Well, actually, the *System* raised him, back when they still had Child Services—taught him skills he's been usin' *against* them ever since." The big man smirked at that. "But he never forgot Nora. Treats her like *family*."

Elizabeth considered this for a moment, then peeked outside the room. Eli hadn't gone far—he sat on the bottom step of the staircase, his head hanging. Drawing a breath, she handed Hannah to a bewildered Derby and stepped toward him.

Finding her words still caught in her throat, she drew a second breath and called gently, "Eli . . . ?"

Eli looked up, his expression torn and dejected. He rose and met her halfway. "Elizabeth," he said, "I'm sorry."

Her own words of apology dried up once more. Instead, Elizabeth hugged him tightly, and this time Eli allowed her to have her moment. She kissed his cheek, looked into his impossibly kind eyes one last time, then retreated back into the room—after reclaiming her daughter from a now *very grateful* Derby.

Derby breathed his relief, then joined Eli. "Okay, Mr. Wonderful," he said with a mischievous gleam in his eye, "even *you* need to sleep. I'll lock up here."

Eli slapped Derby on the arm to say *thanks* in more ways than one, then turned to climb the stairs. At the last second, a thought halted him. "Derby," he called.

Derby faced him once more.

"What *is* Nora's IDC number? It's . . . I've been calling people by their *names* for so long, I can't remember."

Derby searched his own memory and came up with, "Eight-Five—"

Eli joined in as they both finished, "Oh-Eight-Oh." Derby nodded, and Eli agreed, "That's it. All right, thanks." Drudging up the stairs, he began reciting the number aloud to make sure he didn't forget it. "Eight-Five-Oh-Eight-Oh, Eight-Five-Oh-Eight-Oh . . . "

Eli's voice trailed away into the distance as Derby returned to the storage room. He dragged the large door behind him, and its metallic *thud* echoed throughout the basement.

DISCREPANCY FOUND

Another day, another dollar.

The Data Processing Center's usual quiet was broken only by the hacking cough of a Citizen in the grips of a chest cold. Illness in the work place was not an uncommon thing—most Citizens *preferred* to take their chances with whatever ailed them than to enter into what passed these days for their HMO program. Some things changed, some things stayed the same.

Jacob hovered by the assignment rack next to the entrance. A few of his co-workers glanced at him as they collected their waiting gel disks, and Jacob pretended to look his own disks over, supposedly evaluating his assignments. He was merely stalling, biding his time until . . .

Eli emerged from the stairwell, immediately gathered his assignment disks, and strode past his flabbergasted station partner. Jacob had expected at least a *word* of explanation for his tardiness—at which Jacob had been preparing to turn and ignore *him*. With his cold-shoulder attempt thwarted, he could think of nothing else to do or say except, "You're *late*."

"I am?" Eli responded, totally uninterested. He passed Dana as he looked over his workload.

Dana glanced up at him as she worked her hair into a ponytail. "You look beat."

"I am," Eli agreed.

He reached his work station, dropped his gel disks to one side, and took a seat. Without further adieu, he pulled the scrambler's wires from their hidden place up his sleeve, connected it to his IDC, and plunged his hand into the interface gel.

It may not have been the *wisest* move this early in the work shift, while some of the other Citizens had yet to log into their own cyber-limbos, but he'd spent the last few sleepless hours dwelling over his concern for Nora, and he wasn't willing to wait even one more minute—not if he could find out what had happened to her.

>DATA REQUEST: he thought at his cyber counter-part. >SEARCH FOR ANY SECTOR NOTATIONS FOR NON-CITIZEN NUMBER EIGHT-FIVE-ZERO-EIGHT-ZERO WITHIN THE LAST EIGHT DAYS.

>>*NOTATIONS FOUND* . . . his double responded, >>*NONE.*

Reaching across with his left hand, Eli fine-tuned his scrambler.

>DATA REQUEST: he repeated. >*ANY* TRACE OF NON-CITIZEN EIGHT-FIVE-ZERO-EIGHT-ZERO IN THIS SECTOR WITHIN THE LAST EIGHT DAYS—SEARCH LEVEL PRIORITY ONE-ALPHA-BLUE.

>>*SEARCH IN PROGRESS* . . . The image froze for a moment, punctuated by a pseudo-digital flicker. Then the Computer-Eli announced, >>*TRACE SIGNATURE OF SUBJECT'S IDC FOUND IN* DREAM PARLOR *MAINFRAME.*

What the hell. . .?!

>LIST NOTATION OF NON-CITIZEN'S *LOG-IN* TO *DREAM PARLOR.*

>>*NOTATIONS FOUND . . . NONE. SUBJECT DID NOT LOG-IN TO* DREAM PARLOR.

>ARE NCs ALLOWED—?

">>>*WARNING,* Computer-Eli announced, "raising" its voice

significantly and startling him. >>>*DISCREPANCY FOUND IN SEARCH AUTHORIZATION. IMMEDIATE CONFIRMATION—*

>DISCONTINUE SEARCH, he ordered posthaste. >RETRACT DATA REQUEST FROM *DREAM PARLOR* MAINFRAME.

>>. . . *ERROR OVERRIDE. TERMINAL SYSTEMS RESTORED. DO YOU WISH TO CONTINUE . . . ?*

Eli pulled his hand from the interface gel with a jolt. His heart raced, his adrenalin pumping heavily into his coursing bloodstream. His mouth felt dry and his stomach sat heavy and cold in his gut. He wasn't accustomed to underestimating security protocols . . .

Or is that over*estimating the scrambler?*

. . . but he was much more rattled and disconcerted by what his search *had* turned up.

Trace signature in the Dream Parlor *Mainframe?* It didn't make any sense. As far as Eli knew, Non-Citizens weren't even *allowed* to use the *Parlor*, and even if they were, the computer *also* insisted that Nora never walked through the door, never officially logged-in. It was like finding her fingerprints inside a vault that had been sealed years before she was born. So how in the hell . . . ?

Eli felt eyes on him, and turned to meet Jacob's typically disapproving stare. Between his close call with cyber-limbo security and the baffling Nora Enigma, he just wasn't in the mood. "Do your workload," he snapped at his station-partner, throwing Jacob's infamous slogan in his face before he could issue that very platitude.

Miffed, and maybe even a little embarrassed, Jacob stiffened and plugged into his interface gel.

That's right, Jacob. You do your *workload, and I'll do* mine.

Count *on it . . .*

BREAK THE RULES

First things first . . .

The flourescents flickered to life as Eli entered his living unit. Without even closing the door, he strode to his cot, punched the control box, and started purposefully channel surfing . . . seeking . . . *searching*. A couple of *Dream Parlor* commercials flashed by, but he needed one in particular, the one he'd seen just last night. Until recently, he'd never had much interest in or paid much attention to the *Parlor*, so he needed to start by being *sure* . . .

Come on . . . come on . . . there!

". . . go *anywhere*, do *anything . . . no questions asked.*"

As Eli moved to the end of his cot and stared at the image, he realized that it was, in fact, a slightly different version of the earlier commercial. The imagery was the same, climaxing with the giant Citizen's hand, but the words had been reedited and switched a bit, so what had been near the end of the commercial—"no questions asked"—was now closer to the middle.

He listened intently.

The accented woman continued, "*Live for your dreams* here, *at the original* Dream Parlor—or, *experience the* rest *of your life at one of our convenient world-wide outlets.*"

Finally, the send off. The words appeared over the dark IDC, and Eli and the mawkish man said it together: "*For* Confirmed Citizens *only.*"

Bingo.

So, he was right. The *Dream Parlor* was still promoted as a Citizen-exclusive luxury.

But what did all of this *mean*?

Nora's IDC was scanned somewhere inside, but she had *not* logged in as an official customer. She'd interacted with the *Parlor's* mainframe, yet should never have been allowed through the door. And his cyber-limbo counterpart had only reported a *trace* signature, which suggested that someone had then gone back and *deleted* whatever her specific activities had been . . . but what would be the point of *that*?

He sighed, more confused than ever. He didn't trust the *Parlor*—nor would he trust anything promoted so blatantly by the System—but what was the next step? After his *first* close call, accessing the *Parlor's* compumatrix didn't sound particularly appealing . . . although he'd already come up with a few new frequencies he could try. Still, what else was there for him to do?

The *Dream Parlor* had apparently been the last place Nora used her IDC. He wanted, *needed* to know what had happened to her, and the *Parlor* was his only lead. He supposed he could visit the *Parlor* himself and take a look around. Walk right into the lion's den . . .

Well, maybe *that* was an exaggeration. Maybe he was making too much out of the *Dream Parlor*, being a little too *paranoid*, as Jacob was always insisting. He always tried to evaluate these things like he thought his father would, but what he had told Jacob yesterday was true. The NCs, people like Elizabeth, tried to build him into so much more than he really was. Feeding homeless people and planting viruses behind the safety of his scrambler was one thing . . . but he was *not* his father. Mencer Barrett had been a *hero,* had always known what do to and what to think. Eli was just . . . Eli. Without knowing everything involved, *should* he risk a trip to the *Parlor* . . . ?

A shuffle brought his attention to the right. Sara, the waif girl, had wandered into his room. Her attention was on his hand towel—his *clean, white, soft* towel—by the sink, and she gently rubbed its appealing fluff against her young cheek.

"Hey, Sara," he offered with a distracted smile.

"Hey," she returned, drifting deeper into the room. "You left your door open back there."

Suddenly, Eli had a thought. "That's all right. Can I ask you a question?"

She had reached the toilet and casually picked up the roll of toilet paper. "Sure. Go ahead." She began wrapping a large wad of the paper around her hand to take with her when she left—she knew that Eli wouldn't mind.

"You know how you guys don't have the same things that . . . well, people like *me* do. Good food, shelter . . . things like that. Do you know what I mean?"

She tore off the toilet paper and stuffed the wad into her pocket as she walked over to him. "Yeah," was her expectant reply. He knew that if it had been any Citizen other than himself, she would have been more *leery* of such a peculiar, obvious query—for *him,* it was simply, *you* are *going somewhere with this, right?*

Eli licked his lips. "Do you know anyone who *breaks* the rules? Let's you do things you're not supposed to?"

She was beside him now, longingly fingering the knickknacks on his small shelves. She picked up one trinket as she replied, "Is this a trick question? Cause *you* break the rules all the time." Her tone suggested that she'd decided he wasn't going anywhere important with this after all.

Sara (Joey Norcliffe) was beside him now, longingly fingering the knickknacks on his small shelves.

"No, what I mean is, do you know of anybody, any *Non*-Citizens, who've ever gone to the *Dream Parlor*?"

She rolled her eyes. "Why you askin' such lame questions? I thought you was *smart*."

Eli snorted at that. "So did *I*. I don't suppose you've seen Miss *Nora* today, have you?"

"Nuh-huh." She turned his hour-glass over and watched the sand begin its descent. "Why?"

He shook his head. "My *computer* says she's been to the *Dream Parlor*," he said with frustrated disgust.

"Computers suck," she told him knowingly.

Eli chuckled at that briefly, then glanced at his watch. "You'd better get out of here, hon. The Organizers make their rounds soon."

She sighed heavily in resignation. With one last look at the stuff on the shelves, she turned to leave, grumbling, "Maaannnn . . . I *hate* those guys."

She made it all the way to the door before stopping. Stepping back into the room, she got his attention with, "Hey, Mister Eli?" When he turned to regard her once more, she continued, "If you *really* wanna know about the *Parlor*, why don't ya just go check it out for *yourself*?" She then turned and left, closing the door behind her.

Eli had to smile. *Out of the mouth of babes . . .* He glanced over at the hour-glass and its growing mountain of time in the bottom bell.

Of course, all he had to do was picture Nora's face, and he knew that there had never been any real choice at all.

Some decisions you make, and some decisions are made for you.

The sand poured on . . .

SOMEONE WHO ELUDES YOU

The architecture was different.

That was the first thing Eli noticed on his way to the world-renowned *Dream Parlor*. Even before he reached the building, even before he reached the plaza, a completely new flavor stole its way into the decor. The subtrain terminal near his complex was drab and colorless, focused on raw efficiency rather than taste. The platforms, the subtrains, the stairwells leading to and fro . . . all steel, concrete, and somber austerity.

The *Dream Parlor* terminal—and that's literally what it was, as there were no other locations listed for this stop—introduced a new appeal to the standard design. The walls throughout the terminal and along one side of the stairwell were aged brick. The floors were tiled, the ceiling was high, and the colors were earth tones versus shades of gray. There were fewer flourescents and more incandescents.

Organizer visibility was noticeably higher. A trip through most terminals revealed one bored official, maybe two—Eli passed three on his way to the stairs, and two more on his way out to the plaza. As he might have guessed, there was not a single NC in sight.

And then he stepped *outside*.

The expansive plaza offered few distractions. The terminal building was on one end, the *Parlor* on the other. A discreet fountain adorned the very center of the plaza, but other than that there was *nothing* to digress from the grandeur of the *Dream Parlor*.

A hovercraft sailed overhead, its shadow passing over Eli as he halted in mid-stride to gape at the unique sight. The *Parlor* was as different in design from most modern buildings as the terminal had been from its counterparts. It was all arches and bricks, tiles and gleaming metallics. Massive steel letters forming "DREAM PARLOR," with branched girders arching out of their epicenter, slowly circled at the highest elevation. A stylized "DP" symbol—diamond cut and beveled to suggest a reverse "D" back-to-back with a forward "P"—revolved in similar fashion atop a gothic tower over the main entrance, and Eli spied a series of upper-level offices behind monumental chess-piece-like sculptures. The entire complex was full of golds and bronzes, warm yellows and greens . . . colors Eli hadn't seen in mass quantities in a very long time.

The *Dream Parlor* was all arches and bricks, tiles and gleaming metallics.

And there was another major difference, one subtle enough to almost slip past his notice, but obvious enough that he was embarrassed he didn't catch it immediately: *There was no rhetoric.*

"Productive Citizens" this, "Non-Productive Citizens" that . . . the incessant *blathering,* so familiar that he didn't really *hear* it anymore . . . and now it felt as though something essential was *missing.* Funny how a person grew accustomed to things, even when they were *annoying* as hell.

The plaza was far from silent, though. Another voice, also familiar, articulated a different kind of verbiage . . .

"*Welcome to the* Dream Parlor . . . " The same voice from the *Dream Parlor* commercials.

Eli shook himself from his reverie and resumed his stride.

"*You are now entering a world of* pure imagination, *a realm of* lucid dreams . . . "

Near the *Parlor's* entrance, atop a triad of bronze trusses, a holographic sphere within oscillating discs displayed the stylized likeness of an Asian woman. The image was sculpted blue-chrome-and-shadow, a touch that Eli found both engaging and conspicuously high-tech.

"*Journey to the summit of your* greatest hopes . . . "

Eli stared up at the image for a few moments. Citizens passed back and forth, coming and going through three different doors into the *Parlor.*

"*Explore the depths of your most* primitive desires . . . "

What a different world they'd created here. So rich, so enticing. He could see how Jacob and the others found it so appealing, and he hadn't even set foot *inside* the place yet.

Turning, he afforded the briefest glance at the trio of entrances. *Abyss, Sanctuary, Alternative.* At the moment he could only guess at their specific meanings, so he arbitrarily moved toward *Abyss,* simply because it was the closest.

Eli's thoughts were inward, and his head was down, so he collided with the woman who suddenly bolted from the door. The two slammed into one another, but she kept walking. Eli was turning to apologize when he realized who it was.

"Dana," he said, somewhat relieved to see a friendly face in this alien environment.

Dana kept going.

"Dana!" he called, following after her.

Finally she stopped and rocked back on her heels. Eli opened his mouth, prepared to offer a "finally gave in" reference to his first *Parlor* visit, but he stopped cold.

Dana's eyes were glazed over. She appeared breathless and confused at first, but in the next heartbeat she looked as though she were going to cry. She swayed on her feet, her hand pressed to her temple. She was looking at him, but there was no recognition in her face.

"Dana?"

She cocked her head to one side, then gasped. Her expression became both stark and vaguely amused. "H—hhhi, Eli," she giggled. Then she looked lost again.

"Are you okay?" he asked. His eyes flickered past her, around her, for just a moment. Something must be wrong—other people were leaving the *Parlor* in a steady stream, with no hint of the turmoil that gripped his friend.

Dana's arms rose, and she pressed her hands against both temples now. She bit down on a strong chuckle as she wheeled around and continued on her way.

"Dana, *are you okay*?"

She ignored him completely this time, laughing not-so-quietly to herself.

Aghast, Eli stared after her. His impulse was to chase her down and drag her back inside—surely the *Parlor* staff would have some idea of what was happening to her. But then, he'd never been here before, and while no one else leaving the place appeared affected like this, Dana's little display hadn't attracted any undue attention either. Oh, he knew better than to expect anything more than *apathy* from most Citizens, but human curiosity would usually illicit at least a few stares. Maybe Dana's reaction wasn't all that out of the ordinary around here—he just didn't know.

Feeling torn, he slowly turned back to the *Parlor*—his own reasons for coming still stood. Maybe he'd give Dana a call when he got back home.

Just before he entered the door Dana had emerged from, he again considered the title above— *Abyss* . . .

He altered his course and instead opted for the door marked *Sanctuary*.

* * *

Feeling strangely dream-like—which he supposed was fitting—Eli strode into the open, welcoming lobby.

Again, tiles and arches, warm earth tones and glistening golds, this time brushing dangerously close to gaudy. The lobby was spacious, high-ceilinged and inviting, with stained-glass windows at the far end. Dozens of Citizens sat in chairs around the outside perimeter of the room, and more stood randomly through the center, each of those speaking to *Dream Parlor* attendants in royal blue vestments. The room was oddly quiet considering the number of people. A PA system called out various numbers as softly as such a system could. As Eli crossed the room, however, he became aware of one raised voice.

The reception desk seated a single hostess with a massive, multi-ported IDC scanner to her side. IDC scanners were a fact of day-to-day life, but Eli found this one over-sized and over-designed, as if the unit had been purposely restructured to fit into the surroundings, and the result was questionable at best. The hostess, a middle-aged blonde, was receiving a tongue-lashing from an outspoken elderly woman.

"*No*," the older woman insisted. "I don't *like* that young fellow—he's a *pervert*. I want to see *Doctor Corbit*!"

"Doctor Corbit is a very busy man," the hostess explained, sounding very close to the end of her rope. "He has *other* clients. Please take a seat."

The patron *harrumphed*, "Screw you, girly," as she stormed away.

As the old woman retreated, Eli stepped into her place at the reception desk. The hostess regarded him with tired eyes, her manners edged. "May I *help* you?"

Eli hesitated briefly as he noticed the woman's fingernails for the first time—they were garish, each one the length of the finger itself and painted fire-red. The detail struck Eli as extremely odd—he'd never seen anyone wear such a style before, let alone in the hub of such Citizen activity. How strange that such a "prestigious" place as the *Dream Parlor* would allow it . . . unless they were trying to suggest that personal freedoms could run *rampant* in this place. Or maybe . . .

Eli realized the woman was swiftly losing her patience. Not having the first clue about *Parlor* etiquette, he offered, "I've never been here before."

Suddenly, the hostess was all smiles. "Ah, well, good evening, sir. Scan your chip, please." She indicated not the monstrosity to her right, but a more standard port on her left.

As Eli complied, she called out, waving her hand with its extreme nails, "Derek, a new client would like to see you."

A tall, spindly, spotlessly polished man joined them immediately. He did not wear a blue smock like the other personnel Eli had noticed, but a *Dream Parlor* badge—gold diamond letters within a red circle against a black surface—proudly adorned his dark jacket. He elaborately shook Eli's hand. "Great, marvelous. I'll be your host. Follow me."

Eli followed Derek, passing the elderly woman as she stomped back to the desk.

"Damn it," she swore at the hostess, "I was here *first*!"

* * *

". . . uh-huh. I see. Now, *Corbit* . . . he's the man who invented this place, right? I think I saw a documentary on television."

"Ah! No doubt. It seems the *only* place you can see Doctor

Corbit these days is on the dip-chip. But we're here to talk about *you*, Eli. How can I best serve *you*?"

Derek's "office"—if that's what it was called—was another oversized room. The ceiling was painted with billowy white clouds against a perfectly blue sky—perhaps suggesting "the sky's the limit?"—but the walls and decor were the same gold tones as the rest of the building. Two textured pillars rose to a tier of conspicuous spotlights—the center light shone straight down onto the flowery couch, the only furniture the room had to offer, and Eli and Derek were seated together beneath its hot shaft.

"I, uh, I don't really even know what you *do* here, it's just that—"

Derek laughed. Eli shifted uncomfortably, pressing against his side of the couch as Derek scooted closer. This was the first aspect of the *Parlor* that struck Eli as particularly *un*inviting—the air had become thick and uncomfortable to him, almost like a *bad date*, as the sales rep continued to violate his personal space. If Derek noticed Eli's unease, he didn't seem to care as he gripped the small pillow between them and moved it to one side.

"A little *nervous*, huh? I can assure you, Eli, you have absolutely *nothing* to fear."

Eli sighed inwardly. *Well, if I have to* put up *with this, I might as well get something* out *of it.* He moved his gaze from the far corner of the room back to the obnoxious salesman. "Do *Non*-Citizens get this privilege?"

"Only in their dreams."

Derek burst into laughter at his own joke. Eli *had* to look away again as he forced a polite chuckle of his own and rolled his eyes.

Think of Nora, think of Nora . . .

"Now," Derek continued after a moment, "let's pick a setting, and you can tell me what it is that you *like*."

This was the kind of opening Eli had been waiting for. "Actually, I have a *friend* who had this setting that she really enjoyed, but I can't remember what it was." Derek slumped slightly and rested his elbow on the back of the couch to press his hand to his temple—it apparently stole his thunder to lose control of the conversation, but he said nothing, so Eli pressed forward. "My friend's a short woman, a little plump, Hispanic, looks about fifty." Derek's face remained blank, and he shook his head slightly. "She was just here last week." Still nothing—in fact, Derek looked increasingly bored. "*Nora Puente*?"

Derek shook his head firmly this time. "Sorry," he said flatly. "Doesn't ring any bells."

"Can't you just punch up her number?"

Derek sailed right over that suggestion with a muttered, "Confidential," and used it as a springboard to launch back into his arena, "but I'm sure we can make *your* dream as real as your friend's."

Eli clenched his jaw and looked away. *Damn it.*

"Now, is there anything . . . *specific* you would like included in your dream . . . "

Eli wasn't usually one to give up easily, but now he felt *stupid* for coming here. The place was crawling with patrons—did he really expect any of the staff members to *remember* Nora, even if she did somehow manage to get inside?

". . . a *man*, a *woman* . . . someone who *eludes* you in real life . . . "

Someone who eludes *you in real life . . .*

Derek's words suddenly sank in. Eli had only come here to find out what he could about Nora, but as the sales rep continued, *another* possibility occurred to him. He fished into one of his pockets.

". . . *fantasies* . . . *obsessions* . . . anything at all . . . "

Pulling a sheet of paper into view, Eli quickly unfolded it to reveal his unfinished drawing of the woman he had been seeing on the train recently. His heart began to beat faster as he handed the drawing to Derek.

The salesman considered the illustration, his expression somewhere between *confusion* and *amusement.* "I, uh, would *assume* that you would want her to have a *face* . . . "

"This one's not finished," Eli said hurriedly, a new goal now looming before him. "I know what she looks like. I don't want you to *generate* anything, just . . . " God, could this *really* be possible? ". . . *put* her there?"

Derek chuckled and refolded the drawing. "It's *your* dream," he answered assuringly. "Now, let's pick a setting."

"That's *it*?"

Derek smiled knowingly and gripped Eli's shoulder. "We just point you in the *right direction*, and your *own mind* takes it from there." He then stood—taking the folded drawing with him—and waltzed very slowly to the center of the room. "After all, you are a Citizen—why not take advantage of the gratification that you are rightly entitled to?" When he stood aligned so Eli could just see the stone-on-wood "DP" symbol on the far wall, he spun on his heel to face Eli once more. Another of the lights over Eli's head *clicked* to life, spotting Derek perfectly like a showman. Eli glanced up at the source in brief surprise, but Derek didn't let his attention wander for more than a heartbeat. He spread his arms and continued, "Here at the *Dream Parlor*, you can be . . . *every . . . thing* . . . you . . . want. Go *any*where, do *any*thing . . . *no questions asked*."

For the very first time, those words—and the unlimited *potential* therein—*enthralled* Elijah Barrett . . .

DANGER

A pulse. A strobing light.

Drifting off after hours of sleeplessness, and nodding off for the briefest moment while trying to stay awake.

A single heartbeat. A flash.

An endless voyage, and a swift journey.

Natural. Alien.

* * *

When Eli opened his eyes again, he was already standing. Standing on a hillside. A beautiful *hillside.*

He thought it'd been mild culture shock to see the colorful Dream Parlor, *but that experience was nothing*—less *than nothing—compared to* this.

Billowy white clouds against a perfectly blue sky . . . except this time it wasn't painted on the ceiling of a salesman's office. This time it was real *. . . or at least as real as the* Parlor *could make it, and that was enough.*

The sweeping, thigh-high grass rolling against the gentle wind in rippling waves, butterflies the likes of which Eli hadn't seen in a decade,

When Eli opened his eyes again, he was standing on a beautiful hillside.

and the air *. . . so clean, so* pure *. . . As he had acclimated to the endless public ranting of the Organizers' rhetoric, Eli suddenly realized that he'd grown equally accustomed to the stale, sweaty air that was now a fact of life.*

Then he looked down at himself, *down at the vermilion, gold, olive, and tan of his medieval attire. On one side a dirk, on the other a magnificent sword. A ringed vest upon his chest, and a rich cloak draped across the breadth of his shoulders. Searching fingers also confirmed the presence of a neatly-trimmed mustache-and-goatee Van Dyke.*

Just like the Prince on the cover of young Sara's Windsong *book.*

Funny how the subconscious mind works.

With an easy stride, Eli moved down the slope, taking in all of the splendor every step of the way. Birds chirped their sweet song . . . another *aspect of Nature he hadn't realized that he missed until he heard it once more.*

Then, as he neared a plateau, he saw her.

She sat reading a book amongst the grass and dandelions. Her back was to him, but from what he could tell, she was dressed as the Windsong *princess . . . which only made sense. Slowly, he approached her—he wanted to call out to her, but somehow doing so seemed* invasive *to the great, gentle calm about them.*

As he grew near, she closed her book and stood, but she still did not face him. Eli reached out to her . . .

. . . and she vanished in a swirling cocoon of light.

Eli's confusion lasted only a moment, for his attention drifted almost immediately to his outstretched right hand. His clean, smooth, right hand at the end of a leather arm-guard . . . a hand with no IDC.

Eli drew his unsullied hand to him, wide-eyed and disbelieving. In an instant, he recalled something that had never occurred to him before—that in all the adulthood dreams he could recollect, his IDC had always *been there, as necessary as the hand itself.*

But now it was gone. He was free. Free . . . !

Careful, Eli. It's still just a dream—don't get carried away . . .

But that inner voice was difficult to adhere to as he gaped down at the smooth skin on the back of his hand.

Then feminine laughter drifted to him on the wind. With a smile, he pursued the sound . . .

*

Time and space shifted then, as they often do in dreams. In one instant, Eli crested the hillside, and the next, he found himself in the center of an open valley . . .

. . . with the skeletal structure of a subtrain *before him.*

The effect was jarring, *to say the least—an anachronism of the worst kind in that it haunted back to an unpleasant reality from which he had been more than pleased to escape.*

It was far from a complete subtrain—floor plating, hand posts, ceiling grids, stairs. There were no walls or seats, but as Eli stepped into the frame, he heard—just for a moment—the barest hint of the rhetoric he had certainly not missed.

". . . ductive Citizens are the Strength of our . . . " *And then it was gone again.*

Reaching the end of the frame, Eli rested his boot on the first step of the exit stairs. What a strange direction this "fantasy" had taken! If his own mind *really was guiding this dream, why would he suddenly want to include a . . .*

The answer occurred to him even as he became aware of a presence behind him.

Of *course* a subtrain makes sense. Where else have I seen my Dream Woman?

He looked back up the "aisle" toward her *seat . . .*

And there she was. Standing rather than sitting, but present nevertheless. Brilliant yellow gown, salmon-hued bodice, ringlets of blonde hair trailing down her temples . . . she was dressed as he had never seen her, but it was her.

Swallowing hard, reminding himself this was his fantasy after all, he made his way back up the aisle. He crossed around her as she turned, but this time she did not vanish. He reached out and caressed her refined cheek, his breath coming faster. She looked up into his eyes, expectant. Clearly, she wasn't going anywhere.

Eli craned his neck toward her, hesitated, then leaned closer still. She did not withdraw, nor did she move to meet him—she merely waited, but with a welcoming countenance. Taking her face in both hands now, he indulged his months-long desire.

He kissed her.

And as the kiss grew in warmth, he didn't even notice as the subtrain frame dissolved into thin air . . .

*

Kissing *her wasn't the* only *months-long desire engendered within Eli's heart, and as time and space shifted once more, he found that* Parlor *dreams were more than capable of allowing their patrons to* cut to the chase, *so to speak.*

Strewn garments ringed the parameter of the small lagoon, with its high rock facing and meager waterfall. His Dream Woman lazed back in the water, the rippling waves washing over her ex-

posed body as Eli gently turned her through its beautiful clarity. He then pulled her to him, and she proved more motivated in their embrace this time as she wrapped her arms around his neck. They continued turning together as their inner fire flourished, and she drew her legs up and around him. His lips slid down her jaw to the side of her neck, and her fingers gripped the back of his hair. No words were spoken as his kisses developed into love bites, and neither paid heed when they drifted into and under the waterfall. She pulled herself up and then down onto him, and he groaned through clenched teeth—never before this moment had he been so grateful *that he'd never made use of the NC women as his classmates had insisted. They continued to spin through their passion, twisting behind and under and through the cascading waterfall. They gripped each other,* clawed *at one another. His Dream Woman reached out in blind abandon, and he clasped her fingers within his own, squeezing them like a lifeline through his own release . . .*

Afterwards they were floating together, Eli's arms wrapped around her as they nuzzled through their afterglow, when he felt her stiffen against him. He tried to kiss her, to push away whatever change the Parlor *was about to manipulate, but the Dream Woman pulled away and regarded him, almost sadly.*

Afterwards they were floating together, Eli's arms wrapped around his Dream Woman (Alison Storry).

As Eli looked on in confusion, she smiled at him one last time, then backed away. When she reached the waterfall, she lowered as though to sink below the surface, but before that could happen, she was again taken from him in a pulsing chrysalis of light . . .

I don't understand, *he thought.* Why the repeated disappearing act? If *I'm* in control here, the *last* thing I want . . .

"Elijah . . . "

Eli whirled about, seeking the source of the whisper. The water felt suddenly cold as he found no one . . .

"Elijah . . . "

Above him! Eli spun back the other direction and gazed up the rock face.

On the rise overlooking the lagoon, a shaded figure gestured down to him with an open hand. The sun blasted through the open patches in the thick clouds, and Eli could see nothing more than the man's silhouette.

"Elijah, you don't belong here," *the man whispered, his voice impossibly clear given the distance between them.*

But the waterfall no longer made sound—indeed, the entire world had gone eerily mute. There was nothing but the soft lapping of the cold water . . . and the man above him.

"There is *danger,*" *the voice warned. The hand beckoned.*

The voice was hauntingly familiar, *yet he could not place it.* What danger? *Eli wanted to demand, but his tongue felt thick and dumb in his mouth. He shivered.*

The man's head cocked to one side, as though he'd heard the question after all and contemplated the answer. If so, he chose not to elaborate as he instead whispered once more, "Elijah . . . "

* * *

In the *Dream Parlor,* Eli lay upon a dreamslab in one of the many dream rooms, his right hand within a device that was unlike any interface gel he'd ever encountered.

"*Elijah . . .* " the man whispered in his mind, "*listen to the voice . . .* "

There were no *Parlor* attendants in the room—patrons rarely required outside attention once they'd entered enhanced REM—and so no one noticed the consternation that danced across Eli's face. No one noticed his head twitching to one side, then the other.

"*Elijah . . . Elijah . . .* "

No one was in the control station, watching the small monitor scope as it registered the scribbling waveform that charted Eli's status. No one saw the waveform spike off the chart in several places . . . or the *second* waveform that trailed right behind the first.

At least, no one saw it *right away* . . .

SPIKER

Tony Paolino, Senior Technician of the original *Dream Parlor*, did not always enjoy the additional tasks that his coveted position entailed. He had freer access to the *Parlor's* services and wider influence than any of his co-workers, but he also had to answer directly to Doctor Corbit. Sometimes even this in itself wasn't all that bad—Corbit simply *ignored* the staff more often than not, so unless the Doctor was in a particularly sour mood, the most Tony usually had to deal with was disdainful apathy.

It was the *company* that the Doctor sometimes kept that really set Tony on edge.

Said company was with the Doctor tonight, and Tony procrastinated as long as he could in hopes that the "guests" would leave. He hated to interrupt Corbit on *any* occasion, but the man had standing orders that any atypically strong or "unusual" waveform readings were to be brought to his attention *without delay* . . . and Tony certainly had some data that qualified as *unusual.* If he dawdled much longer, Corbit would almost certainly note the time indexes and demand an explanation, but Tony was equally fearful that his unsolicited entrance would provoke just as harsh a response.

In the end, as the Senior Technician—carrying several gel disks and tapping them nervously against the palm of his other hand—strode down the corridor, he decided that if he was going to be damned-if-he-did, damned-if-he-didn't, he might as well take the heat for performing his assigned duty.

At the end of the corridor, Tony reached an ornate, heavily-detailed turret, which split open down the middle to receive him. He stepped inside and waited as the elevator delivered him to his dreaded destination.

* * *

"The government's use of *my Dream Parlor* has left Citizens without the cerebral fortitude to make crucial decisions for themselves."

The elevator opened just in time for Tony to catch the very end of the Doctor's proclamation. In spite of his factual knowledge to the contrary, the Technician had hoped against hope that somehow, some*way*, he would arrive to find the office vacated—he obviously wasn't going to get his wish. Holding his nervous breath, he peeked around the open turret door before actually entering the room.

"We're getting tired of your excuses, Corbit," the government official—the same woman as last time and the time before—responded coldly as Tony approached Corbit's elaborate desk. "We want to move forward on this project, and frankly it looks like you're dragging your feet."

Corbit's office was ostentatious and expansive. It represented the epitome of the *Parlor's* decor, with a row of bronze trusses reaching up to massive golden spheres running down each side of the room. Rust-colored curtains adorned the openings to multiple monitoring alcoves, and a tasteful chandelier hung from the high ceiling. Corbit's mirror-surfaced desk reached outward on oversized legs that were an amalgamation of girder and claw. It was dark now, and search lights from the plaza below raked periodically through the French doors leading to the slender balcony.

Tony advanced toward the desk. The official was a severe woman somewhere in her thirties—Tony would have found her attractive were he not so intimidated by the threat she represented. Dressed in a tight, black outfit, her hair pulled back in an austere bun, she gripped her leather gloves in one hand—Tony caught an oh-so-brief glimpse of her extremely rare *chrome* IDC. Tony had never learned exactly what her capacity within the System actually was, but he knew she was one of the few who held sway over the Doctor—*Corbit* referred to her as the "Chief Suit," but Tony was fairly certain that this was a derogatory term the Doctor had labeled her himself . . . the Doctor called her a *lot* of derogatory terms when she wasn't around.

The Doctor's second regular guest stood near the French doors. The husky Organizer's helmet was in the crook of his left arm, leaving his mostly-bald head exposed. He was the first to notice Tony, but he said nothing.

"I'm busy," Corbit muttered when the Technician finally came to a stop beside the official. He fixed Tony with a stare that, for a moment, unsettled him more than the presence of the Suit or the Organizer.

But it was far too late for any kind of retreat, so Tony pressed onward. "I've brought you the dailies, sir," he said—it came out shakier than he would have preferred.

"Fine," Corbit grunted.

From the corner of his eye, Tony saw the woman stiffen in irritation. It suddenly seemed prudent to stress the *importance* of his errand. "You asked me to let you know if there was anything interesting," he explained. He moved around the desk—the Organizer increased his stress by waltzing after him—and stopped before the mirrored mantel. "The usual, mostly. A few climbers." With all the confidence of a rabbit in a den of wolves, he placed the gel disks on the desk one at a time—the large Organizer brushed past him to glance at the disks, although Tony suspected that no *real* interest was involved. "There's one in here that's *especially* noteworthy," he said as he reached the final disk. "He's a real *spiker*, off the grid at times." That almost seemed to *annoy* the Doctor, for what baffling reason Tony could not imagine—he thought Corbit *wanted* to know about spikers. He placed the last disk on top of the Doctor's data reader, and added with emphasis, "He has some odd readings that I've *never seen* before."

The woman suddenly interjected, " 'Spikers' are good, *right*?"

Corbit further surprised Tony by completely ignoring the official's remark. To his Technician he said, "I'll get to it when I have time."

The official leaned forward, placing a firm hand upon the edge of the desk. "*Corbit . . .* " she snapped in warning.

Corbit glanced back at her, appearing as innocent as he ever could, "I *said* I'll look into it."

Tony slowly began to suspect why the Doctor had responded negatively to the spiker reference . . . but before he could absorb any more of this exchange, the Organizer nudged him firmly. He retreated toward the elevator, and the large man stayed right behind him to insure his step was fleet.

"You'd *better*," the woman was saying as she leaned back. "We don't want any fringe lunatics to oppose us as we finalize the global contract."

"Stages One and Two are rock solid," Corbit assured her. "I'm testing Stage Three's effects on Citizen Five-Five-Six-One-Seven." Now Corbit leaned forward, and he stopped when he felt the reflected light from the table upon him at just the proper angle. "Soon you can play your pipe for the *rats*, and Rome will never fall." The Doctor laughed at himself, sure that even the Ice Bitch would appreciate the propriety of his analogy.

But the Chief Suit maintained her mask of impassivity. "We're not interested in the details, Corbit," she stated without the slightest humor. Corbit's smile dropped away as he drew back into the folds of his hooded chair. "We don't want excuses, or any more of your *pointless* metaphors. Get it done." Abruptly, the bitch stood and slipped into her gloves. "If we haven't started admitting Non-Citizens by the end of the month, you lose your funding and you're off the project." She spun on her heel and headed for the elevator.

Something akin to a growl exuded from the back of Corbit's throat as he leaped to his feet and took a half-dozen steps after her. "The Dream Parlor is *mine*!"

"Only so long as *we* say it is," the bitch replied coolly. She stopped as she reached the waiting elevator. The Organizer stepped back and away from her, but her focus was still on Corbit as she glanced over her shoulder. "You've got a spiker there—*use him*." She then marched into the turret with Corbit's horrified Senior Technician, and the doors closed.

Corbit stared after her for a moment—his calm exterior was deadly.

The Organizer shrugged and spoke for the first time. "I don't see why you can't just grab a couple of Citizens and—"

"*Kirk*," Corbit barked. "*Hush*." The Doctor let his frustration overflow onto his only remaining guest as he returned to his seat behind the desk. "If only your *IQ* were in proportion to your *body*. Try to *retain* the things I tell you from time to time."

The Organizer—Kirk—sighed inwardly, lowered himself into the chair the official had occupied just moments ago, and stared out the French doors.

"As I tried to explain to the *Ice Bitch*, the first two stages have turned almost all *Citizens* into *damaged goods* . . . it's difficult to find remotely useful test subjects for either their projects, *or* mine. They're nothing but *cattle*—why do you think *your* job is so *easy* these days, huh?"

Kirk glanced at Corbit, then back out into the night.

Corbit clasped his hands together on the table before him, bitterness seeping into his lowered voice, "*Social deprivation* has left the dreg Non-Citizens *almost* as useless . . . but not quite—that Hispanic woman lasted longer than most. But the NCs . . . they're pretty much all I have left . . . and now even *they* won't last much longer." He turned a meaningful eye to Kirk. "I need you to get me *more*, and *soon*."

Kirk ground his teeth. "I'm not your *errand boy,*" he spat.

Corbit's only reaction to the rebuke was a knowing smile. He swivelled his chair to one side and rose to his feet, moseying around behind Kirk as though he suddenly had not a care in the world.

Kirk resisted the temptation to keep a watchful eye on the Doctor.

Slowly, Corbit reached out and placed a firm hand upon Kirk's right shoulder. "Kirk . . . " he began, and then he squeezed much harder than necessary. Kirk again ground his teeth, but otherwise refused to acknowledge the abuse—Corbit admired that. The Doctor's left hand rose to his other shoulder, and the grip on both sides casually transformed into a massage. "Kirk . . . haven't I always taken care of you? Hmm?" Kirk finally looked up and back at the Doctor . . . as Corbit knew he would. He lowered his face a touch closer. "Now do *this* for *me.*" He smiled.

Without a word, Kirk placed his helmet upon his head. He drew a fresh breath, then rose and headed for the turret.

Corbit smiled again, and returned to his desk.

Now, he thought, feeling far more satisfied and in control than he had in hours, *what about these odd readings that my techy has never seen before . . .*

Popping the disk into the reader, he punched a few buttons on the control panel. Multiple beams of green light flashed across and through the mirrored surface of the desk, and a holographic representation of the standard waveform grid appeared.

"*System profile:*" the desktop computer announced, "*One-One-Eight-One-One . . .* " Corbit noticed right away that there was only a single reading on the disk—the techy had taken the trouble to isolate it—and he could see why: This *was* a spiker, the strongest Corbit had seen in some time. Although there was nothing particularly odd about—

Corbit froze, then leaned forward as a *second* waveform appeared.

"*Discrepancy: Dual-waveform pattern,*" the computer reported as it analyzed the anomaly. "*System Error . . . negative.*

Pattern echo . . . negative. Explanation . . . none. Subject generating two *waveforms . . .* "

Two waveforms?! The notion was as unlikely, and *shocking*, as listening to a person's chest and hearing two *heartbeats*.

Doctor James Edward Corbit was practically *salivating*.

. . . SAME AS BEFORE . . .

. . . Eli was at his workstation, his pencil strokes gracing yet another drawing of his Dream Woman—this time around, her features were distinct, and she wore flowing renaissance attire . . .

. . . after a while he set aside his rendering. He slipped the scrambler into place and reached into the interface gel . . .

>ACCESS EXECUTION CHANNEL— he began, but then Cyber-Limbo suddenly flushed sharply red, and a stabbing pain lanced through Eli's left temple . . .

. . . Eli withdrew his hand from the gel, rubbing his forehead against the abrupt headache. He rolled his neck around and worked his jaw until, slowly, the headache subsided. He stared at the interface gel . . .

. . . then simply removed the scrambler and returned to his drawing . . .

. . . at the workstation to Eli's right, Dana Levy left Cyber-Limbo as she struggled with barely suppressed laughter . . .

. . . Eli didn't notice . . .

. . .

. . . as the television screen displayed its usual programming, Eli placed still another illustration of his Dream Woman in the growing stash under the mattress . . .

. . . Eli eased back onto his bed. He stared at the ceiling, unable to sleep, until he finally reached over and flipped his control box to COMM . . .

"*Sector?*" a weary and somewhat impatient voice asked from the TV speakers.

"Local," Eli muttered just loud enough to be heard. "Connect me to the *Dream Parlor.*"

The voice virtually sighed as it prompted, "*Corporate or franchise?*"

"Corporate."

. . . after a momentary delay, a different, far more energetic voice came from the speakers. Absently, Eli recognized it as the same voice from the "For Confirmed Citizens Only" bit on the *Parlor* commercials . . .

"*Thank you for accessing the* Dream Parlor. *To schedule a session, say 'One,' now. To leave v-mail, say 'Two,' now. For operating hours, say 'Three,' now. To speak with—*"

"Three."

"*. . . in accordance with sector ordinance, code FHT-four-five-one . . .* "

Eli sat up, listening.

"*. . . the* Dream Parlor *offers services between the hours of oh-six-hundred and oh-two-hundred daily . . .* "

Eli checked his watch—it was just before one in the morning. If he hurried . . .

"*. . . for more options, say 'dot,' now . . .* "

Eli rolled off his cot . . .

. . .

. . . Eli rolled onto the dreamslab . . .

"Same as before, please," he said to the technician, then slipped his hand into the unusual interface port without waiting to be prompted . . .

. . .

. . . *snippets of the dream* . . .

. . . *Eli walking down the hillside* . . .

. . . *Eli passionately entwined with his Dream Woman* . . .

. . . and for some reason, that's all it *was* this time around—a pale imitation of the first time. Not *bad*, mind you, but . . . *weaker* . . .

. . . *and, again, the man in silhouette* . . .

. . . maybe Eli wouldn't come back here anymore . . .

. . .

. . . the next day, Eli slowly ascended the stairs leading from the *Dream Parlor* terminal to the *Dream Parlor* plaza . . .

. . . and this time it was much better, much closer to the first time . . .

. . . so he came back later that night . . .

. . .

. . . and the next evening, he returned again . . .

. . .

. . . and early the following morning . . .

. . .

. . . and again . . .

. . .

. . . and again . . .

. . .

. . . and every time, without fail—whether the dream was as deeply satisfying as the first experience, or the hollow echo that he sometimes found it to be—there was the man . . .

. . . and the *voice* . . .

"*Elijah* . . . " it whispered, ". . . *you don't belong here* . . . "

"*Elijah* . . . *Elijah* . . . "

. . .

HE KNOWS YOUR NAME

"Elijah . . . Elijah . . . "

. . . walking down the hillside . . . passionately entwined with his Dream Woman . . .

"Eli . . . *Eli.*"

Eli finally shook from his reverie and looked to the sound . . .

. . . and realized that he was sitting in the middle of the Food Park, with Jacob standing over him.

It was a bit jarring—hadn't he just been at work?

"I thought you were mad at me," he said to Jacob before returning his gaze to the fascinating spot at the center of his food tray.

"I *was,*" Jacob admitted, moving to sit next to him. "But you've been so *out of it* all week . . . " The sentence trailed off, as though that were explanation enough. Eli was vaguely aware of Dana sitting across from him as Jacob slipped onto the bench seat to his right. "You gonna eat your lunch?" his station partner probed.

"I'm not really hungry," Eli answered, then leaned back so that Jacob could take the plate of mush for himself.

"You're not missin' anything," Dana muttered.

Jacob apparently disagreed. He jammed spoonfuls of mush into his mouth as Eli slipped back into his thoughts. Jacob stole a glimpse at his brooding friend, evaluating his uncharacteristic mood. Eli really *had* been out of it this past week, hadn't he? He'd never known Elijah Barrett to behave so . . . *sedate*. If he didn't know better, he'd swear . . .

Jacob looked at him again, this time openly. Eli didn't even notice—he just sat there, his eyes vacant and his fingertip absently tracing the manufacturing imprint at the center of his now-empty food tray.

"You've been to the *Parlor*."

Eli's head snapped toward Jacob. Dana froze, her spoonful of food halfway into her mouth. How could Jacob have known that? He hadn't said anything about his new habit. Maybe Dana . . . but no, one glance at her discounted that possibility, as she seemed almost as surprised as Eli himself.

Jacob took Eli's lack of denial as an affirmation. "I *knew* it! One-One-Eight-One-One, Elijah Barrett, converted at last."

Eli looked away, embarrassed—he felt as though he'd been caught in the middle of a very common but very private act. Dana giggled, while Jacob's honest enthusiasm grew by leaps and bounds.

"This is *great*, man," Jacob told him with an assuring hand on the back of his friend's neck, "this is *great*. You know, I didn't know if I was gonna like the *Parlor* at first, either. Oh, but that look! I remember that look—man, I would sell my *nuts* to get that first rush back!" Eli smiled, and Dana giggled even *harder* this time. Feeling as though he were on a roll, Jacob suggested, "Hey, maybe we could all go *together* some time. You know, maybe they can do some kinda dream-*link*—"

And that was when Dana *really* cut loose. She barked a loud, boisterous laugh that drew several stares from the Citizens around them. She caught herself almost immediately, covering her mouth, then gesturing an apology with the same hand. She closed her eyes and forced the titter inward.

Her friends gaped at her—even Jacob knew that the insinuation had not been anywhere near *that* funny. And . . . there was something *else*. Something nagging at Eli, *itching* the back of his mind, like a sneeze that wouldn't come. Something about Dana and laughter . . .

After the long, abashing moment passed, Eli decided to change the subject—now that his *Parlor* visitations were out of the closet, so to speak, he might as well take advantage of it. To Jacob, he asked, "After you went to the *Parlor* the first time . . . the first *couple* of times . . . did you feel . . . " He searched for the right word. ". . . *apathetic*?"

"Hell no—I felt *great*! Still do!"

"But is it the *same* for you?" Eli insisted. "*Every* time?"

Jacob shrugged. "It's whatever you want it to be."

"But sometimes it *isn't*." Dana's giggling was growing louder again, but this time only Jacob noticed. Eli was furiously grasping for the best way to describe his on-again, off-again relationship with the *Parlor*. How could he make Jacob understand if he didn't already? "Okay, *sometimes* it's like any dream I have *outside* the *Parlor*, and other times there's . . . *more*. It's *too* real. And it's like it's not even *my* dream, like I'm not—"

"No one's *dickin'* with your head, Eli," Jacob snapped, and Eli was surprised by the sudden anger behind the words—he'd been so wrapped up in articulating his feelings that he'd missed the irritation that had swelled up in Jacob's eyes. His station partner continued, escalating sarcasm dripping from his tongue. "There's no *conspiracy*, no hidden *agendas*, no little *demons* running the *Dream Parlor*." His heat faded a bit, but he still sounded as though he were explaining to a small child that the boogeyman is just make-believe. "It's—a—*joyride*. That's *all*—nothing *more*. It's a *funhouse*—"

Dana *exploded*. Dwarfing all of her previous outbursts, she threw her head back in uproarious mirth and slammed her hands down onto the table. Her wrist caught the edge of her spoon, sending mush high into the air and showering her co-workers. She found this terribly amusing and somehow laughed even harder.

"What the hell's the *matter* with you?!" Jacob snapped furiously.

Dana lurched away from the table, ignoring Jacob and stamping her feet. She could barely catch a breath—her face reddened as the convulsions consumed her. Citizens around the room gawked at the spectacle.

A deep chill snaked its way into Eli's gut. As Dana's control slipped away, the memory pried its way to the forefront—*laughter*! That first day, his first trip to the *Parlor*, came back to him, and he remembered his bizarre encounter with her. She had been really spaced out, and giggling . . . *laughing* to herself.

God, how could I have forgotten *that? I was going to call her, talk to her, but . . . what's wrong with me? What's* been *wrong with me?*

What else *have I forgotten?*

Jacob, now more concerned than angry, rose and shuffled past Eli. Eli reached out to him, tried to grab him, but he was in a daze and his reflexes weren't up to the task. "Jacob," he warned, "d-don't touch her . . . "

Too late—Jacob grasped Dana by the shoulders and turned her to him. He'd barely gotten a few murmured words out before Dana exploded in an entirely *different* fashion.

In a heartbeat, her jocularity mutated into severe screams of panic and rage. She dug her nails into the side of Jacob's neck and shoved him away. Jacob, totally unprepared for such an assault, lost his footing and tumbled. His forehead struck the edge of the table—not hard enough to draw blood, but Eli could see that he was stunned. Floundering, he slid to the floor.

"Don't you *touch me*!" Dana was screaming.

Eli was moving now. He closed the distance between them and seized the raging woman from behind, deliberately pinning her arms to her sides, even as she descended upon Jacob. He dragged her back, pleading, "Dana! Calm down!"

"Don't you *ever touch me*!" Dana continued. She twisted about, pulling Eli along for the ride with desperate strength that he almost underestimated. "You're *evil*! You're *all evil*!!"

"Calm down! Dana—!"

Across the breadth of the Food Park, the attendant watched the action. Only seconds had passed, but beads of perspiration trickled down his forehead as he stood torn between duty and loyalty, nausea washing over him all the while. Eli was a good kid, and until recently, he'd honestly enjoyed helping him, but . . . well, he had a wife and child to think about. Eli had gotten careless enough lately, and now *this*! *This* sort of thing could mean *death* for the people involved . . .

. . . and other people *involved* with *them*.

In that moment, his decision was made—even his nausea subsided a degree. He slipped behind the mesh barrier and grabbed the nearest food server on the line. "Hey!" he whispered harshly to the bewildered man. "Get an *Organizer*."

Completely unaware of this—or almost any *other* aspects of the world around her—Dana continued to struggle against her friend and co-worker. She finally coiled and turned sharply enough to spin within Eli's arms. Without warning, she suddenly became *enraptured* by Eli's familiar face—Eli, surprised by the sudden change but sure as hell not letting go, stared down at her.

Dana managed to lift her hands, however, and stroked his cheek. She trembled, and when she spoke, her voice was raspy from screaming. "He's *right* . . . you were *there*." Her hands began stroking his face in alternation—left cheek, then right, then left again. "I remember. I *saw* you. I saw you go into the *pit*. The Devil—the Devil *took my soul* . . . "

Eli's breath came hard—he didn't know what else to do but stroke her hair and pull her to him. Dana cried against his chest for a moment, then raised her lips toward his ear.

"He knows your *name*," she whispered. "The Devil . . . he *knows* your *name* . . . "

Dana (Lia Jett) lifted her hands and stroked his cheeks. She trembled, and when she spoke, her voice was raspy from screaming. "He knows your *name,*" she whispered. "The Devil . . . he *knows* your *name* . . . "

Despite himself, Eli felt a totally different kind of tightening in his chest. Every bit of common sense *insisted* that this was all part of whatever psychosis gripped her, and yet . . .

"*Who?*" he heard himself asking.

"He knows *my* name, too . . . " Dana cried.

"*Who?* Dana, *tell me* who the Devil is."

That touched her in an almost endearing way. Her eyes brightened just the slightest bit, and he could almost hear her thinking, *Finally, someone's listening to me.* She stroked both cheeks this time, and her right hand lingered. She glanced over at her IDC . . .

but only she *could see that the IDC was no longer an IDC—it was something else, a* thing, *a tentacled creature that had slithered under her skin into her body and threatened to devour her from within*

. . . and she opened her mouth in a bellowing howl of abject *terror!*

Eli had finally relaxed his grip, so when Dana raked her fingernails down his cheek, tearing deep trenches of pain into his flesh, he lost his hold and fell back. Clutching his maimed face, he stumbled against the table bench.

Dana thrashed and screamed, clutching her wrist as she gaped at whatever she saw in place of her IDC. She rushed over to the condiment stand and began smashing the chip against its metal surface as hard as she could.

Despite his pain, Eli gathered his strength for another effort . . . until a new scuffle behind him drew his attention.

No. Oh, no.

A trio of Organizers bounded down the stairs into the Food Park. The two larger men marched straight toward Dana, while a third official blocked Eli's way even as he struggled to rise.

"*Down*!" the man ordered, his regulation-issue shock-rod—Eli didn't know what their official designation was, but Derby had jokingly dubbed them "submissioners"—brandished menacingly in Eli's face. "Stay *down*!"

With the exception of Eli, who merely held his ground, the other Citizens gave the Organizers a wide berth—they continued to watch the action, of course, but from a greater distance. The first Organizer to reach Dana casually prodded her in the shoulder with his submissioner. He clearly expected that to be the end of things, and his eyes widened when Dana merely twitched and then continued smashing her IDC against the table. Grunting, he gave it to her again. The second Organizer zapped her as well, this time giving it to her squarely between the shoulder blades.

It was unheard of—Citizens would be gossiping about it for months—but rather than dropping, Dana actually whirled and *attacked* the first Organizer. Both men were clearly shaken—a woman her size should have been stunned by the first shot, and twitching in drooling paralysis by the second—so Dana got in several good hits.

Eli moaned as he looked on—there was no way of knowing *what* Dana perceived before her, but it most likely *wasn't* an Organizer, unless this was her way of committing *suicide*. He tried to rise again, and the third Organizer brushed the tip of his rod against Eli's chest. Every muscle in his body clenched, and he fell back onto the bench. The man didn't bother with a follow up, as he, too, watched the incredible, impossible scene before him.

The Organizer Dana was striking finally got tired of the abuse and reacted. This time he braced her with his other hand as he rammed the submissioner into the nape of her neck. This *finally* registered through Dana's fury, and she stumbled around—she was still staggering when the other Organizer cracked his rod across her face as hard as he could.

the Organizer's arm was a blur of violence as his club cracked against the back of Mencer's skull

A low moan escaped Eli's lips, and his heart thundered wildly in his chest.

Dana fell hard against the condiment stand, scattering its wares in all directions. The angered and indignant Organizers moved in. As the second pinned the still-moving Dana to the stand, the first again pressed the business end of his shock-rod against the nape of her neck—and *held* it there! The smell of burning flesh quickly filled the room, and *still* Dana struggled.

The Organizer standing guard over Eli—his hands trembling uncharacteristically for a man in his uniform—stepped away. He produced his palm-sized communicator and called for back-up.

Eli seized the moment, rising shakily to his feet. Bracing himself against the table, he prepared to thrust himself into the thick of it. Some part of him screamed out against such *stupidity*, but he didn't care—his every thought was centered on saving Dana. He shifted his weight . . .

the Organizer's arm was a blur of violence as his club cracked against the back of Mencer's skull

. . . and then Jacob resurfaced. "No! Eli!"

Jacob grabbed Eli by the shoulders. He tried to pull away, but Jacob held on. "They're going to *kill* her!"

"You can't help her—not now!"

The Organizers were too distracted to notice as Jacob wrestled with Eli. Dana was hemorrhaging now, blood trickling from her nose, ears, and eyes, but the Organizers were beyond caring—the voltage continued.

Eli shoved at Jacob, but his friend would not give in. Jacob grasped Eli's face with both hands—heedless of the bloody gashes on Eli's left cheek—and *forced* Eli to make eye contact with him.

"There is *nothing* we can do!" he insisted vehemently. Eli didn't listen—didn't *want* to listen—and tried to pull away. Jacob held fast. "Do you hear me, Elijah? There's *nothing* we can *do*! There—is—*nothing*—we—can—*do*!!"

It wasn't the words, or even how he said them—it was the look in his eyes. Eli saw it, knew it. He stopped fighting and—oh, so slowly—collapsed against Jacob's shoulder. Jacob held his friend close and tight as the sobs came.

And even through the burning tears, Eli watched as the Organizers electrocuted Dana all the way to the floor.

HERE COMES THE SANDMAN

"Doctor Corbit?"

"I'm busy."

"He's here again."

Corbit paused, the gel disks he'd been cataloging momentarily forgotten. He took a sip of coffee, then smiled. "Good," he spoke to the intercom. "Go prep him in Room Two-Twenty-Two. I'll be there shortly."

Setting his coffee cup upon the desk, Corbit rose from his august chair. Carefully, almost anxiously, he strode to his cloak room, reaching past the casual piece he wore most of the time to select a fresh, crisply-white lab coat. He then moved to the mantel and picked up his personal *Dream Parlor* badge—not the standard design of those beneath him, but a gold-plated "DP" diamond that adhered to the magnet sewn into the coat's material.

Finally, he considered his reflection in the mirror. He straightened his posture and smoothed his mustache. He wanted to look his professional best—after all, this was the day he'd meet his ticket to *Paradise*.

Smiling at his own grandiloquence, Doctor Corbit headed for the turret elevator.

* * *

Slipping through the back hallways of the *Parlor*, Corbit managed to arrive at his destination relatively unmolested by the brainless throng that worked under him. He stepped into Room 222 unannounced, which also suited him just fine.

There he was, sitting on the dreamslab and staring off into space as the *Parlor* technician prepared his session. The woman must have heard the Doctor after all—she looked over her shoulder . . . then did a double-take. Corbit could see the confusion on her face as she looked at Eli, then back to Corbit once more. *Who is this Citizen*, he imagined her thinking, *that Doctor Corbit* himself *would actually come downstairs to meet him?*

He's far, far more, my dear, Corbit answered the unasked question in his own mind, *than* you *could ever hope to be.*

The technician made one final adjustment to the IDC port, then hurried from the room with a muttered, "He's all yours, Doctor."

Corbit stood his ground, watching Eli. The young man with the mysterious abilities finally glanced over apathetically, then did his *own* double-take. "You're James Corbit," he observed, obviously surprised but not as intimidated as Corbit was accustomed.

"You're Eli Barrett," Corbit returned. When Eli turned his head to look at him straight-on, Corbit spotted the large bandage on his left cheek. Eli appeared drained, strung-out, with dark circles under his eyes. Surely he wasn't completely addicted so soon? Corbit hoped not—no, he *refused* to accept the possibility. Something else *must* have happened to him—Corbit hadn't waited all this time simply to have his opportunity ruined by the System's interference! "You look like *hell*," he commented. "How do you *feel*?"

"Like hell," Eli admitted.

"I guess you *can* judge a book by its cover," Corbit mused, stepping closer to the dreamslab. What was the best way to proceed? Perhaps he should try to bond with the boy on a personal level. "What happened to your face?" he tried. "You want to talk?"

"I wanna dream," Eli answered, looking away.

So much for ingratiation, Corbit thought. "I figured *that* out all by myself." He turned away, biting down on his anger at being dismissed. If he had any hope of convincing Eli to help him of his own *free will*, he couldn't allow them to get off on the wrong foot. He didn't know how such a proposal would be received, but if it *could* possibly work out that way, it would surely prove better than having Kirk drag him kicking and screaming into Corbit's domain.

Corbit moved into the enclosed control station, peering into the mass-production version of his own scope down in the basement. "I understand you've been spending a lot of time here over the last week. More than most," he added, driving the point, "except for the *junkies*." He headed back toward the bed. "Scan your chip."

Corbit had the boy's attention again. "I hear you're a busy man," Eli commented as he slipped his right hand into the interface. "How do *I* rate?"

"Lucky, I guess. I was reading your preference file—who's the dame with no face?"

That touched a tender spot. The boy stiffened and his weariness reared its ugly head. "Look," he said with a feeble attempt at a smile, "I just wanna *dream*, all right?"

"Suit yourself," Corbit chuckled, but not for the reasons Eli probably thought. *How ironic*, he ruminated. *Two distinct brainwaves loose in that skull of his, and he turns out to be so* single-minded. "I suppose you know the routine by now: Pick a dream, any dream. Where do you wanna go?"

Eli sighed heavily, his frustration evident. "I don't *care* . . . a *funhouse*. It doesn't matter as long as *she's* there."

" 'Funhouse,' " Corbit repeated with a smile. *Interesting* response—perhaps it was an opening he could *use*. "I used to love amusement parks." Slipping his hand into his pocket, he sauntered down to the foot of the bed, talking all the while. "Had a favorite one, you know. Went there all the time. Had one of those 'annual pass' things." He turned back to Eli, who listened begrudgingly. "The world around us was *crumbling* to *dust*, getting so rundown and overcrowded—we weren't *used* to it then like you kids are today . . . "

"Look," the boy interjected, and this time he forced the insincere smile all the way to the surface, "the other guy just flipped a *switch* to put me to sleep."

Corbit grunted good-naturedly. "Don't piss me off," he advised, returning to the side of the bed, "I might flip the *wrong one.*" He pointed ominously to a lock box near the head of the bed—a kill-switch for those rare times that a dreamer reacted *violently* to his *Parlor* session. Of course, it would take deliberate meddling for it to actually *harm* the dreamer . . . but *Eli* didn't know that, didn't know *what* it was, and that made it all the more foreboding. The boy looked at the box, then into the Doctor's eyes—Corbit *really* had his attention now. He smiled and leaned in close. "All I'm saying is: Don't *shoot your wad* all at once."

Eli stared back at him, but said nothing.

Corbit straightened, then returned to the control station. Checking the scope, he continued as though uninterrupted, "I went to that park so often, it lost its *magic*, and I never wanted to go back. Oh, I heard they added some great new rides just before the plug got pulled, but I'll never know." He fingered the initiation switch, but he wasn't finished just yet. "Anyway, my *point* is . . . I'm working on my *own* ride, and *you* are turning into a great new client." He stepped out of the station. "I wouldn't want you to miss out . . . "

Eli lay on the dreamslab, fast asleep.

Corbit grunted to himself. *So much for perking the interest of my little* Wunderkind.

Stepping into the station once more, he sang to himself, "*Turn out the lights, boys and girls,*" then grumbled, "here comes the *Sandman.*"

Click!

WAKE THEM

Click!

With a jolt he was completely unaccustomed to, Eli's eyes snapped open.

He knew immediately that something was different, and it was more *than just his unusually abrupt transition. Every other dream he'd had—the* good *ones and the* not-*so-good—he'd appeared upon the same hillside.* This *time he was in some kind of sparse woodland. Also, even though a few birds sang in the distance, they and the other natural sounds—wind, crickets, rustling leaves and grass—he'd come to associate with these dreams fell . . . not silent—hushed,* muted. *It was a lot* hotter, *too. Slowly, he cast about for his Dream Woman.*

He didn't have to look far. He spotted her, kneeling beneath a tree, some twenty meters away. She held a bundle in her arms—a bundle that suspiciously resembled a child*—and he could hear her crying.*

Cautiously, he approached her. He was concerned, yes, but he was also . . . irritated. *Desperate for an escape from Dana's tragic fate, he'd returned to the* Parlor *as soon as he was able. If the salesman or technicians had decided to add a little spice to his fantasies, now was most certainly* not *the time! Or maybe* Corbit *had something to do with this. Why would the creator of the* Dream Parlor *want to—*

His foot bumped into something. His gaze had been leveled at the crying woman and her unsettling burden, but he knew *that when he had first spied her, the path had been completely clear. He looked down . . .*

His breath caught in his throat, and his jaw clenched, then dropped. Spread like a barrier between him and his Dream Woman, dozens of covered forms lay across the ground—forms that had not *been there before! The bodies—that's what they were,* bodies!*—were covered by blue-green bed sheets. The buzzing of horseflies punched through the stillness he'd noted earlier.*

Eli again looked to the woman. She was no more than ten meters away now, and she was slowly rocking the still child. As she turned his direction, the child's head slipped from the crook of her elbow. The neck bent backward at an unnatural angle, affording Eli an open view of the raked claw marks—not too different from those Dana left on his cheek—running across the cavities where the youth once had eyes. What's more, the bloody fingers on her limp hand suggested self-mutilation.

Eli's guts seized with icy dread.

His Dream Woman looked up, tears streaming down her grimy, dirt-smeared face. "Help me," she wept in a delicate, British accent.

At a loss, Eli gestured helplessly at the wall of bodies—he couldn't bring himself to just clamber over them, not yet. "What is *this?"*

The woman shook her head numbly. "They're dead," she said, almost too low for him to hear. "They're all dead."

Not knowing what else to do, Eli bent on one knee. He reached out to one sheet at random and drew it back, then recoiled from the sight of the putrefied skull shrouded within, its jaw rotted completely away and its remaining tissues mummified.

Repulsed, Eli dropped the sheet back in place and almost stood when the barest movement from another form caught his eye. This time he did not pull the sheet back right away, but reluctantly placed his hand where the upper-torso appeared to be. Sure enough, the chest slowly rose, then fell, and he felt the faintest of heartbeats within.

Calling across to the woman, Eli assured her, "They're not all *dead. Only some—the rest are . . . sleeping."*

"Wake *them," she replied, almost as a challenge.*

You heard the lady, *Eli chided himself. Holding his breath, he pulled the second sheet away . . .*

. . . and gasped. "Jacob?"

Lying before him, Jacob's head fell sluggishly to one side, but he did not respond.

Anxious and confused, Eli shook his friend and co-worker. "Jacob? Come on, Jacob, wake up." When Jacob still did not stir, he shook him harder still. "Come on, Jacob, wake up. *Jacob—!"*

In spite of his efforts, Jacob did not move—but one of the other *bodies* did.

Eli's heart leaped into his throat, then proceeded to race like a sprinter against the tape as, one by one, the covered bodies sat straight up, and their heads turned in his direction.

A scream crept its way up the back of Eli's throat—he was fairly certain it would have found its way past his trembling lips had his attention not been diverted in such a timely fashion.

"Elijah . . . "

As perturbing as the voice had been over the past week, it was

Eli's heart leaped into his throat as, one by one, the covered bodies sat straight up, and their heads turned in his direction.

comforting in that it was, at least, familiar. Eli spun on his knee to face the source of the sound.

He was disappointed, though not surprised. The recognizable shape of the man from his previous dreams stood on open ground, in clear view, yet nevertheless somehow *managed to remain in shadow.*

"Elijah," *the man continued,* "*you* must wake them. You must *free* them."

Eli gritted his teeth in frustration. "They don't hear *me," he told the man sharply, allowing his vexation to flow through the words.*

"You don't belong here, Elijah," *the man chided gently, seemingly unaffected by Eli's acrimony.* "You must find the *truth.*"

So fixated was Eli on the verbal exchange, he didn't notice as the Dream Woman rose and slowly approached him—nor was he aware that the disfigured child, Jacob, and the rest of the faceless assembly had now faded away. "What is *it?" he insisted. "What are you trying to* show *me?!"*

The man answered Eli . . . but not in words.

As Eli looked on, the man spread his arms. For the briefest instant, Eli thought a wind was gusting through his trench coat, but that illusion didn't last long enough for the thought to fully form. The man's entire body rippled, as though viewed under water, and expanded. In scant seconds, his humanoid form disappeared entirely.

In the man's place loomed some sort of . . . portal*—at least, Eli couldn't think of what* else *to call it. Roughly pentagonal in shape, the monstrosity rose over two meters high to its peak. Its body was a twisted unification of stone and steel, with what looked like hoses and pipes running up, through, and around the outside and facing of the structure. A red sphere, suspiciously similar to the retina scopes used for cyberlimbo interfacing, perched at the highpoint of the structure's open center—a center which swirled and writhed like some kind of gossamer membrane. On top of this, the aperture's arrival was marked by echoes of faint, whispering* voices, *too low and run together for Eli to understand.*

Gaping, Eli rose to his feet as the Dream Woman, also staring wide-eyed at the bizarre structure, joined him. There was something

The man spread his arms. His entire body rippled and expanded. His humanoid form disappeared entirely, and in his place loomed some sort of . . . *portal* . . .

about this portal, something . . . yes! It looked very similar to the gateway on the cover of Sara's Windsong *book—but instead ofsmooth stone it had come out looking like half of it belonged within the DPC computer core! Eli supposed its resemblance was somehow fitting—after all, his subconscious had chosen to clothe himself and his Dream Woman as the heroes of that same publication—but* why *was it here* at all?

And what were those voices?

Very slowly, Eli approached the portal—his Dream Woman followed. As he drew closer, the voices, accompanied by a low wind-like moaning, increasing in intensity.

"Listen," Eli said, more to himself than his aerial companion. "Do you hear that?"

Before she could respond, a single phantom voice rose above the others. ". . . rivate Entry . . . vember Sixteenth . . . *" It was garbled and distorted, but it was the* only *one even remotely discernable.*

"Do you hear *that?" Eli insisted. He gestured vaguely to the mist swirling through the portal's center. "Do you* see *it?"*

He was very near the portal now. The voices rose and fell, more and more of them joining the cacophony every second—it was like standing in the center of the Food Park and trying to listen to every single person all at once. Eli wasn't sure how *or* why, *but every fiber of his being was screaming out that this was* not *coming from anywhere in his subconscious, but from some unknown external source. Hadn't Jacob joked about trying a* dream-link? *Was something like that* possible? *Was he somehow linking to the other Citizens using the* Parlor *right now?*

"I . . . I-I can hear *them," he breathed in wonder, "*all *of them—in there . . . "*

The singular voice broke through again for just a moment. ". . . having trouble establishing bio-feedback with Non-Citizen number . . . "

This *time it was clearer than before—yet again, Eli found himself confronted with some new dream-twist that seemed completely* alien *at first but then proved itself* familiar *instead. "And there's something else . . . " he spoke aloud to his Dream Woman, still using her as a sounding board. He could almost swear . . .*

". . . by manipulating the mainframe's neural net, it may be possible to *control* people's dreams . . . "

Now Eli recognized the voice beyond any doubt . . . and it left him more confused than ever.

". . . or even their *conscious* thoughts . . . " *it added, taunting him.*

Eli stopped short. "Corbit."

* * *

Sitting in his office, Corbit studied the data from Room 222 in pure rapture. He was so fixated on the magnificent display that he didn't even mind when the Senior Technician burst from the elevator unscheduled and unannounced.

"Doctor Corbit—!" the man stammered urgently, out of breath.

Corbit ignored him, beaming with undisguised glee. "*Look* at this kid! He's generating *two* waveforms—"

"Doctor Corbit," the Technician interrupted, "something's happening to the *mainframe*."

Annoyed, Corbit shut off the holographic display. Turning on the younger man, he demanded, "What *kind* of 'something?' "

It was almost *more* telling of the seriousness of the situation that the tech *ignored* Corbit's incising tone. "It's sustaining *power surges* and *fluctuations* across the board," he said in a rush. "We've never seen *anything* like it! And now it's starting to affect the *other* systems, all the way to the outer-compumatrix!"

This *was* serious—and unprecedented. The outer-compumatrix? Those systems and files were barely related to the *Parlor*'s mainframe, and had *nothing* to do with the induced dreaming process. Of course, Corbit had *theorized* that if he could accomplish his goals, such influences would be possible . . .

Then *another* thought occurred to him. It was a long-shot danger at best, but the outer system was also where *Parlor* employees secured their private research . . .

. . . and their *personal logs*.

Corbit stared straight through this messenger of bad tidings. "What *parts*?"

"*All* of them!"

Pondering considerations both exciting and dangerous, Corbit turned his thoughtful gaze out toward the early-morning sun . . .

* * *

His Dream Woman stood before the portal as it fell silent. The voices—both Corbit's and those of the multitudes—trailed away, and the mist through its center faded altogether. The portal itself, however, remained.

"It's stopped," she said. "I don't hear it anymore."

Kneeling off to one side, his back to her and the portal, Eli barely heard her. He muttered, "What does 'bio-feedback' *have to do with the* Dream Parlor*?" The woman joined him, dropping to her own knees in front of him as he now spoke to her. "And what the hell is a* 'neural net?' "

But the woman wasn't listening to him. Wearing a befuddled expression, she reached out and touched his face . . . which no longer sported a VanDyke, but was clean-shaven.

But Eli hadn't realized this yet. Bewildered, he allowed her to turn his head to one side as she inspected the three deep scratches that now graced his left cheek. She stretched forth a probing finger . . .

. . . and Eli winced in pain.

The woman leaned back, gawking. Eli stared at her—she *had changed as well. Gone were the ringlets of hair and the opulent Renaissance attire. She knelt before him, dressed in modern-day clothing, and appeared not at all dream-like or enthralled by his very company, but focused and very . . . present. And he didn't have to inspect himself to surmise that* his *fantasy outfit was gone as well.*

"Lucid dreams my ass,*" he spat as he rose and strode over to scrutinize the mysterious portal.*

"You're real,*" she said to him.*

Eli didn't respond. Thinking furiously, struggling to make sense of it all, he planted himself before the portal and remained silent.

"I don't understand this," she continued, pacing around behind him. "What's happening to me? What do you want *from me?"*

Eli didn't answer, didn't even look at her—but he hung on her every word.

"Out there, outside the Parlor, *I can't* think straight . . . "

That struck a chord that he could not ignore. Eli turned and approached her. "Nothing matters *anymore?" he added for her, testing. "It's like you're* fading away?"

His words left her badly shaken. "I don't want *to fade away," she said angrily, marching a few steps away. "I* can't. *The children* need *me. I* like *who I am . . . and I* like *being their Guardian Angel."*

Eli's heart skipped a beat. "What?!"

The woman merely stared at him, perplexed and a little intimidated.

Eli's mind snapped back to the last feeding session, when he'd noticed Sara's Windsong *book. She'd observed his curiosity and told him . . . she told him . . .*

"My Guardian Angel gave it to me."

Very deliberately, while endeavoring to remain as outwardly calm as possible, Eli crossed to her. "Tell me who you are,*" he said. When she didn't answer immediately, he closed his eyes briefly against his precarious control, but continued to approach her. "I* need *to know who you* are.*"*

She still *didn't answer—she just kept staring at him with that same jittery expression on her face. Didn't she realize how* important *this was?* Didn't she?!

Eli's temper snapped, and he seized her too roughly by the shoulders. "Tell me!" he *blurted.*

It was too much for her. Gasping, she knocked his arms away with surprising strength and ran from him. Eli started to pursue, but that damned voice brought him up short.

"Elijah . . . "

Eli spun around, ready to challenge the man to reveal himself once and for all, but the shady figure was nowhere to be seen.

"Elijah . . . *" the voice resounded, ". . . find* her . . . find her . . . find her . . . "

In the distance, thunder rolled . . .

THE HARD WAY

Jacob stepped numbly through the threshold into the DPC. Like a robot, he plucked his assignments from their disk slots. He turned . . .

Eli strode purposefully down the stairwell. He was focused, determined—far more so than he'd been in over a week, that was for sure. He emerged into the DPC . . .

Eli and Jacob laid their eyes upon Dana's empty seat at almost the exact same moment. Both froze—Eli barely in the doorway, Jacob a step closer at the assignment rack. In that instant, neither was consciously aware of the other's presence . . . yet, somehow, they shared this sorrowful interval. Neither would have been surprised if they were the only ones to even notice Dana's absence—and they were certainly the only ones who knew her *name.*

Then Eli was moving once more, if somewhat slower. He brushed past Jacob, bumping him harder than he'd intended, and strode toward their work station. Jacob glanced at him, then back to Dana's vacant spot before following. As Eli passed by her chair, he allowed his fingers to trace its rough surface, but he did not stop again.

Eli dropped into his own seat and, without preamble, reached into his sleeve and plugged the scrambler's electrode into his IDC. Jacob watched him as he dove into cyber-limbo without having so much as touched his assignment disks. For once, Jacob withheld his judging comments.

>CITIZEN DATA REQUEST: Eli thought. >IDC NUMBER UNKNOWN—NAME, DANA LEVY—SUBJECT OF ORGANIZER CONTAINMENT IN LOCAL FOOD PARK, SECTOR TWO-ONE-EIGHT, WITHIN LAST TWENTY-FOUR-HOUR PERIOD. CONFIRM AND IDENTIFY SUBJECT IN QUESTION.

The Computer-Eli hesitated only briefly before reporting, >>*SUBJECT IDENTIFIED: FIVE-FIVE-SIX-ONE-SEVEN. TERMINATED CITIZENSHIP—SUBJECT HAS BEEN DELETED FROM SYSTEM.*

Tell me something I don't *know.* >CONFIRM REGISTERED CHARGE AGAINST DANA LEVY WHICH LED TO TERMINATION.

>>*FIVE-FIVE-SIX-ONE-SEVEN: CHARGED WITH DESTRUCTION OF GOVERNMENT PROPERTY.*

>*WHAT* PROPERTY?

>>*ASSIGNED IDC.*

Bullshit. >CITIZEN DATA REQUEST: BACKGROUND CHECK. FREQUENCY OF *DREAM PARLOR* LOG-INS FOR DANA LEVY.

>>*ACCESS TO* DREAM PARLOR *MAINFRAME IS RESTRICTED. IDC AUTHORIZATION INADEQUATE . . . REQUEST DENIED.*

Again, as he had experienced earlier in the week when he'd tried to access the Execution Channel database, cyber-limbo pulsed oddly red, and Eli's jaw clenched against the sharp ache that spiked behind his left eye. On top of that, he was also *painfully* aware that this was the computer system that almost *caught* him the last time he'd come knocking.

This time, however, he did *not* let it distract him from his intended goal. He indulged himself a quick massage of the left temple, then adjusted the scrambler's combination and pushed forward. He repeated his request.

>>. . . *PROCEED*, Cyber-Eli stated almost begrudgingly.

>REQUEST MONTHLY REPORT FROM SUBJECT'S FIRST ENTRY. ROTATE SEARCH LEVEL PRIORITY BETWEEN ONE-ALPHA-BLUE AND ONE-BETA-RED. With a little luck, the rotating frequencies would buy him the time he needed.

>>*SEARCHING . . . LOG-IN FREQUENCY FOR FIVE-FIVE-SIX-ONE-SEVEN:*

>>*FIRST MONTH: SEVEN LOG-INS . . .*

>>*SECOND MONTH: SEVENTEEN LOG-INS . . .*

>>*MONTH-TO-DATE: FIRST SIXTEEN DAYS, THIRTY-FIVE LOG-INS.*

Oh, my god, Eli thought as he listened to the tale of addiction . . . a tale that struck a far-too-familiar chord.

>>*NOTE*: Computer-Eli added. >>*THERE ARE* NO *LOG-INS FOR SUBJECT WITHIN LAST EIGHT DAYS. SUBJECT RESTRICTED FROM* DREAM PARLOR *FOR REMAINDER OF MONTH.*

This brought Eli up short—it meant that Dana had actually been *denied* access the day he'd seen her there. But . . . how did that track with his building suspicions about the *Parlor's* side-effects?

>REASON FOR SUBJECT'S RESTRICTION FROM *DREAM PARLOR*? he asked.

>>*DECLINE IN WORK PERFORMANCE.*

Uncertain what to make of this monkey wrench, Eli switched to another track.

>BUSINESS DATA REQUEST: ALL INFORMATION ON *DREAM PARLOR* MAINFRAME. SPECIAL SEARCH PARAMETER: *BIO-FEEDBACK* AND *NEURAL NET.* PRIORITY ONE-GAMMA-GREEN.

>>*SEARCH IN PROGRESS . . .* Then Computer-Eli assumed a flatter, more rote-sounding tone of voice as it recited,

>>*BIO-FEEDBACK. RE:* DREAM PARLOR *MAINFRAME, DESIGNED BY JAMES EDWARD CORBIT, IDC CODE RESTRICTED.*

>>*BIO-FEEDBACK: A SYNAPTIC LOOP GENERATED BETWEEN DREAMER AND MAINFRAME. LOOP CREATES AN INTERACTIVE BIO-LINK BETWEEN* DREAM PARLOR *PATRON AND—*

Computer-Eli froze in mid-sentence, closed its eyes, and tilted its head back, almost as though it had suffered a sudden attack of *narcolepsy* and collapsed into a deep sleep. Then cyber-limbo itself shrank out of existence, leaving only darkness . . .

Eli's chest clenched into a vice grip so tight he had trouble breathing. Hesitantly, he reached out and tapped the computer lens twice, then four more times in rapid succession. Deep inside, he knew that it would do no good, but denial was a comforting blanket against the cold truth threatening his very existence as the person he was today. The sounds of the DPC closed in on him as he nervously chewed his knuckle, his thoughts and his heart racing frantically.

All right . . . he'd always known that this might happen someday—

But you never thought it actually would, *did you, Eli?*

—but, slave to bureaucracy as it was, the System wouldn't just step on him without "processing" him first.

You sure? They stepped on Dana *without much pause, didn't they?*

Ignoring the nagging inner voice, Eli removed the scrambler from its strap on his sleeve. Disconnecting the wire, he started to drop it into his pocket until he thought that maybe that wasn't the smartest place either. Sure, no one would know exactly what it *was* to look at it, but why take the chance? Maybe leaving it on his wrist was the best—

Then another idea occurred to him and he pushed away from his station. Bending over, he opened the zipper on his right utility boot and shoved the scrambler inside. And even as he resealed the opening, the call—which denial had been suggesting *might* not come after all—rang throughout the DPC.

"One-One-Eight-One-One: Report to Citizen Processing . . . "

Eli froze. No, it *couldn't* be—not really. He was just so scared he'd imagined it, they hadn't actually—

The imposing, bass voice repeated, "*One-One-Eight-One-One: Report to Citizen Processing.*"

It was real. He hadn't imagined it. The day he'd feared for so long, the horrible theme of so many nightmares . . . was here. Now. And there was no going back.

He'd *thought* he'd been prepared—thought he'd known the risks he was taking to force his way into the *Parlor's* compumatrix. Reality proved a lot less noble than it had seemed *before* they called his number.

As he rose shakily to his feet, Eli glanced over at Jacob. His friend's concentration was deeply entrenched into his cyber-limbo . . . but Eli knew that he'd heard—he'd had to have been *deaf* not to. Still, what could Jacob *do* for him now? Nothing.

Turning away from his station partner, Eli's eyes slid past the hand he'd used to steady himself, his right IDC hand . . .

Oh . . . God . . .

(I will not vomit, I will not vomit, I will not vomit)

He hadn't even been to Citizen Processing yet . . . and his formerly *opaque* IDC was already fading to the *clear* of a Non-Citizen.

Refusing to linger on the horrific sight and irrelevant mystery of the change—he hadn't known they could change your status by remote, but it probably took place when his station lost power and his hand was still in the gel—Eli forced his legs to move. He circled around the perimeter of the DPC, passing co-workers who steadfastly ignored him.

He lingered at the foot of the stairwell, then continued forward and up. Emerging onto the ground level, he trudged down the corridor toward Citizen Processing . . .

* * *

Kirk and an Organizer subordinate marched up the corridor toward the DPC. He turned into the stairwell without lingering and continued forward and down.

Descending into the room—turning slightly sideways so that the tight walls could accommodate the breadth of his shoulders—he took stock of the hapless Citizens sitting in their little chairs in front of their little computers. Gesturing with his head for his adjutant to follow, he ambled around to the station belonging to 11811.

When they arrived, of course, they found only Jacob. Kirk bent, resting his hands on his thighs as he considered the younger man. He glanced at the computer lens—which revealed nothing without the gel interfacing with his IDC—then shook his head and shared a disgusted smirk with his colleague. Leaning forward just a bit, he spoke quietly, even *gently*, into Jacob's ear. "Excuse me."

Jacob withdrew his hand from the gel, blinked away cyber-limbo's mild disorientation, and glanced over his shoulder. When he saw who had spoken, every muscle in his body jolted to rigid attention. He whipped his head around to the other side, taking in the second Organizer who leered down at him. With no other safe recourse, he fixed his gaze straight ahead as though he were still in cyber-limbo.

"How long has One-One-Eight-One-One been away from his work station?" Kirk asked in a perfectly congenial manner.

Don't tell him anything! screamed a long-forgotten voice, the voice of a man who cared deeply for Elijah Barrett . . . but the thought of resisting made Jacob literally ill. Swallowing against the bile rising in the back of his throat, he stuttered, "I-I don't know. It hasn't been very long. He went to Citizen Processing." The words came out weak and pathetic.

Kirk glanced at his colleague, who shrugged. He placed a friendly hand upon Jacob's right shoulder . . . and then squeezed much harder than necessary. Jacob cringed, but he managed to bite down on the cry that rose from his quivering diaphragm. Kirk studied his writhing features a moment longer, then commended, "You're a *good boy*."

Releasing Jacob with a little shove, Kirk strode back toward the stairwell with the other Organizer in tow. When their threatening figures ascended from sight, Jacob slammed a frustrated, angry, and guilty fist onto his desktop. He noted Eli's empty seat from the corner of his eye and fought against the tears that wanted so badly to come . . .

As the Organizers reached ground level, a soft *beeping* emitted from Kirk's jacket. He turned to his companion and nodded toward the far end of the corridor. "Go ahead. I'll catch up."

Apathetic, the other Organizer sauntered on his way.

Kirk reached into one of his many uniform pockets and pulled out the undersized communicator that begged his attention. Sighing, he thumbed it on. "This is Kirk, reporting from DPC. One-One-Eight-One-One isn't here, and he didn't show up at Citizen Processing."

"*Surprise, surprise,*" Corbit's biting sarcasm seeped through the tiny speaker. "*I told you* he *isn't* stupid."

Kirk clenched his jaw, and *almost* responded to the implied insult. Instead, he ignored the comment and responded, "It's not a problem, Corbit, it just means we have to do this the *hard* way."

"*No head injuries, Kirk. Do you understand me?*"

Kirk clenched his jaw even harder. "What if he *resists*?"

"*I said—no—head—injuries. I* mean *it.*"

Disgusted, Kirk broke the link without signing off. Disgruntled on levels that he wasn't entirely *comfortable* with, he stormed away from the DPC.

BOY MEETS GIRL

On the floor of the storage room where—until recently—he fed the NCs on a weekly basis, Eli dozed in and out of a fitful, dreamless slumber. His DPC coat was tucked under his head as a makeshift pillow, and his mind longed for rest, an escape from the demands of conscious thought, a chance for his *sub*conscious to come to terms with just how drastically different his life would be from now on . . . but deep sleep eluded him.

Was it worth it, *really* worth it? He hadn't learned very much from the *Parlor*'s mainframe, and now it was all gone. There was no "Plan B." There would be no more Execution Channel viruses, no meal credits . . . and, selfishly, no more trips to the *Parlor*, no way to find *her*, ever again . . .

When he finally slipped away from sheer exhaustion, dozing just deeply enough to snore, a *thumping* rang from outside the storage room door, and Eli snapped back awake immediately, adrenaline flowing into his bloodstream like a river. The noise came again—it sounded as though someone were trying to open the door but having difficulty getting it moving. He snatched up the length of pipe he'd kept near—his only chance would be to strike the person while they were still struggling with the heavy door. He took a breath and shoved the door open as hard and fast as he could, the pipe poised and ready to crack skulls.

He held back just in time when he realized who it was.

"What're you, *nuts*?" Sara scolded from behind arms raised to protect her face.

Shaken on several levels, Eli lowered his impromptu weapon. Tension made him snap at her more than he normally would have. "I *locked* this door!"

The waif girl marched into the room. Plucking the pipe from his hand as she passed him by, she explained, "Derby went out to patrol the area." She dropped the pipe onto the crate from which Eli had taken it.

"And he left *the door open*?" Eli seized it in anger and made to drag it shut. "*Now* I feel safe," he grumbled.

Sara grabbed his arm before he'd moved the hunk of metal a half-meter. "There's an *Organizer* lookin' for you."

Two thoughts occurred to Eli as he met the girl's concerned eyes. The first was that they'd already *taken* his Citizenship. Despite his own fear of discovery just now, if he *really* thought about it, he hadn't committed any crimes *dynamic* enough to warrant a trip to the Execution Channel . . . so why send an *Organizer* after him? What more . . .

Which led him to his *second* thought—*Sara* didn't yet know that he was an NC now. Even if Derby told her Eli was in trouble, the big man wouldn't have discussed that kind of detail without his permission. In that moment, Eli felt pity for himself and for her, and most of all, *shame*.

Not knowing what exactly he hoped to accomplish by putting it off, Eli casually covered his right hand with his left, hiding his clear IDC from her view.

"I know a better place you can hide," she was telling him. She reached out, took his arm again . . . and looked down at his covered right hand. She paused for the briefest moment before pulling him from the storage room.

She already knows, he realized. *Derby didn't* have *to tell her, and neither do I. She's a smart kid.*

Now embarrassed by his clumsy attempt to protect her—

Or was it to protect yourself, *Eli?*

—he allowed himself to be guided over to the stairs. As they ascended, she glanced over her shoulder and teased, "Did you know you *snore*?"

Eli smiled back, finding it quite endearing that *she* was trying to cheer *him* up. Shrugging absently, he followed as she led the way.

* * *

"It's not much further now," Sara assured him.

Eli would have replied, but he was too focused on *not* slipping on the wet, slime-covered concrete. There was barely enough light to allow him to *see* the slick surface, but Sara seemed to know exactly where she was going.

Given the "underground" nature of many of his activities, Eli was surprised he hadn't previously heard of this place. Back at his living complex, Sara had taken him up one level, only to lead him to the opposite side of the building and then back *down* again, this time through an old, dilapidated grate, the kind used to evacuate the water into the storm drains in the event of flooding.

The grate had proven itself the entrance to an amazing *labyrinth* of concrete and rusted steel—a maze with which Sara was clearly familiar. As they moved forward, every sound was amplified through the tunnels. They came to a T-junction and the girl made her turn without hesitation.

She glanced back at him, then asked the question that had probably been on her mind since she'd found him in the storage room. "What'd you *do*? *Kill* someone?"

Moss was growing everywhere, and water dripped endlessly. As Eli glanced up toward an unexpected source of moonlight, he was treated to several drops right in the eye. Wiping it away before it could run into the bandage on his cheek, he gave her the simplest answer he could think of: "I rocked the boat."

She snorted and smiled. "You *are* nuts." Eli was unable to refute her analysis. Then, just as he noticed another light source at the far end of the tunnel, she declared, "It's there, up ahead."

Even before they emerged from the tunnel, a woman's voice drifted to them on the damp air.

". . . and deep from within Galgoth's lair, they could hear a sound . . . "

As they stepped through the archway, Sara turned to him and raised a *shushing* finger to her lips. Eli stood, grateful to straighten his back.

". . . but twas not the sound of the monster's heavy footsteps, which they had become so terribly used to . . . " Now he could hear the woman's British accent, so much like . . . like . . .

His mind struggled to accept what his heart already knew.

Sara had brought him to some sort of *tunnel cavern*—a junction point of several storm drain tunnels, with old pumps and processing machinery. Several algae lines upon the walls indicated that the room had flooded to more than one level at more than one time in the past, but now the place was relatively dry and unused. A fire burned in a metal barrel across the room, and an open grate far above allowed more moonlight to add further illumination.

". . . no, this time it was something different . . . some*one* different . . . "

In the center of the spacious grotto, a woman sat with an open book on her lap. Her feminine hand brushed over the yellowed pages, keeping place as she read to the group of about a dozen wide-eyed NC children, who sat in a circle around the storyteller with practiced discipline. They hung on her every word—even the youngest children were silent and attentive.

" 'Finally, my prince has come for me,' the Princess whispered with fear and hope," the woman read in her lilting, familiar voice, "Nimbus quickly replied, 'It's probably nothing more than a field worker. Nothing more!' "

Well-behaved though they were, some of the children were looking past their storyteller now, studying the visitor Sara had brought. As she turned the page of her aged *Windsong* book, the woman finally became aware of the watching eyes behind her. She glanced over her shoulder, then lost her breath at the sight of Eli standing in the mouth of the tunnel.

Eli was equally aghast as he gawked back at her, his blood rushing even faster now than it had in the storage room. Mindless of the drama she'd inadvertently created, Sara smiled widely and waved largely. "Hi!" she called out.

To *her.* The woman from the subtrain. His *Dream Woman.*

Dressed exactly as his Dream Woman had been at the end of his dream that morning, the woman snapped her divided attention around to her listeners.

"Okay, children," she choked through a constricted throat, "story time is over, and I'll see you all back here tomorrow." Dropping the book, she stood shakily.

The children exchanged confused reactions.

"You . . . " was all Eli managed to say at first as he took a step closer.

She bolted into an uncertain trot, slipping into another one of the side tunnels.

"Hey, hold on a minute!" Eli called, gaining speed. He ducked under a massive pipe that barred his way. "I want to talk to you!" The bewildered children cleared a path as he stormed past them.

Upon reaching the second tunnel entrance, he spotted the woman immediately. In her flustered haste, she'd chosen a junction with a closed gate not five meters inside. She pounded on the metal in frustration, then turned to him while backing into the corner. "Leave me alone!" she demanded, hardly making eye contact with him. She was far more out of breath than her short run justified.

"What the hell's *wrong* with you?" he gasped. How could this be, that she didn't *want* to talk to him? Didn't she have as many questions as *he* had?

"I said, leave me *alone*!" she repeated, her voice trembling. As he moved forward, she worked her way to the opposite corner, trying to keep as far from him as possible.

"I *won't* leave you alone," Eli snapped, "I want *answers*!"

Now she tried shuffling back toward the tunnel cavern. "I don't know you," she insisted without authority, "and I don't *want* to know you . . . "

Eli leaped forward, slamming one hand against the wall on either side of her and cutting off her escape. He was desperate, *speechless*.

"Get out of here . . . " she told him in the weakest tone yet. She still wouldn't even look at his face.

At a complete loss, the only thing Eli could think to ask was, "What about the *dream*?"

She mumbled, "I have to go," and tried to push past him, tried to run from him just as she had in the last dream.

Eli grabbed her shoulders and forced her to face him. "Not this time."

Back in the cavern, the children gathered around to watch the bizarre show, but neither Eli nor his captive noticed. The woman panted, desperately short of breath. She fought not to look at him, but Eli stood strong—it would *not* end like this! He reached up and took her face in his hands. Finally, her wandering blue eyes were drawn to meet his.

"You know me," he whispered. Then he launched his final attempt to reach her: He tried to kiss her.

Their lips touched, but before anything more could happen, she shoved him away as hard as she could. Eli missed a step and stumbled back against the opposite wall.

The children gasped.

But though she now had her escape route, the woman did not run. Instead, she looked across at Eli, at his bewildered, frustrated, and *hurt* expression . . .

. . . and then *she* came to *him*.

While Eli had intended a soft romantic kiss, a kiss to tug on her heart strings, she smothered his mouth with passionate *longing*.

As advanced and lucid as the *Parlor* dreams were, they could not match the reality of their embrace—and yet, at the same time, the earlier dreams now gave them a sense of destiny fulfilled upon reaching this true, genuine kiss.

The children giggled heartily, pointing and ogling. The woman heard them first, and she pulled away. Eli tried to keep her close, but then he also realized that they had an audience and blushed.

On cue, Sara appeared, moving to the front of the pack and urging them away. "What're you, the *media*?" she chastised them. "Break it up. Take a hike. There ain't nothin' to see here. Come on, move it. Let's go, everybody—back upstairs." The children all laughed and scattered, followed by Sara, who herded the youngest NC ahead of her. She stopped to collect the old suitcase the woman had been sitting on as she read, then took a brief moment to regard Eli and his companion. "Don't do anything *I* wouldn't do," she advised with a wink.

The woman was slumped against the gate, her breath finally slowing. Eli leaned back against the wall and tried to tame his own racing pulse.

"*How*?" she whispered, so softly that Eli almost didn't hear her. "How is this *possible*?"

Eli grappled for an answer, when he knew in truth that he had none to give. Still, rather than pop off with *How the hell should I know?*, he opted to take a shot in the dark. "We . . . we must have been using the *Parlor* at the *same time* and . . . I don't know . . . *bonded* somehow . . . " He nodded his head. That didn't sound too far fetched at all. In fact, it made quite a bit of sense.

Beside him, his Dream Woman stiffened. She stood up straight, and said, in a flat tone of voice, "What, are you suggesting that we're *soul mates*?" She headed out into the cavern without waiting for a response.

Eli was taken aback by the sudden return of her standoffish side, but he stepped after her. "I thought I *lost* you," he said as he followed her toward the fire.

"You almost *did*," she admitted, folding her arms and stopping before the welcome heat. "I wasn't going back there."

Leaning against the wall on the other side of the fire, Eli considered that. He also considered Dana's—and his own—drastically increased *Parlor* usage over such a short period of time. "I don't think you could've stayed away," he commented.

His Dream Woman smirked sardonically. "You weren't so *cocky* in my dream." Eli looked from the fire to her face. It was on the tip of his tongue to explain that she'd misunderstood him, but her attitude put him off and he merely stared. "I suppose your name isn't 'Elijah' either?"

He continued his cool stare. "My *friends* call me 'Eli.' "

"I think we passed 'friends' in our first fantasy," she pointed out. Eli blushed and returned his gaze to the fire. After a moment, she added in a softer tone of voice, "I prefer *Elijah.* It's a good name."

To Eli's chagrin, he suddenly realized that he had *no idea* what *her* name really was. With a self-depreciating grin, he admitted, "I've always referred to you as my 'Dream Woman.' "

"I'm flattered," she stated in a tone which said that she really *wasn't.* "Now you can refer to me as *'Susan.'* "

This time Eli didn't allow her chill to pass unnoted. "*Susan*," he said as he stepped away from the fire, "you weren't so *brash* in *my* dream."

Susan stared after him, and her tone was again softer, and even a little apologetic, when she offered, "Well, this is hardly your conventional 'boy meets girl.' "

Eli paused, taking casual hold of a dangling chain and sighing, but also keeping his back to her. She was right, of course, and was probably coping as best she could under these bizarre circumstances—the heat of their first real kiss indicated how she felt *somewhere* inside . . . but her repeated sarcasm still stung. Part of him yearned for the *fantasy* that the *Parlor* had offered: The "perfect" relationship, without friction or consequences . . . but that's all it had been—a *fantasy*, and he knew it.

"Since I . . . started using the *Parlor*," Susan was saying, "everything seems so . . . *disjointed*." She moved behind him, and he heard her sit on the platform upon which the children had listened to her rendition of *Windsong*. "The System's neglect of the Non-Citizen children bothers me to no end . . . but now even teaching them, which I *love*, has become a daily chore. *You* out of everybody must *understand*."

Still facing away, he asked, "What do you mean?"

"*You* must be the one who's been feeding them, right?"

He turned sharply, somewhat aghast. "You *know* about that?"

She didn't answer him in words, but merely looked back at him with a far warmer expression on her face. Cautiously, lest she lash out once again, he moved to sit next to her.

"Sara thinks the world of you," she told him as he reached her side. "You're like a father to her." Then her smile slipped away. "Tell me . . . has feeding them meant the same to you since you started using the *Parlor*?"

Eli shifted uncomfortably. "I lost my food connection, so it's a null point, but . . . *no*. And I haven't even really tried to find a *solution*. I haven't had the *drive*."

"*That's* what I mean," she pointed out urgently. "See, *that's* what I'm talking about. It's as if somebody's ripping out my *soul* and my *heart*."

Eli asked, "Then why do you *go*?" but he was pretty sure he knew what her answer would be—she'd become fixated on the dreams to the exclusion of common sense . . .

Instead, she surprised and unnerved him when she answered, "I just started working there."

Eli pulled away from her slightly without realizing that he was doing it. "The *Parlor*?"

"Yes." She noticed his discomfort, but didn't seem to know what to do about it. After a short pause, she started talking again. "Use of the service is mandatory protocol. It's meant to be *safe* . . . so *why* do I feel like this? I'm convinced that everything is *connected* . . . "

Before Eli could wonder what exactly she meant by "everything," another thought cut in. Sure, he was startled when she first said that she worked at the *Parlor*, but he could also see several *advantages* to this new development. His efforts to break into the *Parlor's* mainframe—the same efforts that cost him his Citizenship—had proven painfully *fruitless* . . . but maybe *she* could learn something from the *inside*. If he could teach her how to use the scrambler, she might be able to—

Again, the sharp, piercing headache, lancing through his temples and behind his eyes without warning. He pinched the bridge of his nose and tried to breathe the pain away.

". . . I mean," she was still asking, "could it be *possible* that—?"

The pain ground on his nerves, and he waved her silent a little more rudely than he intended. "I—!" he started to snap, then swallowed the surliness and began again, "I . . . don't know. But there's a *lot* more to the *Dream Parlor* than just 'lucid dreams.' "

Susan stared wide-eyed at him for a moment, then said, "There's a lot more to the *Parlor* than you even *realize*." She stood, and offered him her hand. "Follow me. I have to show you something . . . "

Confused, Eli took her hand and she helped him up. She led him across the breadth of the shadowy space. Upon reaching the far corner, she took hold of a hanging switch box and depressed the control with her thumb. With a laborious creaking, a rusted plate which Eli had mistaken for a permanent fixture slid up the side of the nearest wall, revealing a dank, dark tunnel less than half the size of the ones Sara had led him through to bring him here. Eli peered into the gloom, but he could make out nothing . . . nothing with his *eyes*. His *nose*, on the other hand, detected a putrid *stench* coming from somewhere within.

Without a word, Susan crawled into the waist-high tunnel. A second later, Eli followed.

PRECISE KIND OF MAGIC

"*Total synaptic hemorrhage. Link to mainframe severed. Session terminated.*"

With a tired sigh, Corbit leaned heavily against his work table and growled into his hand-mike, "Private Entry: March Twenty-Eighth . . . " He paused briefly, then spat bitterly, "Another wasted day in the secret life of Doctor Corbit . . . watched another *fry* in the *pan*."

Glancing over his shoulder, Corbit considered the lifeless husk stretched out upon the dreamslab. Straightening, he ambled back to its side, mindful of the blood and carnage spread from one end of the slab to the other.

"Every one of these feeble-minded lab rats either wakes up *dead . . .* " Reaching out, he took the former NC's gore-soaked heart from the corpse's clutched hand and looked it over, feeling its texture and smelling its aroma. ". . . or *at best,* severely *lobotomized* . . . which is never a good thing."

Disgusted—by another disappointment, *not* the ichor of the prominent organ—Corbit slapped the heart back into the cavity from which it had been torn. The surrounding tissues had since swollen and thickened, so the heart only slipped halfway in, but Corbit left it where it lodged.

What did this *one dream?* he wondered idly. *An army of fire ants crawling through his chest? What possible vision could give the man the strength to tear through his own flesh and bone and rip his beating heart from his chest? So pathetic . . . yet so fascinating.*

But these days, Corbit had found something—some*one*—a lot *more* fascinating. He lowered the NC's up-stretched arm across its chest, then pulled the IDC hand from the gel to do the same as he continued his dictation in a lighter tone.

"My boy, *Eli*, is the only bright spot in my research." Casually, almost without realizing what he was doing, Corbit stopped speaking into the microphone and started talking to the blood-covered corpse. "His inbred resilience to external forces kind of turns me on . . . in a *professional* way, of course." The carcass offered no feedback, so Corbit continued with an encouraged smile. "And now that his *social status* makes him eligible for my personal *draft list*, I can go so far as to say: I have *faith*."

With a final grin and nod, Corbit carefully wrapped the body in its blue-green sheet. Picking those sheets up had been one of his wiser moves—it certainly helped with the clean-up.

Still smiling, Corbit sauntered around to the other side of the slab. He still held the small microphone in his hand, but for the moment, his dictation was forgotten. It had been some time since he'd felt this optimistic, what with the pressure from the Ice Bitch and other *Powers That Be*. The noose was tightening a lot quicker than he'd cared to admit—once the System allowed NCs into the *Parlor* . . .

But all of that might be neither here nor there at this point. If his astonishing performance during his last dream session was any indication, Eli Barrett had the precise kind of *magic* that Corbit had been looking for every day for the past five years. The Chief Suit wanted him because he was a spiker . . . she had *no* idea.

Following the incident, Corbit had pulled every string and called in every favor he could to get Eli brought in. After all, he had the Ice Bitch's personal approval to start working him over, right? And, lo and behold, when they tapped into his cyber-limbo outlet at the DPC, it turned out that *Eli* was in the middle of some questionable activities anyway, trying to access the *Parlor's* mainframe . . . *if* the records were correct. It was hard to tell—it looked like the boy had some kind of frequency scrambler. Corbit *told* that idiot Kirk that he should nab Eli right in the DPC, that Eli was beyond your common Citizen in more ways than one and wouldn't just waltz down to Citizen Processing like a good little automaton.

Sure enough! Eli dodged the authorities . . . which pretty much put him on the ordained *shit list.* Corbit's knee-jerk reaction had been to snap at Kirk, but later he got to thinking that this *could* be a good thing after all. A spiking *Citizen* was one thing . . . a spiking *NC* was another. If all went as planned, if Kirk could hunt him down as efficiently as he claimed, then it would not only be novel but *exhilarating* to look his savior child in the eye and make him an offer he couldn't refuse.

With a grunt, Corbit opened the hatch leading down to the drainage system. Leaving the lid open, he turned back to the task of hefting the latest bit of rubbish into its final reward.

The System is under the erroneous impression that it can have whatever it wants, he thought. *They took my* Dream Parlor . . . *they will not have my* Eli.

MY REASON

"Cover your face . . . it only gets worse from here . . . "

When he first entered the tunnels with Sara, Eli recalled, he'd thought that the dank, moldy smell of rust, slime, and stagnant water had been fairly unpleasant. Now, as he and Susan forged their way on hands and knees through the dark tunnel, he was smacked with an indescribable stench that made the tunnels smell like sweet perfume. This new fetor reeked of utter *decay*, and he found himself unnerved as well as revolted.

Although it made his crawl more laborious, he heeded Susan's advice and covered his nose and mouth with his sleeve.

After a few more grisly meters, Eli slowly became aware that Susan was now climbing out of their current burrow and into a larger cavity. Bluish moonlight was again filtering in from above into this next area, and Eli could see her silhouette quite clearly now. She stopped at the threshold. "I would prepare you," she informed him flatly, "but I don't have the words."

Eli nodded his vague understanding, but she didn't wait for his response. As he clambered out after her, she navigated her way deeper into the rancid dugout. The walls on either side of them sloped outward from the half-meter area where Susan's feet found tedious purchase, and she was using the sides for balance.

For Eli to drop down and join her, he had no choice but to move his sleeve away so that he could use both hands. The unfiltered effluvium elicited a grunt of disgust, but Susan again gave no indication that she even heard. Eli stumbled after her, now holding his entire forearm against his face—the stench was unspeakable! As she led him into the open area, however, he found himself more than a little distracted. A chill ran up and down his spine, finally settling like ice water in his bowels as he took in the ghastly scene before him.

Lined up—no, *piled*—along the sides of what appeared to be an old maintenance junction were at least a dozen or so bodies covered head-to-toe with blue-green sheets. They were arranged upon some sort of shelf-units, with the scant floor-space left mercifully clear. The moonlight was coming through grates strewn with moss, rust, and grime, and Eli could sense rather than see the inevitable rats and other interested vermin. Short of the deaths of his father and Dana, it was the most nightmarish thing Eli had ever seen. The scene harkened back to his—*their*—last dream, where the bodies had blocked the way between them. At *that* point, at least, as unnerving as it had been, Eli had taken some comfort in the knowledge that it was, after all, a *dream*.

But this was *real*.

Roboticly, Susan bent over one of the smaller shapes nearest the entrance. "I discovered this one not long before my last visit to the *Parlor*," she told him as she drew back the cover and revealed the sadly familiar child with the mutilated eye-sockets. Eli's resolve slipped, and he whirled involuntarily, gagging and trying desperately not to vomit against the wall.

"Are you okay?" Susan asked, only semi-concerned as her concentration seemed to remain on keeping *herself* emotionally detached from the sights within the room.

Eli nodded that he would be fine . . . or, at least, that he would survive.

Susan replaced the blood-stained blue-green sheet. "No surprise *this* crept into my dream," she commented sardonically. She glanced to her right and observed that, somewhere along the line, another corpse's feet had come uncovered. Like a nurse, or an undertaker, she stepped over and straightened the sheet appropriately. "I don't know what drew *you* to the *Dream Parlor*, but what you see here was *my* lure. *This* is why I took the job."

Distracted and queasy, Eli didn't follow. "What do you mean?" He stayed as close to the center of the walkway as he could.

"I've been teaching down here a while," she explained in a halting, stilted voice, "but I had to find a place of safety for the children in case the Organizers raided us. So I familiarized myself with all the tunnels . . . and that's when I discovered my first bodies." She gestured around her. "I've done the best I can to give them a better resting place, but . . . "

Eli still wasn't getting it. "How did you connect them to the *Dream Parlor*?"

"I didn't, at first. But then I found *another* one in the same place, and so . . . I stayed down here a couple of nights, and that's when I witnessed my first *dumping*."

" 'Dumping?' "

She nodded. "They drop the bodies through a drainage pipe just outside this room. I traced the geography of the tunnels. This spot is right beneath—"

"The *Dream Parlor*," they said together. Eli was with her now.

"Right," she affirmed. "But I've checked *everything* at work, and *nothing* leads back here . . . but still the bodies *come*!"

Her frustration evident, she turned on her heels and strode to the other end of the room. Reluctantly, Eli trailed behind her. She stopped at the far end of the shelves, indicating one of the last bodies.

"This is the most *curious* one. She has *blisters* like no burn I've ever seen before." She lifted the sheet for Eli to look without asking whether he really *wanted* to. Feeling backed into a corner, Eli indulged her by sneaking a peek under the . . .

His breath caught in his throat, then slipped free as a wordless, mindless groan. His eyes shifted away, looked back, then away again. His stomach churned, and while a part of him realized that he might vomit after all, the rest of him neither knew nor cared. He stumbled back a step, gasping.

This time Susan could not ignore his distress, although the intensity of his reaction baffled her—true, the sight was terrible, but after everything else he'd gone through recently, surely . . . She dropped the sheet quickly, stepping after him. "What?" she asked, concerned.

Eli was rocking back and forth now, his mind and body in utter turmoil. Heaving and groaning, he finally turned and stumbled back into the sloped area, retreating all the way to the tunnel entrance before collapsing against the wall, his head against his arms.

"What's *wrong*?" Susan implored. "What *is* it?"

Finally, Eli began to get a hold of himself. He straightened, but did not quite face her as he said, "Nora . . . "

The burned body, the burned *woman* . . . it was Nora Puente. *His* Nora. The Nora he had so boldly followed to the *Dream Parlor* . . . and then virtually *forgotten* about.

How could he have *done* that? How could he have been so selfish, so *heartless*? Nora, the grandmother he never had, the caring soul who had saved his *sanity* when he had nothing else to live for . . . and after he'd waltzed so easily into the *Dream Parlor's* loving embrace, he'd barely even *thought* about her—until faced with this hideous, seared *carcass*.

Susan gaped at Eli in confusion. "*Who*?"

She couldn't understand, of course. "A friend," he explained in a choked voice.

Susan sighed in empathy, folding her arms and dropping her head.

Slowly, Eli forced himself to turn and face the covered form, face his *guilt*. Guardedly, he stepped back into the shelved area, his eyes skimming Nora's oh-so-familiar shape. *Nora* . . .

"Family, really," he corrected himself. Susan had turned to contemplate the concealed body in a new light, but when Eli said that she again closed her eyes. Eli had to step around her. Kneeling, he tenderly placed his hand upon Nora's blanketed shoulder. "She was *my* reason for coming to the *Dream Parlor.*" He bent closer, as though the deceased woman might hear him better as he whispered, "I'm sorry . . . "

But "sorry" wasn't enough, and he knew it. He'd failed her—her, Sara, Derby, Elizabeth, and everyone else he was supposed to protect and care for. He'd failed his father and his mother, and every ideal he'd worked so hard to maintain in this abysmal world . . .

Slowly, the pain mutated into seething *rage.* Rage at himself, and rage at the nameless, faceless entity that was the *Dream Parlor.*

Trembling more with anger than distress, he worked his clenched jaw just enough to state, "Someone's gonna *pay* for this."

He felt Susan's hand fall gently upon his shoulder. "What can I do to help you?" she asked.

At first he thought she was offering emotional support, but then he realized that she was suggesting *action.* Yes, *action*, that's what he craved right now. He needed to do *something*, something working toward their ultimate goal of bringing this horror—*whatever* the hell it all meant—to a consummate and unequivocal *end.*

And he had an idea where to *start.*

PHASE THREE

"Most assuredly, I have never *heard* of such a thing!"

Ruth Davis, department head of the DPC, would have been right at home in any library . . . when libraries were still around, that is. Rigid, austere, and puritanical, she lorded over her domain like a lower-class version of Corbit's Ice Bitch. She wore duplicate gray dress-suits every day of the week—an effort in efficiency that no one around her seemed to appreciate—and her hair was always in the tightest bun above her taut face and horn-rimmed glasses.

She found it a bit harder to maintain her dignity, however, in the middle of the night. Roused from bed by the frantic night watchmen, she now found herself escorting an intimidating Organizer into the data-entry pit. The pit wasn't her favorite place these days either, what with her losing *two* workers in two days. As she reached the bottom of the stairwell, she brought her hands together in a sharp *clap-clap!* to turn on the overhead lights.

Standing obdurate as the large Organizer joined her, she continued trying to explain that his notion that *one* of those former workers—11811—could be lurking on the premises was preposterous . . . *without* trying to suggest in any way that *he* was preposterous.

"As a matter of fact," she clarified, "I have worked at this facility since it opened, and we have *never* had any intruders of *any* kind."

The Organizer consulted some sort of device in the palm of his hand. He gave no indication that he was even listening to her as he slowly began circling the perimeter of the room.

"No," Ruth pressed on, "none at all!" Her next words were arrested as the man actually kicked aside one of the work chairs to glance under the terminals. Choking on her dismay, she thought about how she would react if this man were any one else *but* an Organizer. "By the very *nature* of processing data, we are *required* to maintain the—" She swallowed hard as he knocked over more furniture on the far side of the computer core. "—the *utmost* in security standards. Now . . . " More furniture tossed aside. ". . . if a discharged employment were to even *set foot* on these premises . . . " With a final commotion, the Organizer was back at her side, scowling at his device more than ever. ". . . he would be dealt with, *swiftly* and *severely*." The man—clenching his jaw hard enough for the muscles in his cheeks to twitch—lowered his instrument and cast one more hard look around the cold room. "I *assure* you."

Without so much as glancing at her, Kirk said, very politely, "Thanks for your help," before bumping her aside on his way back up the stairs.

Ruth stole a moment to compose herself. She thought briefly about straightening up the room the Organizer had left in such disarray, but then decided that she'd had enough for one night. She moved for the stairs herself, only remembering at the last moment to double-clap the lights back off.

Holding her work pad close to her chest, Ruth Davis ascended the stairs . . .

. . . never suspecting that the "discharged employment" was crouching beneath the risers the entire time.

Releasing the mutual breath they'd been holding for eternity, Eli and Susan slid up the wall, appreciating the support until they reached their feet. Eli released the death-grip he'd held on her hand, knowing that the sweat left behind belonged to both of them.

"It's clear," he said when he heard his former department head reach the ground level and shuffle away. At that moment, he almost wanted to *kiss* his scrambler!

"Okay," Susan exhaled, "let's get back to work."

Nodding, Eli led her back to the end of the access way. There wasn't much work left to do, at least as far as getting them *inside* the maintenance room. He'd been seconds from overriding the scanlock before Ruth and that huge Organizer interrupted them.

"You work here?" Susan asked idly, unable to envision the man in her dreams laboring in such a frigid, stale environment.

"Used to," Eli reminded her just as he nullified the lock. The door slid open, and they entered the dusty, claustrophobic room. Vents bled heat from the core's primary cyber-link trunk, but they both appreciated the relative warmth.

Eli popped open a housing server without bothering to consult the technical diagram below. "Never thought I'd have to do *this* without the gel-interface," he remarked. "Are you watching this?"

"Yeah," she affirmed.

"Good. I want you to know how to run the scrambler if we get into trouble. It's like I showed you—it's all a matter of *combination* and *frequency*." To reiterate, he indicated the scrambler's small switches with his thumb. "If 'one' and 'two' are *up*, then 'five' and 'six' are *down*. If *'four'* is up—"

'Eight' is down," she finished.

"Right . . . " Satisfied, he began the tedious task of hardwiring the scrambler's electrode tip into the server.

Almost immediately, as he slipped into the intricate but otherwise wearisome task, his mind began to wander. He attempted to lose himself in the job, but it simply wasn't engrossing enough. Nora never drifted far from his thoughts.

How ironic that you can't stop *thinking about her now, huh, Eli?*

It didn't *help* matters either that his *splitting headache* had returned. He tried focusing on the mission that lay ahead once he accessed his cyber-limbo terminal. The best way, Susan had agreed, to get to the bottom of this mystery was to take another crack at the *Dream Parlor* mainframe, and—regardless of his previous failures—the most surreptitious entrance was still through cyber-limbo. Eli pointed out that Susan was still a Citizen, and their only *official* link to the *Parlor*—his initial thoughts of using *her* access to the mainframe now seemed premature. After all, *he* was already in trouble, and therefore had less to risk. He even suggested that perhaps she shouldn't join him on his raid of the DPC, but she would hear nothing of it . . . in fact, she seemed almost *insulted* that he'd even made the suggestion. They were in this together, she notified him—had been, truthfully, since their first dream.

As they had cautiously made their way through the underground to the DPC, Susan had confirmed Eli's suspicions that, like his experiences, there had been times when her dreams had seemed exceptionally lucid and realistic, and others when they were nothing but an *echo*. As near as they could surmise, those special times must have been on the occasions when they had, in fact, utilized the *Parlor* at the *same time*—an increasingly plausible coincidence when they compared their schedules.

Their dreams became a *collaboration*, he'd realized. In their last venture, she provided the covered bodies and mutilated girl, and he supplied Jacob . . . *and* the Mystery Man, as Susan could not recall that image or voice from any previous visit—apparently that oddity was Eli's trademark. The dreams became their *bond*, but for such a bond to possibly occur, there *had* to be a presiding, paramount *nexus* through that damned "neural net" to which they'd overheard Corbit referring. That, and the question of exactly *how* they'd tapped into Corbit's private journals from their dreamslabs, demanded *answers*.

And even if the System *were* using the *Parlor* to manipulate its users, *nothing* explained all the butchered bodies Susan had discovered, including . . .

Damn. Right back where I started. Nora . . .

Eli glanced at Susan, who waited patiently for him to finish his work. At least *he* had something to do, something to accomplish. "So, Susan," he spoke gently to avoid giving her a start, "I've told you a little about *my* background. How did *you* end up as a Citizen who actually *cares* about other people?"

Susan smirked. "Interesting way to put it." She folded her arms, her eyes downcast. After several seconds of silence, Eli had decided that she wasn't going to indulge him when she suddenly continued. "*Unlike* you, my parents raised me to *believe* in the New World Order. My father was neither a politician nor a government employee, back *then* at least, but he would go on for hours at a time about what a great idea it was, the one-world government. No more war, no more strife, no more Middle-Eastern countries or old Soviet states screwing everything up for the 'civilized world.' When the . . . revolution finally happened, my father actually volunteered for service. He was much too old and out-of-shape for any kind of active duty, but his *jingoist attitude* was appreciated, and he was transferred from maintenance mechanic to Organizer detail . . . " This brought raised eyebrows from Eli until she quickly added, ". . . working *dispatch.* I remember Mum crying over the move, her tears a mixture of joy and pride and apprehension. So, from the beginning, I was a particularly *well-cared-for* Citizen, just over that never acknowledged but firmly recognized line above the working-class Citizen. I was so naive . . . trusting . . . *oblivious.*"

Her self-repugnance tempted Eli to reassure her, but he bit his tongue and let her continue.

"Then late one night, when I was still a teenager, I awoke to use the water-closet. On my way back to bed, I overhead my parents talking through the open crack of their door. I wasn't normally given to *eavesdropping,* but for some reason I found myself stepping closer, holding my breath furtively, both to hide and to listen. I can't remember all the exact words that were spoken, but the *story* marked me forever. Earlier that evening, my father had issued an Organizer alert involving the ever-unwanted presence of those 'lazy Non-Citizens' in a Citizen-Only area. I remember . . . as Dad kept talking, his words reflected pride of efficiency, but his *tone* sounded more like *contrition.* I learned that the offending NCs had been children, younger than *I* was, and they'd ended up in the forbidden area simply because they *couldn't read the signs* that designated the zone off-limits." She smirked bitterly and spat, "Well, *illiteracy* was no excuse to the Organizers, of course, and the children were punished accordingly—not deleted from the System, but the two boys were beaten quite severely, and the *girl* . . . apparently the Organizers still hadn't finished *using* her by the time Dad signed off for the day. What did it really *matter*, he muttered to Mum at the end, why was he *talking* about it, she was just an inconsequential *Non-Citizen* . . . he apologized for keeping her up so late and rolled over to go to sleep in his nice, warm bed.

"*I* returned to *my* nice, warm bed undetected, and spent the rest of the night thinking very *hard* about life. Three children, scarred forever because their IDCs had been the wrong color . . . and because they hadn't been *educated* enough to watch out for themselves. How could I live with myself so *comfortably* with that sort of injustice going on? How could I make a *difference* . . . ?"

Her words trailed off, and an awkward silence filled the tight little room. Eli's gaze drifted back toward her. He started to say something, to offer some comfort . . .

A brief spark shot from the scrambler link and into his IDC. Eli grunted loudly in pain, spinning away from the server and cursing under his breath as he gripped his injured right hand.

"You okay?" Susan asked, concerned. She also took his hand and examined it for visual injury.

On edge, Eli pulled his fist away. "Bad combination," he muttered, turning back to his task. His hand smarted, and his headache was worse than ever!

"Look, maybe we should do this *later*," Susan suggested, her hand on the small of his back. "You need to *sleep*."

"I'm fine!" Eli snapped, twisting out of her touch. She said nothing, merely folded her arms and stared at him. Eli quickly backed down. "Sorry . . . " he sighed. "I don't think *rest* would do me any good anyway. I haven't been sleeping well."

"I know the feeling," Susan sympathized.

As if Eli had now paid his dues, the scrambler hooked in and the server hummed into activity on his very next try. He reached over and opened the auxiliary computer lens. "Okay. Here we go."

"*Good* combination?" she asked.

"Good *frequency*."

He activated the lens, and was mildly surprised to find himself facing a *blue* globe rather than the customary red. The link cycled, and he was in . . .

But when he opened his eyes in cyber-limbo, he found himself facing not his usual counterpart, but the computer-likeness of *Jacob*.

Damn! "I plugged into the *wrong terminal*," he informed her through sluggish lips.

"There's no time to go through this *again*," she insisted urgently.

Torn briefly before realizing that she was right, Eli inwardly pledged to be exceedingly careful—for *Jacob's* sake—and pushed on.

>DATA REQUEST: he thought at the familiar and yet *un*familiar image. >ALL INFORMATION ON *DREAM PARLOR* MAINFRAME. ROTATE SEARCH LEVEL PRIORITIES BETWEEN ONE-ALPHA-BLUE, ONE-BETA-RED, AND ONE-GAMMA-GREEN. MAINTAIN CONSTANT ROTATION ON SEQUENCES UNTIL FURTHER NOTICE.

>>*AFFIRMATIVE,* Computer-Jacob acknowledged after a brief pause.

>SPECIAL SEARCH PARAMETER: Eli added, >BIO-FEEDBACK AND NEURAL NET.

>>*SEARCHING . . . BIO-FEEDBACK. RE:* DREAM PARLOR *MAINFRAME . . .*

"This could take a while," Eli slurred to Susan.

"Just relay the information to me as you get it," she told him.

A moment passed. "So far . . . it's nothing we haven't figured out on our own . . . the *Dream Parlor* induces a *passive mentality* in its clients . . . it feeds signals through the IDC into the nervous system . . . "

Unconsciously, Susan rubbed at her inky chip. "So, they *sting* people whenever they visit the *Parlor*."

"Not just when you visit the *Parlor*," Eli clarified. "The pacifying signals are *reinforced* every time you use your IDC in *any public outlet* . . . "

"That's insane, but doesn't *explain* why they—"

Eli cut her off with a wave of his free hand. "Wait, wait, hold it . . . "

"What?"

"Great . . . everything I just described was 'Phase One' . . . "

>>*PHASE TWO,* Computer-Jacob continued, >>*INCREASES GOVERNMENT CONTROL OF THE POPULACE. ONCE SEVENTY-FIVE PERCENT OF ALL CITIZENS ARE ATTENDING THE* DREAM PARLOR *CONSISTENTLY, AN ADVANCED ENDORPHIN STIMULANT/SUPPRESSANT WILL BE INTRODUCED.*

>>*ANY CITIZEN WHO VIOLATES WORLD ORDER LAW OR POLICY WILL SUFFER ADVERSE PHYSICAL SIDE-EFFECTS PROPORTIONATE TO THEIR LEVEL OF ADDICTION AND THE DEGREE OF INFRINGEMENT. THE SIDE-EFFECTS WILL HAVE A VARIETY OF NEUROLOGICAL AND PSYCHOSOMATIC . . .*

". . . a variety of neurological and psychosomatic manifestations, relative to the individual . . . "

Beside him, Susan folded her arms as she absorbed what Eli was saying. "That explains my *nausea*," she lamented.

"And my *headaches*," Eli agreed with equal realization. "That's the end of Phase Two . . . Phase *Three* . . . will provide total assurance against any *opposition* or *uprising* when the World Order solidifies its *one-world power*. As soon as we're thoroughly addicted, the *Dream Parlor* will be officially opened to *everyone* . . . " Then, despite the usual slack-jawed numbness of cyber-limbo, Eli's brow furrowed in concern as he stated, ". . . and users of the *Parlor* will *lose* the ability to enter REM sleep without *Parlor* assistance."

"That's *dream deprivation,*" Susan stammered, her voice both skeptical and appalled. She'd once read an old psychology textbook that contained a chapter on dream deprivation. A number of volunteer students were permitted to sleep all they wanted but *not* to enter REM so that the researchers could evaluate such denial's effects. The test was *supposed* to run for one month, but after two weeks the students were in such bad shape they had to call the whole thing off. When she thought about everything that those students went through . . . "Can they *do* that?"

"We have to assume that they can. There's no safe release from this addiction—according to Corbit's charts, it would take a person's nervous system four-to-six months to readjust without the IDC signals . . . "

It was a *horrifying* concept. The bastards had created an addiction from which no one could escape. Even if people figured out what was happening to them, there would be nothing they could do about it!

Susan was dumbstruck. Realizing that the nausea that had plagued her was artificially induced almost seemed to make it worse now, and learning that she could either continue to submit to the *Parlor*'s claws or stay away and wait for her cognitive abilities to fall apart . . . She stepped back into the access way, leaned her head against the wall, and held herself.

Through it all, Eli's dismaying rendition never stopped, although by now he wasn't telling her anything that she didn't already know. ". . . and without the ability to *dream*, it's only a matter of weeks, maybe *days*, before the person begins suffering from intense hallucinations, paranoia, disorientation . . . the person's expected to either *commit suicide* or become *hopelessly insane* . . . " Slowly, his voice trailed off.

Hallucinations, paranoia, disorientation . . .

Susan glanced over and saw that, although the blue light was still on, Eli had leaned back out of its retinal grasp. Slowly, she made her way back to him as he disconnected his IDC. When she reached his side, she asked hesitantly, "When does Phase Three begin?"

"*Dana*," Eli whispered.

"What?"

He looked down at her, sick with comprehension. "It's *already begun.*"

JAM HIS SIGNAL

"*Nothin'*. Not *one* damn lead. I can't find him *anywhere* . . ."

Corbit stood at his office's French doors, leaning casually against the frame and staring out at a glorious sunrise. Gripping his helmet in the crook of his arm, Kirk paced in front of Corbit's desk—the husky Organizer could not see the tempered amusement on Corbit's face. Oh, Corbit was equally frustrated that Eli had thus far escaped their—*his*—grasp, but he also recalled how *cocky* Kirk had been about tracking the Wunderkind down. If anything, Corbit's respect for Eli *grew* with each hour of evasion.

He considered the mini-gel disk in his hand. He'd intended to fill Kirk in on this latest development as soon as he entered the office, but then Kirk had gone off and Corbit couldn't resist letting the tirade play out.

". . . I follow his chip to where he outta be and he ain't *there*!" Kirk continued.

Corbit casually observed, "He's learned how to jam his IDC signal."

"Yeah," Kirk muttered, "well, if I get close enough to *tag* him, *I'll* jam his signal. I don't know who this guy *is*, but he sure knows how to *dig a hole*."

The sun crawled up the horizon, clearing the lower structures at the opposite end of the plaza and flashing its intensity into Corbit's face. The Doctor did not look away, but embraced the warmth. It had been a long night for him as well, and it was time to bring Kirk up to speed.

"Ever hear of *Mencer Barrett*?"

Kirk paused at the change in subject, then slowly moved toward the French doors himself. ". . . sure. The lunatic who tried to stop the New World Order."

"I've been doing some digging myself. It seems that *Eli* has quite a *lineage*."

As the full implication of that statement sank in, Kirk reached Corbit's side. Corbit glanced over at him, and Kirk saw none of the harshness that usually clouded the Doctor's gaze when their eyes met lately. For the first time in quite a while, Kirk felt the *bond* that had kept him at Corbit's side these past couple of years. He wasn't *comfortable* with that bond, however, and he stuck to the subject at hand. "What idiot gave *him* a job handling classified documents?"

Corbit shrugged one shoulder. "Regardless . . . some *yahoo* accessed my *computer* a few hours ago. I doubt it's what it *seems* to be . . . but he *did* work with Eli." Corbit held up the mini-disk and grinned. "Here's the stats. Go *chat* with him, will you?"

Kirk took the disk. Both of them knew this meant two things to Kirk: A possible *lead* . . . and a chance to blow off some *steam*. Kirk returned Corbit's leer, turned on his heel, and slipped his helmet onto his head.

Corbit returned his gaze to the rising sun and took a long sip of his luke-warm coffee.

Eli, Eli . . . where are *you, my boy . . . ?*

A BETTER PLAN

Eli's pencil sketched back and forth across the paper he'd found in his pocket, and for once it had *nothing* to do with his artistic renderings. Situating himself where the sun shone through from overhead, Eli struggled to yield a concrete depiction of the subjective *Dream Parlor* "neural net."

The clicking of heels on concrete stirred him from his frustrating-yet-exhilarating task. Once Susan appeared, ducking under the cross pipe to join him in the tunnel cavern, he returned to his drawing, but when she stood directly in front of him with a water bottle in one hand and a wrapped cloth in the other, he glanced up once more.

"I brought you something to eat," she told him with a slight smile.

All at once, the ravenous pit in his gut overwhelmed his senses. Throwing both pencil and paper from his lap, he bolted to his feet and took the glorious boons from her . . . remembering only at the last moment to peck a kiss of thanks on her cheek before racing to use the shelf of the nearby machinery as a lunch table.

As he unwrapped the gifts in a flurry matching his pre-World Order Christmas mornings, Susan wandered over and plucked the paper from its fallen spot on the grate. "What's this?" she asked.

Never thought carrots and an apple could look so good, he mused. *Now I understand the NCs' reaction to the feedings.* It then occurred to him that she'd asked a question. He glanced over his shoulder briefly and mumbled, "Neural net," as he crammed a carrot stick into his mouth.

Susan sat on the stool, considering the bizarre, web-like sketch. "A what?"

Eli forced himself to speak more clearly while continuing to wolf the food. "*Dream Parlor* neural net . . . I got the image while I was plugged into the system . . . "

"And this?"

When he saw what she was pointing at specifically, he grunted. "Mainframe." She still looked confused, so he elaborated. "See, the *net* is fairly localized. Turns out that the *Parlor*'s surface and shape aren't just *aesthetic design*—the place is a huge *satellite link.* All the neural patterns are stored, monitored, and managed from *one* central computer." He was still devouring his food, but his enthusiasm also grew as he spoke. Listening, Susan joined him at the ancient apparatus. "All the other *Parlor* outlets, all the IDC ports that zap us answer to this one location. The whole damn *building's* part of the mainframe . . . "

"Yes," she agreed, starting to catch on, "so if we can penetrate *this* system . . . "

Eli nodded. "*Exactly.*" He seized the water bottle and stated boldly, "I want to plant a virus into the core," before taking a heavy swig.

"But you said that it would take *months* for the victims to detox . . . ?"

Now Eli was shaking his head. "I used to create *time-delay* viruses that would delete people's IDC numbers from the Execution Channel. If I can replicate that virus in my *mind,* and design it so that it mutates so quickly they can't get a fix on it, then it can hide in the *peripheral links* while it weans people off of their addiction."

Eli popped another carrot in his mouth. The ardor and hope that Susan had felt briefly in her chest began to wane as her damned nausea grew . . . or perhaps it was the *magnitude* of what he was describing sinking in. "And you think you can achieve this through a *lucid dream*," she observed skeptically.

For the first time since he began outlining his intention, Eli's confidence slipped. "I'm not sure," he admitted as he took another drink of water.

Susan turned and sauntered away, not wanting him to see the doom-and-gloom that she knew was on her face. Drifting over into the sunlight, she contemplated Eli's drawing of the neural net.

". . . I have to get a closer look inside the mainframe itself," Eli was saying.

Susan held the paper up, turning it in such a way that the sunlight shone on the back of it. Slowly, the drawing on the *reverse side* of the paper caught her attention.

". . . I have to get back into the *Dream Parlor*. Back inside *my head*."

Susan flipped the paper around, revealing an illustration Eli had drawn of her an eternity ago. Unexpectedly touched, her face lit up in a smile as she gazed at Eli in a different light.

Warmed, but somehow embarrassed, Eli reached her quickly and took the paper, lowering it gently. He touched her cheek, and for a moment, neural nets, *Dream Parlors*, and Phase Threes seemed worlds away. "I told you before that you were my Dream Woman," Eli whispered. Susan's heart leaped, and she remembered exactly why she had fallen so heavily for this man, why the dreams had been so irresistible, System-addiction be damned! She gasped heavily, her lips parting . . .

And then the moment passed. Eli was suddenly all business again, and he actually turned away from her as he continued chattering about his reckless plans! Susan didn't know whether to be hurt, angry, or both . . . so she tried to swallow *any* reaction and follow his studious example.

"Before I went into that last dream, Corbit—the man *himself*—told me about some great, new experiment he was working on.

And he almost seemed to be warning me *against* overusing the *Parlor* . . . are you listening?"

Susan shook herself. "Yes . . . I, uh . . . I don't understand." Now it was *her* turn to pivot away. How could he *ignore her* while she was feeling so vulnerable?

"Well . . . what if he needs *me* for something he's working on?"

"What does he need *you* for?" she probed. Part of her motivation behind the question was selfish—they'd linked in their dreams *together*, and now he acted so sure that this all revolved around *him*. Not only was he dismissing her, but he seemed determined to get himself killed. Didn't he *care* about her, her *feelings* on the matter? She was being petty, and she knew it . . . and she didn't bloody well *care*! "You're not a *Citizen* anymore. The Organizers are looking for you . . . exposure in public is *not* a good idea."

Eli, for his part, was baffled by her lack of support. He touched her shoulder and returned, "Look, just get me to a dreamslab, all right? Now, once I'm deep enough in my dream, I'm going to *need* you monitoring *with* the scrambler from an *inside* port . . . "

She pulled away, her hand rubbing at the sweat building on her throat. Wasn't it usually *cold* down here? "I'm just a low-level *tech*," she groused, once again pacing away from him. "I can get us inside the *Dream Parlor*, but not inside the mainframe."

Eli rolled his eyes, his confusion giving way to irritation—talk of storming the *Parlor* had also brought his headache back. "Try using Corbit's *office* then."

"You're not thinking this through clearly."

"No, if you think about it, it makes *sense*—"

"It doesn't make *any* sense!"

Without even being aware of it, they began to circle one another as they argued back and forth.

"If Corbit's got some—"

"*No.*"

"Susan—"

"What are you gonna *do*—"

"—if Corbit's got some kind of private operation—"

"—break in there and say, 'Hey, Doc, I'm here—"

"—he's got to be running it from his own office!"

"—and I wanna sabotage your mainframe?' " When they finally came to a halt, they were in a virtual stand-off—Susan's arms folded across her stomach, and Eli's left hand pressed against the side of his temple. While Eli had run out of verbal steam, Susan pressed on, "*No!* You need a *better plan.*"

"Like *what*?" Eli snapped. "Climb up the *drainage pipe*?!"

The moment held, each one staring daggers at the other. But before either could say anything else to make the tension *worse* . . .

"Mister Eli! Mister Eli!"

Both their eyes widened, the argument forgotten. "Sara!" Susan gasped as they moved as one toward the tunnel from which the familiar voice had emerged.

"*Mister Eli*!" Sara gasped, out of breath, as she burst into the cavern. She barely had to duck her head to clear the cross pipe.

"What *is* it?" Susan asked the panting girl.

"You gotta help him!" she insisted. "He's in *trouble*!"

"*Who's* in trouble?"

Sara took his arms, shaking them. "The guy who used to hang out with you!"

Flustered, Eli looked to Susan for help. " 'The guy who—?' "

Sara shook his arms harder, forcing him to face her. "From your *work*!"

"*Jacob*?!" Eli gasped. But he couldn't really say he was *shocked*, and that was a terrible feeling. Hadn't he unintentionally used Jacob's DPC terminal to access the *Parlor*'s database?

"An Organizer dragged him to your place lookin' for ya," Sara explained in a rush. "They're gonna *kill* 'em!"

It was so obviously a *trap* of sorts that even Sara herself might have seen it if she weren't so shaken. Even if Eli's break-in *had* been traced back to Jacob's station, why would an Organizer *bring him along* on a manhunt for a former Citizen?

If Eli's *Parlor* addiction had left any brains *at all* in his head, he would stay far, far away . . .

. . . and the frustrated Organizer just might end up killing Jacob after all.

Eli did not think—did not *allow* himself to think. He ducked under the pipe and dove into the tunnel at a full run.

"Don't do it!" Susan called after him.

"I'm going *with* you!" Sara cried, moving to follow him.

"No!" Susan wrapped her arms around the struggling little girl. "You're staying right *here*!"

Sara stared into the dark tunnel longingly. "But what if he *needs* me?" she pleaded.

TAGGED

Kirk *loved* his job.

From early childhood, Kirk had been bigger than his peers, but he hadn't *learned* to use his size to his selfish advantage—that had come quite *naturally*. By the time he hit puberty, he'd even started a game of acting very *polite* at times when he knew such behavior could unsettle his victims the most. It was cold and sadistic . . . and it *amused* him.

While Corbit's genius went unappreciated by the world at large, Kirk's predisposition toward cruelty was preciously *savored* in his position as an Organizer. But Kirk *wasn't* much of a thinker—as Corbit *reminded* him more and more frequently these days—and therefore did not rise in the ranks. He remained the favored foot-soldier, in many ways little more than a glorified *thumb-breaker*. This didn't bother him at first, but it did serve to stifle what little chance he had for upward mobility in a society that already specialized in preventing individuals from bettering themselves.

Kirk's social life was equally stagnant. He had his share of "buddies," co-workers who wanted to hang out with the toughest hombre ever to don an Organizer's uniform, to ingratiate themselves to him in case they ever found themselves in a tight spot . . . but he found himself forever alone in the *romance* department. Sure, he occasionally helped himself to NC women whenever the sexual pressure got too high, but how could he ever really be satisfied with dirty, unkempt, human garbage?

That was all his life had amounted to: Forever praised but never taken too seriously in his occupation, the companion everyone wanted . . . so long as they were heterosexual *males.*

Then came the *Dream Parlor.*

Unlike the working-class Citizens, encouraged to visit the *Parlor* as frequently as they desired, the Organizers' access to the *Parlor* was strictly regulated—it cost them double-credits, they weren't allowed to visit more than once a week, and *never* on duty days. Regardless, it didn't take the *Parlor* long to sink its habitual teeth gum-deep into Kirk.

The attraction was very love-hate. In his dreams, he was already at the height of his ambitions: An Organizer *Commander.* Issuing orders, setting mandates, answering only to the very top brass of the New World Order. There was only *one* Commander per sector, and they didn't get involved with footwork for anything less than assault on an Organizer. And when he was off-duty, he had women—dozens of beautiful, over-sexed women—who yearned for nothing more than to worship him. Yes, the dreams certainly were great.

At the same time, Kirk didn't care for how he felt *after* each trip to the *Parlor.* Following each dream, he felt . . . sluggish, less *aggressive.* A day or two later he was usually back to his old self, bad to the bone and aching for another visit to the *Parlor*, but that lackadaisical sensation was almost enough to keep him away.

Then came his meeting with James Corbit.

Corbit had noticed him, allegedly, from his "waveform pattern," or so he was told. Kirk was something Corbit called a "haphazard spiker," whatever the hell *that* meant. Apparently he wasn't exactly what Corbit was looking for, but he *had* stood out enough to draw special attention.

Corbit made him an offer: About twice a week, Kirk reported to Corbit directly, giving him little tips, bits of information, names of people who had given the Organizers and the System any trouble and therefore lost their Citizenship. Sometimes Corbit asked Kirk to bring these new NCs to him—again, on the sly—and Kirk never saw them again. Other times, Corbit just asked for any old NC off the street, and Kirk didn't *care* if he ever saw *them* again.

In exchange for these services, whenever Kirk made his semi-regular reports, he was given preferential treatment at the *Parlor*—off the record, and more often than not handled by Corbit himself. That meant up to *three Parlor* visits a week . . . and not just *any* visits. Corbit fine-tuned Kirk's dream experience, aligning the mainframe to his individual waveform patterns. Now the dreams were not only more vivid than ever before, they also left him feeling, *not* placid, but stimulated, aroused, charged with energy . . . in short, *high as a kite!*

Kirk wasn't exactly sure when his relationship with Corbit . . . *changed.* Sometimes, when he allowed himself to dwell on it, it seemed as though they'd been co-conspirators one minute, and then the next . . . they were . . . *more.* Kirk had never considered himself open to such . . . *possibilities*, but when he tried to *resist* Corbit—hell, his very first impulse had been to knock the older man's head clean off his body—he found that he could *not.* It was a bizarre, *frightening* sensation . . . not quite like being physically *ill*, but close enough that Kirk found himself melting like butter under the heat of Corbit's whims.

Now, while Kirk wasn't "much of a thinker," he wasn't completely *stupid* either. He'd sat in on enough of Corbit and the Chief Suit's conversations to figure that Corbit had done something to him through his *Parlor* usage. But *knowing* a thing and being able to *do* something about it were often very different, and so . . . things continued.

Kirk *thought* that he secretly hated Corbit for it . . . and so found himself shocked and appalled by how he felt about Corbit's attention to this *Eli Barrett* fellow. So long as his *Parlor* access wasn't threatened, Kirk would have expected to feel *relief* when Corbit's focus finally drifted so far from him. Instead, he felt . . . *jealous*, and that realization made him feel *worse* than his initial efforts to hold Corbit at bay.

So when Corbit—in a good mood for a change—"suggested" that Kirk use Barrett's former co-worker to drag him out of hiding, Kirk heartily seized the opportunity for some much-needed stress relief. While Corbit was sickeningly protective of his new treasure-child, he wouldn't care less what happened to this Jacob Moore loser.

And that meant Kirk could play *dirty.*

* * *

A sharp blow across the side of his head sent Jacob tumbling across Eli's living unit. As he went down, his face collided sharply with the COMM box next to the cot, and the television projection whirled to life even as Jacob found himself almost wishing for death.

As Jacob writhed on the floor, Kirk deliberately crushed the Citizen's glasses beneath his heavy Organizer boot. He made sure the lenses cracked and shattered with as much noise as possible.

It produced *exactly* the effect he was looking for: The wimp's attention shifted from his latest pain back to the *source* of that injury, and his eyes widened once more in gratifying *dread.* Kirk almost laughed when the pantywaist, leaving a thin trail of sweaty blood behind him, actually tried to crawl under Barrett's bed to get away from him.

Almost laughed.

"Don't know why you're holdin' out, friend," he spat, suddenly *irritated* by the display of total cowardice. He stepped across the small room and grabbed Jacob by his ankles. "You're in deep enough as it is."

Jacob cried out as he was dragged from his perceived shelter. He clutched desperately at the cot's legs, to no avail. Kirk pulled him up just long enough to slam him back down on the edge of the bed, the wooden ridge under the mattress fracturing his collar-bone in the process. Jacob gasped, his mind reeling with such pain that he couldn't even give it proper voice.

"You go to the *Dream Parlor*, right?" Kirk asked in a terribly casual voice. "There was a *security breach* there earlier. And guess whose work station it got traced back to?" The big man jerked Jacob up only to shove him back down on the opposite edge of the bed. The impact on his cracked bone almost made him black out—tears rolled down his cheeks, leaving relatively clear streaks through the blood on his face. "Listen, you idiot," Kirk continued, his annoyance now evident, "you haven't got the *balls* to pull that stunt, but we both know who *does*. Your buddy, Barrett, left you out to dry."

Even through the thick haze of misery, Kirk's words struck Jacob. Jacob didn't know exactly how the scrambler worked, but he knew far too much about the sorts of things that Eli used it for. The security breach *had* to be caused by Eli—*he* certainly hadn't done it—but *why*? *Why* would Eli do this to him? *Why*?!

"If you help me find your pal," Kirk whispered seductively in his ear, "*maybe* you'll keep your Citizenship. Hell, *maybe* Doctor Corbit will even let you keep your D*ream Parlor* privileges. What do you say?"

In that moment, Jacob was more than willing to give up the ghost and let Eli fend for himself amongst the wolves. What did he owe that bastard anymore anyway? Jacob turned his head just enough to gaze up at the Organizer . . . but even as he opened his mouth, fully intending to help this cruel man find his former best friend through whatever means possible, a spark of the *old* Jacob, the Jacob who *did* once agree with Eli that things needed to change, flickered through his heart. He hesitated.

Kirk saw the indecision, and his temper snapped. He spun around and hurled Jacob across the room—the Citizen flattened against the large television screen, the projected image and sounds of martial dancers swirling around him. He held his footing for just a moment before slowly sliding down to the floor.

Shaking his head, Kirk pulled his submissioner from his belt. "Too late, friend," he chided as he extended the shock-rod and snapped it into place.

Jacob cowered . . .

. . . until Eli burst into the room, throwing himself bodily against Kirk with all of his might. His momentum carried both of them headlong into the screen—Jacob twisted in confusion just enough to avoid getting trodden upon.

"Jacob, get out of here!" Eli snapped as he struggled with the surprised Organizer. He'd managed to pull the side of the shock-rod—regretfully, *not* the business end of it—across the man's throat, but he had no delusions about the size of his opponent, or how long he could maintain any advantage.

Jacob scrambled to his feet, moving in the general direction of the door.

Enraged, Kirk twisted around until he had Eli between him and the wall. He then thrust himself backward repeatedly as Corbit's wonderful new trophy struggled to hold on and keep his breath . . .

In the hallway, Jacob could not help but pause—his mind and body raced to catch up with one another, and they weren't doing a very good job at it. So much had happened in such a short period of time. Less than an hour ago, the Organizer—the *same* Organizer who'd shown up at the DPC—barged into his living unit, ranting about Eli Barrett. Jacob knew nothing of Eli's whereabouts, but the Organizer had refused to believe that. Regardless, Jacob—God forgive him—had been on the cusp of agreeing to help the man find Eli when—

Jacob *thought* he'd only stopped for one second, *two* at the most. But when a grimacing Eli suddenly sailed out of his living unit only to crash against the door on the opposite wall, Jacob realized it had been *longer* than he'd thought, and that the difference might prove to be a *critical* one.

Kirk emerged from the room, his inflamed gaze fixated upon the Citizen who had *dared* to assault him. Trembling movement caught the edge of his vision, and he whipped his head over to glare down at the quivering idiot who hadn't escaped when he had the chance. Clenching his jaw tightly, he swung his shock-rod at Jacob. His bloodied target barely managed to duck as it struck the wall behind him, but Kirk drew the charged club over his shoulder next, and there was *nothing* that would keep him from splitting the wimp's head in *two*.

Without thinking, Eli leaped to his feet and stepped under the Organizer's descending arm—maybe Mencer Barrett had never placed a great emphasis on physical combat, but *Derby* had shown him a few moves over the years since his pounding by the three older boys. Eli seized Kirk's wrist and added the man's strength to his own as he brought the arm down across his shoulder. Kirk's bellow of pain and shock echoed down the hallway, drowning out the horrific *crunch* of his hyper-extended elbow. The shock-rod missed Jacob, dropping from Kirk's hand and clattering to the floor instead.

Kirk, however, was *thoroughly* trained in hand-to-hand, and Eli's brief advantage again slipped away. Despite the distress involved, Kirk used Eli's hold on his injured arm to toss him back across the hallway. Before Eli had even bounced off the wall, Kirk

Eli seized Kirk's (Peter Hendrixson) wrist and added the man's strength to his own as he brought the arm down across his shoulder. Kirk's bellow of pain and shock echoed down the hallway.

forcefully buried his leather-clad elbow into Eli's right kidney. Eli stiffened, then dropped. Barely able to breathe, he clutched his crippled, *screaming* side and fought to stay conscious.

Jacob's bare feet slapped against the floor as he *finally* escaped down the corridor.

" 'No head injuries,' " Kirk spat from above. "That's the deal. But I'd *crack your skull* if I could!"

Eli glanced over at Kirk's open right hand, then looked up defiantly at the Organizer. Between gasps, he asked, "How's the arm?"

Kirk clenched his jaw so tightly he could barely speak. "*Screw* Corbit," he muttered as he bent forward . . .

. . . before crying out as his own submissioner was placed against the back of his neck.

Derby followed him forward as he stumbled into the wall. He kept the rod against the base of the Organizer's skull—and his thumb against the activation switch—as he gestured to his little partner that *now* was the time!

"Mister Eli!" Sara called as she dove forward to help him stand.

Eli's mind was tumbling as crazily as Jacob's had been as he tried to absorb the fact that Derby and Sara had just saved his life. He tried to stand on his own, but found that he did, in fact, need the young girl's assistance. Slowly, she helped him work his way down the hall in the opposite direction from which Jacob had fled.

"You're making a *mistake*, friend," Kirk threatened Derby.

"I've made'em before," Derby acknowledged casually. He then added, in a significantly heavier tone, "*You're* on the wrong side of town, *friend*."

But Kirk had meant to do more than just frighten Derby, and while he had failed in that arena, he succeeded in the other—*distraction*. As Derby returned the caveat, Kirk had reached back with his good arm to the duty padd on his belt, which still had Citizen 11811 locked in for tracking . . . and *tagging*. Before Eli could get too far away, he flipped the switch, and Derby realized too late what had happened.

Down the hallway, Eli grunted and stopped as his IDC suddenly gave him a small but unpleasant jolt. He and Sara looked on in horror as the housing tube suddenly shifted from *clear* to a definite *red glow*.

"Hey, Eli!" Derby called. "You okay?!"

But he *wasn't*, and everyone present *knew* it.

"Believe me," Kirk continued, a gleam of satisfaction in his eye, "you can't handle a trained *Organizer* by yourself." He got no further, however, as Derby thumbed the shock-rod. Kirk's entire body went completely numb this time and he collapsed, unable to even raise his good arm to cushion the fall.

"I believe you," Derby assured him.

Down the hall, Sara urged Eli onward—he continued to gape at his glowing IDC as she led him toward the freight elevator.

Kirk stared after them, unable to so much as speak . . . or even clench his jaw, as he was so prone to doing. It slowly began to dawn on him that this might very well be his end . . . and it struck him that he had no Maker with whom to make peace . . .

* * *

Her name was Sara. That much she knew.

But that was her only real knowledge of her greater *self*, of her background or origins. She had no last name, no parents, no siblings—none that she could *remember* anyway. It was as though she had been born right onto the streets, maybe even *of* the streets. Always and forever, a Non-Citizen. An *NC*.

Then she met Miss Susan, and later, Mister Eli.

Both so caring in their different ways. Susan the teacher, the Guardian Angel, Eli the provider. They treated her so affectionately, so special. Oh, the other NCs treated her *all right*, especially Derby, but in the end they *were* Non-Citizens, and had their own oppressed lives to look after. Eli and Susan were caring, sensitive, *loving*. She wanted so much to open up to them, to let them be the parents she always longed for, especially now that they were actually together for *real*, and not just in her dreams. But it was so difficult for her to let down her guard, to shed the thick skin of cynicism that had protected her from pain for so long. Her answer to most problems was a smart remark, a life-sucks-but-what-does-it-matter flippance, and she wasn't sure she could approach things any other way.

Even *now*, standing beside Eli in the freight elevator as they descended toward the basement, when she wanted to hug him and tell him how much she loved him, all that came out was, "Got tagged, huh? That sucks. You're in *big* trouble now." Eli, still gripping his side as he rode the waves from his tortured kidney, barely nodded his agreement. Sara *hated* seeing him in such pain, and she unconsciously folded her own arms in sympathy. "I thought you were supposed to be *smart*," she admonished. Then, half-surprising herself, she added in a softer tone, "I'm glad you're *okay*."

Eli straightened as best he could. "Where's Susan?" he mumbled.

"Right after you bailed, another stiff came through the chute. Miss Susan went to check it out." She was, of course, downplaying the *lengths* she'd actually gone to in slipping away during Miss Susan's moment of distraction, but Mister Eli didn't really need to hear about that right now.

Eli nodded but said nothing as he gazed down at his glowing chip, his expression sickened for more reasons than kidney discomfort.

Tagged. It sounded like such a colloquial term, and yet if there were any other, more *official* designation, Eli had never heard it.

Everything had changed now. When he was a mere NC, Eli's scrambler—which he wore even now—had been enough to keep that big Organizer from getting a solid lock on him. NCs were a dime a dozen, and an Organizer would have to program his tracker to his prey's distinctive IDC number in order to hunt him down for any given reason.

But a *tagged* NC was entirely different—Eli was now flagged as a *wanted fugitive.* Whereas before an Organizer would have to be looking *specifically* for him to glimpse his location, a tagged IDC was a *beacon* that would set off an alarm on *any active tracker* he came within ten meters of—*thirty* meters, if the area was relatively clear of other IDCs. While he wouldn't necessarily have to worry about Organizers who were off-duty or engaged in other assignments, he would now have to go far out of his way to avoid the regular patrols that frequented all Citizen-populated areas. And what if his number had also been transmitted to the Central Organizer Network? If he were *correct* about Corbit's desire to get a hold of him, then he *might* not have to worry about that just yet. But if he were *wrong* . . .

Sara was also staring at the red chip, and she shook her head. "We gotta get you back down to the tunnels," she advised, thinking of the layers of thick concrete and steel. "It'll make it harder for the Organizers to track you . . ."

Eli was already shaking his head. "No . . . no place will be safe for very long . . ."

* * *

"You got *that* right," the rookie agreed—the younger NCs *were* better, probably because of the archaic taboo against an adult sleeping with someone under the age of "consent." Such laws didn't apply where the Non-Citizens were concerned, and even with the *Citizens*, Organizers could do pretty much whatever they wanted—that was one of the perks that had drawn him to this life in the *first* place.

The rookie Organizer and his *slightly* more veteran partner were enjoying a casual moment to themselves. They were between scheduled rounds and, although *technically* no Organizer was *ever* supposed to relax on duty, there simply was nothing important for them to do at the moment. They were leaning against opposite walls of the basement hallway, the rookie with his helmet off and resting casually in his left hand. As such, they were caught completely off guard when their sector Commander suddenly appeared with two SWAT-Organizers, their rifles at ready, in tow.

They scrambled to make themselves more presentable, dropping their propped feet and coming to attention, the rookie quickly slipping his helmet into its proper position. But the Commander marched right past them, and the rookie and his partner, unsure of what else to do under the circumstances, fell in with them.

"Hey," the barely-senior Organizer whispered to one of the SWAT officers, "what's up?"

"There's a situation," the SWAT officer answered curtly. "An Organizer's involved."

The two patrolmen followed the special unit down the corridor towards the freight elevator.

* * *

Eli's kidney finally eased its assault, allowing him to breathe more freely. As his thoughts flowed more coherently, he slowly became aware of voices drifting up from the level below them, which happened to be their destination.

". . . the Organizer in question is *not* assigned to this area," the sharp, imposing voice snapped. "I want to know *why* he's here."

The freight elevator lowered into position. Eli looked out through the grated door . . . and his heart skipped a beat.

Oh, no . . .

A squad of Organizers stood at attention just outside, apparently waiting for this very elevator to open. The two younger ones in the back wore standard Organizer uniforms, and two others wore some variation of assault garb. Eli didn't recognize the outfit of the apparent leader . . . even as that leader, a rough-and-rugged black man, turned toward him.

Eli froze. Sara, however, did not.

As the door slid up, she moved across the elevator and took Eli's right hand in both of her own, effectively covering his glowing IDC. The parts of Eli's brain that were still working understood what she was trying to do, but if any *one* of these military men had their trackers on . . .

The Organizer unit merely glared at them, waiting impatiently for them to clear the way. Another second of delay would have brought random, arbitrary retribution, but Sara was again moving. She pulled Eli from the elevator and into the hallway.

Eli dropped his gaze from the Organizers' leader to the floor, but even as the rest of the troop marched forward, the Commander stared after the two apparent NCs. His business was upstairs—business involving an officer whose movements and behavior had become increasingly suspicious over the last few months—but some killer instinct still reared its head as he studied the adult being led away by the little girl.

Suddenly, a commotion from above seized the attention of the Organizer unit and its two tag-alongs. The Commander was still outside the elevator, but the others had to scramble as a body tumbled down the shaft, passing through the open ceiling of the elevator car and crashing loudly onto the floor.

Even Eli and Sara turned back, startled by the explosive interruption of silence.

The lower ranked officers gaped at the fresh corpse, but the Commander calmly took in the situation: It was the body of an Organizer. He'd landed on his stomach, but judging from the portion of his face that was visible, the Commander assessed that this was the very Organizer he'd been about to rescue and then interrogate. The Citizen informer who'd called in the confrontation provided little information about this officer's opponents, but his tracker was still active and relatively undamaged. Although the screen was cocked at an angle, the Commander could see that one of this Organizer's last actions had been to *tag* an NC. The Commander looked closer at the IDC number and profile headshot—"11811" blinked boldly over a picture of the adult NC who had walked past them seconds ago.

As the Commander spun around, the man and girl were already sprinting for the end of the corridor. He hefted his rifle, firing from gut level.

Shrapnel stung Eli's back as first one shot, then three more in rapid succession shattered the wall behind them—the highly-charged rounds partially melted the concrete, and smoldering fragments sizzled where they made contact. Eli grit his teeth but swallowed any vocalization—he didn't want Sara to slow down even for a second! Keeping his body between her and their assailants, he lunged for the bend in the hallway.

The Commander raised the rifle to his shoulder. The tagged NC was about to clear the corner, and he wanted to make the next shot count.

Sara, smaller and lighter, cut her turn much sharper than Eli, whose feet slid just enough to carry him past her.

The Commander fired.

Sara shrieked as the explosive projectile intended for her tagged companion slammed into her side. The force of the impact knocked her right off her feet and into Eli, who staggered into the wall but managed to throw his arms around her and keep moving.

She slipped she just slipped it was close but they missed I know they missed . . .

The Commander glared in frustration—he hated missing his prey. He whipped a finger around to the rookie they'd picked up. "*You*, call for back-up! The rest of you, fall in!"

Eli turned another corner, holding Sara tight and shaking both her and his head in denial. "No, no, no," he panted as he ran. "Sara? *Sara*? No . . . "

I'll give her a moment she's just stunned she'll be fine she'll catch her breath any second now . . .

The blood flowed over his fingers . . .

The rookie was on his knees beside the body, his helmet tossed aside. "Um, um, Organizer down! Organizer down!" he rambled into his communicator. He was badly shaken—he'd seen this Organizer around Sector HQ, knew him even better by reputation.

He was supposed to be the baddest of the bad-asses—*how* could this have *happened*?! "Section, uh, Charlie-Three . . . uh, Peter-Ocean! The, uh, uh, the Gray Team," Was that right? Gray Team? If the Commander was involved . . . oh, *please* let that be right! ". . . in pursuit of tagged NC, uh . . . " He seized the tracker on the body's belt. "One-One-Eight-One-One! Possible accomplice upstairs! Uh, requesting back-up, *repeat*, requesting *back-up* . . . uh, to lock down the building . . . "

As he wrapped up his blundering call, the rookie flinched at the sound of breaking glass that echoed from the twisting hallways of the basement. Was it Gray Team, or 11811? Should he join them, or hold his position?

Near the opposite end of the building, Eli, his sleeve tugged protectively over his right hand, leaped as he ran and smashed every flourescent bulb he passed.

The Commander's tracker flickered with each crash as Gray Team and their Organizer tag-along passed the body of the little girl. The Commander smirked—this 11811 was brighter than most. The body would only slow him down, so he'd dumped it. Still, the girl was carefully positioned, and streaks of blood down her cheek suggested a tender caress before abandonment. Those extra seconds would *cost* their prey—the Commander would *not* miss again . . .

Collapsing behind a crate, Eli struggled to keep his sobs silent.

Sara . . . why Sara . . . ?

The Commander now discovered the source of the breaking glass they'd heard—the next few corridors were dark, would have been pitch black if it weren't for light seeping through in various places from the maintenance shafts, basement-level windows, and so on. This guy *was* brighter than most . . . not that it would save him.

Sara . . .

Eli tried to regain control of himself . . . then asked himself *why*? Dana, Nora, Sara . . . everyone he cared about was being taken from him. Why go on? So that he could lead them straight to *Susan*?

Maybe he should just sit here and wait for death—Susan could go on without him . . .

The SWAT-Organizers fell into position as the Commander indicated which junction he wanted to take. The rookie's partner brought up the rear, but the Commander simply *ignored* him for the most part. This stretch was not only dark, but a light source from the ventilation duct at the far end was aimed right at them, throwing what they *could* see into glared silhouette.

The Commander didn't like it. From what he'd seen, the fugitive appeared unarmed, but he didn't care for this unfamiliar environment. Despite their apparent advantage, he decided they would proceed with caution. With the small spotlight on their rifles helping to lead the way, they pressed forward . . .

. . . and the Commander grunted as his boot came down on glass from the broken light bulbs.

A couple of meters from the turning ventilation duct, Eli heard the crunch. Peering carefully around the edge of the crate, he drew back when he saw the lights of the Organizers' rifles. All thoughts of waiting for death fled his mind as he cast about for some escape from this dark junction which he suddenly realized was a deathtrap.

The SWAT-Organizers' search was frustratingly slow—there were simply too many nooks and crannies among the various crates, pillars, and cross beams where the fugitive could be hiding. Their small spotlights scanned dirty walls and littered corners as the beams reached through the hall like probing fingers, finding every sort of filth and grime as brown water dripped onto their helmets from rusted pipes in the exposed ceiling. If the fugitive *did* have a weapon, surely he would have fired upon them by now. If the Commander's tracker said he was down this junction, why weren't they just pressing down on him? But they were too well conditioned to voice such an insubordinate question.

Eli's frantic gaze swept past a metal hatch . . . then returned to it. It was so small—but what if it led into the maintenance duct? Still, how was he supposed to open it and squeeze through without immediately alerting them to his exact position?

The Commander's small light came to rest on a larger crate—the very crate behind which Eli crouched. The Commander smirked and moved forward, the SWAT officers noting his stance and falling in . . .

Behind them, the rookie's partner bumped into a stack of old boxes. A metal coupling toppled and fell, clattering loudly on the ground.

Eli bit his lip.

The Commander spun, shadowed by the SWAT officers. His finger relaxed on the trigger a split-second before he blew the patrolman's head off. He gaped back at them in horrified chagrin, unable even to vocalize his apology.

The Commander shook his head in disgust—he'd have to remember to deal with that idiot when this was over—and turned back to the crate. The SWAT officers exchanged an amused look.

The Organizer closed his eyes. How could he make such a stupid move in front of—?

"Hey!" came the stage-whisper from behind him.

Crying out, the patrolman whipped around and fired before the tagged fugitive could attack with his make-shift weapon.

The SWAT members realized that they'd severely underestimated their opponent. They shouldered their rifles and fired past the idiot Organizer, striking the figure beside the crate repeatedly.

"Cease fire!" the Commander roared. "*Cease fire*!"

The SWAT members obeyed instantly—but the Organizer continued to discharge his weapon.

"*Wait*!" the Commander bellowed, prepared to smash his rifle against the back of the idiot's head if he didn't obey . . . which he finally did.

As the echoes of the gunfire still reverberated throughout the junction, the metal hatch behind the crate closed, bloody fingerprints the only indication that it had ever been disturbed.

At the opening of the junction from where they had come, the rookie looked down at the smoking, sizzling holes throughout his torso . . . then died before his body hit the ground.

The Commander glared at all the Organizers, SWAT or otherwise, making sure they could *feel* the heat of his disapproval. After a few seconds, he gazed down at his belt, and his face dropped. He blinked, let his eyes scan the small area and the crate he'd reached just as the chaos had erupted, and then looked back down.

The death of the rookie was an unfortunate waste of manpower, but it could be cleaned up. What he *wasn't* sure how to handle was the information on his tracker . . .

As impossible as it seemed, 11811 was gone.

THE VOICE

Sara . . .

Eli held his hands away from him, particularly the hand Sara had so quickly covered with her own to hide his tagged IDC from the Organizers. He rested his right forearm on the rung of a maintenance ladder in the storm drain cavern and peered down at the blood on his palm and fingers . . . *Sara's* blood.

Sara . . . little Sara . . .

Sniffling, Susan leaned back against the wall beside him. "It's not *your* fault," she told him in a broken voice. "*I* should have watched her closer."

"It doesn't matter," Eli mumbled. He continued to stare at his still-wet hand. "It really doesn't."

"Don't do this to yourself. She's *gone*, and this won't bring her back."

Eli glanced up at her briefly, his tears blurring his vision.

Susan wiped the tears from her own cheek and drew a shaky breath. "Elijah," she said as firmly as she could, "I need you to be *strong*. I . . . I can't fight the *Parlor* on my own." Her sobs rose again, but she forced herself to continue. "And if you quit now, their deaths mean *nothing*. Nora . . . Dana . . . and S-S-Sara . . . what was it all for . . . ?"

Eli shut his eyes, leaned forward, and not-too-softly banged his head against the next rung of the metal ladder, as if he could *beat* the painful thoughts and feelings from his mind. It didn't work. "I'm tired," he muttered as he turned his back on Susan and leaned against the ladder while facing away.

That nearly broke Susan. She covered her face briefly, allowing herself just a moment of unrelenting, unadulterated crying, then she reached out and struck Eli on his shoulder. "*Damn it*," she sobbed, "*I'm* tired, *too*. But if we don't stop the *Parlor*, then everything we've ever *worked* for means *nothing*. You *know* what I'm talking about—you *know* it's true."

Eli *did* know what she was talking about. It wasn't just about the latest threat that the *Dream Parlor* represented—both of them had dedicated their adult lives to righting the wrongs the System had perpetrated. Eli sheltered and fed; Susan educated. The *Parlor* was the *greatest* danger in its ability to produce a world that was *incapable* of change, but that was a change the two of them had stood for since long before the *Parlor* opened its seductive arms.

At this point, however, Eli's understanding of her meaning almost *angered* him—he didn't *want* to play the hero anymore! What he wanted was to curl up into a little ball and *die*.

Still, Susan would not stop—she joined him beside the ladder. "That *man* in your dreams . . . the one who told you to 'wake the people' and 'find the truth . . .' "

Eli stiffened—why wouldn't she just leave him alone? Why was she bringing up that man—what did *he* have to do with anything?

Unfortunately, Susan noticed his reaction, and it encouraged her. "What *is* that truth?" she insisted. "When he said that you 'don't belong here,' what did he mean?"

Eli snapped, "That I never should have gone to the *Parlor*," and turned away again, facing the ladder.

But Susan wasn't letting him off the hook. "Or did he mean *here—now—*in *this* world as it *is*? *Trust* that voice, Elijah! *Listen* to that voice, and trust it with *all your heart*!"

Eli clung to the ladder as if it were his lifeline.

Listen to that voice

What the hell did *she* know? What did *she* know about the voice in his dreams?

Listen to that voice

There was only *one* voice that Eli had ever listened to, *one* voice that ever mattered to him, and that was the voice of . . . the voice of his . . .

Father . . .

*

" 'Trust in the Lord with all your heart. Lean not on your own understanding. Acknowledge Him in all your ways, and He will make your path straight.' "

Young Eli thought hard before saying, "Proverbs Three . . . verses Five and Six." He was just *confident enough not to phrase it as a question.*

Mencer turned away from his work table—and the dissected prototype for the Identification Chip the government was promoting so extensively—and nodded at his son, who sat across the room on the basement steps. "Good," he praised before moving on to the next test. " 'Live as free men, but do not use your freedom as a cover-up for Evil. Live as servants of God.' "

Eli had to think even harder about this one. When it finally came out, he couldn't help but add a question mark to his punctuation. ". . . First Peter Two . . . verse Sixteen?"

Mencer nodded again, beaming proudly at his son. "Yes."

Eli smiled back.

Mencer swivelled his chair back to the table, then decided to test his son on one more. " 'This is your hour, when Darkness reigns.' "

Nothing but silence from Eli.

When Mencer looked back, his son was fidgeting uncomfortably, his eyes downcast. "You have questions," he observed.

Eli's expression was almost guilty.

Dropping his tools next to the IDC he'd been studying for the past few weeks, Mencer rose and crossed the small basement to where his son sat. He scratched thoughtfully at his face, carefully pondering how to handle this moment that he had always known would come.

Finally, he placed a warm hand on his son's shoulder. "Don't be afraid of questions, Elijah. Question everything. *Authority, faith, love, motives . . .* everything—*question it* all. *How else do we find* answers?"

Eli relaxed enough to ask, "How come Evil reigns?"

Mencer nodded his approval of Eli's curiosity. "Because people don't want to believe in God anymore. It's easier to justify your actions when you don't have to consider the consequences."

Mencer paused and looked down at Eli with a peculiar expression on his face. Eli would think of that expression in the years to come—that deep wisdom *dancing hand-in-hand with pained* regret.

Then his father suddenly said, "Come here, son." They shifted so that Mencer could sit on the step with Eli on his knee. The boy was getting a little too big for that, and they shared a sentimental, self-conscious laugh at the awkwardness of the arrangement. Mencer looked into his son's eyes, and spoke the words Eli Barrett would never forget: "It will be difficult, *Elijah, to grow up and try to fit into the world as it is, as it's* going *to be. You may find it easy to forget who you* are. *You can't let that happen—you* must not *forget who you* are, *who* God *made you to be. And there will come a time when you will have to remind others of who* they *are as well. When people lose faith, and hope . . . they'll accept* any*thing to make them feel good, even when it's* wrong. *But if* you *do what's* right *and* true, *you will* give *them hope. You will be a* light *in the darkness . . . "*

The adult Elijah didn't remember any more words after that, or even whether his father returned to his work bench or followed him up into the house. All he remembered was the next few moments, when he reached out with his young hand and touched the wooden cross around his father's neck—the same cross he would later wear around his own *neck—just as he would do the night his father would be murdered before his eyes . . .*

*

Eli stood away from the ladder, looking down at his father's cross and gingerly touching it so as to avoid getting Sara's blood on it. Susan had given up for the moment, retreating to the far corner and holding herself through her pain. Her eyes were closed, so she did not witness Eli's . . . experience.

Staring at the cross, Eli slowly became aware of a new light source. Lifting his head, his eyes widened as he gazed at the figure before him.

In his dreams the man had always maintained a shroud of shadows, but now he radiated as if from within, a glow that was almost blinding after the dim of the storm drain. Amazingly, Susan didn't seem to notice.

Although the effulgence served to obscure the man's features almost as well as the shadows had, Eli no longer had any doubts as to who this man really was. He reached out, wanting to touch his father—to convince himself that it wasn't an illusion—but at the last moment he hesitated. If it *were* a hallucination, he didn't *want* it to be dispelled.

The ghost of his father—if that's what it was—waited patiently for him to speak.

And Eli had so much that he *wanted* to say . . . so much that eluded him somehow. In the end, he spoke the only words he could find. "I've . . . tried to help them . . . " Eli whispered, his voice thick with emotion, ". . . but I'm not . . . *you*."

"*I never meant for you to neglect* yourself, *Elijah*," his father said as though from afar. "*I wanted you to serve God while living the* human experience. *But that is something that you and everyone else risk losing* forever. *There* is *a greater purpose*."

Eli sagged. Just as his father seemed about to say the words he'd always wanted to hear—that he'd pushed himself *too hard*, that he should spend more energy on his *own* life—it came back around to the danger at hand.

Mencer observed his defeated demeanor. "*Your* faith *will be your strength.*" And then the glow dimmed, and Eli could see his father clearly, as he had appeared his last day on this Earth. When he spoke next, his voice sounded far less other-worldly, and much warmer. "Go now, son. Water the *seeds* you have planted."

The glow returned as Mencer stepped away. Eli wanted to grab him, to cling to him and never let go, and yet he found himself unable to move. "Stay with me," he pleaded through numb lips.

Mencer looked back, "*Now that you've found me, I will* always *be with you.*"

Then the light faded altogether, taking his father with it.

Eli stared into the empty space and sighed deeply, a sigh born both of pain and of *peace.*

Now that you've found me, I will always *be with you.*

Suddenly, Susan's hand was on Eli's cheek. "What is it, Elijah?" she asked, her eyes filled with deep concern. "What's wrong?" Then she looked ill as she whispered, "It's Phase Three, isn't it? You're *hallucinating.*"

"*No,*" he stated firmly. Suddenly filled with new strength, he took a deep breath and squared his shoulders. "We have *work* to do . . . "

PARLOR AFTER-HOURS

cling . . . *clack* . . . *cling* . . . *clack* . . .

Slowly, excruciatingly, Eli dragged himself steadily upward, hand-over-hand, through the drainage pipe.

It started out as a flippant remark during his argument with Susan. He didn't recall the exact exchange, but he remembered that she was criticizing his unpolished plans for assaulting the *Dream Parlor*—specifically, the overlooked element of *how* to get him inside. One thing led to another, and he popped off with some smart-ass comment about climbing up the drainage pipe.

Now he would have *kicked* himself . . . if only he'd had any *room.*

cling . . . *clack* . . .

The drainage pipe—which was really more of a narrow, metal *shaft*—had a *smaller* pipe running along the inside of it. The shaft was extremely steep, but it wasn't *quite* straight up-and-down—by gripping this smaller pipe, and bracing himself at each point with his legs against the opposite wall, Eli was able to pull himself up, one half-meter at a time. Each movement shook the small pipe in its housing, and the repetitive noise was already grinding on Eli's nerves.

**cling* . . . *clack* . . .*

The cold metal shaft was just wide enough so that Eli could touch the opposite side with his back while propped on his hands and knees. He'd first tried to *scoot* up the shaft in that fashion, but the very first meters—and *screaming* muscles—had shown the folly of *that* approach.

Not that *this* way was much easier . . .

Man, his head was hurting . . .

**cling* . . .*

If nothing else, the mindless monotony of movement allowed his fatigued mind to wander somewhat. He thought about his *experience* earlier, and part of him *had* to wonder if perhaps Susan were correct: Was it a hallucination? His impulse had been to deny that possibility outright, but now . . . *was* it a hallucination, or was it a *vision*?

When Eli had washed Sara's blood from his hands in a pool of standing water, he'd thought—for just a moment—that the entire basin had been filled with blood. The effect had lasted only a second, and then he'd blinked it away. *That* was the sort of side-effect he would expect from dream deprivation at this early stage—the encounter with his father had been on a wholly different level.

Now that you've found me, I will always *be with you.*

No. He *refused* to accept that his mind had been playing tricks on him. Either way, he knew that the longer they waited, the more his cognitive abilities would deteriorate—and Susan could either go through the *same*, or continue to *use* the *Parlor* and watch her will-power drain away. And now that he was actually *tagged*, time was even *more* of the essence.

Lacking any apparent alternative, they'd suddenly looked upon the drainage pipe in an entirely new light. Susan expressed concern that another body would be dumped while he was halfway up, but Eli pointed out that they really had no other choice. Any hope of a more orthodox entry into the *Parlor* had burned away in the red glow of his IDC.

**clack* . . .*

The drainage pipe creaked and groaned as Eli paused for a short respite. At times it seemed as though the pipe were going to collapse inward at any moment . . . but Eli forced such claustrophobic thoughts from his mind as best he could. If only his headache would ease up for just a minute . . .

He reached up for his next half-meter drag . . .

. . . and that's when he lost his grip.

Eli cried out in terror as he slid back down the pipe at break-neck speeds. The slight incline saved him from a straight drop, but at the rate he was skidding, he'd be unspeakably lucky if he *only* shattered both legs at the bottom. Helpless, all he could do was scream as he plunged toward his probable death.

In the end, it was instinct rather than thought that saved him. His arms flailed up and out and his legs kicked out and forward . . . until finally they coordinated their effects and did both at the same time. In a burst of friction-burned flesh, Eli wedged his back, forearms, knees, and shins against all sides of the pipe, bringing him to a fierce, tearing, and agonizing halt.

For the first few seconds, all he could do was hold his position, groaning in pain and marveling at the blessing of his life. When he could move again, he *very slowly* shifted his arms around toward the smaller pipe . . . then took the leap, letting go with his legs as he pulled himself back into his original position. The maneuver almost wrenched his hands loose again, but somehow he managed to hold on.

As he panted and shook his head, movement flapped in the corner of his eye. A surge of arachnophobia drove him to swat at it with one desperate hand, which *again* nearly caused another fall. Seizing whatever it was, he tossed it away—it wasn't until he saw the bandage from his scratched face fluttering down the shaft that he realized how much he needed to regain control of himself.

Taking several deep breaths, he resumed his climb.

**cling* . . . *clack* . . .*

* * *

"*The* Dream Parlor *is now closed . . .* "

Slipping her work smock securely onto her shoulders, Susan approached the main entrance to the *Parlor*. She'd never been here this late before, and it was an odd sensation to see the place devoid of bustling patrons coming and going through the three doors. Their plans for the evening flashed through her mind, and she swallowed bile as her nausea rose sharply. For once, however, the effect served as an *incentive* rather than a deterrent—*damn them* for doing this to her!

She passed the revolving hologram, which never ceased its chatter. "*Our normal operating hours are—*"

Susan was within arm's reach of the entrance when, without warning, the verbiage suddenly stopped, and bright illumination flooded her area. She looked back to find several spotlights targeting her, and the now-stern hologram swivelling to face her *directly.* Not in the mood to be intimidated by tricks of *light,* she pressed her IDC to the *Parlor*'s scanlock.

The hologram recollected its smile, but the spotlights remained focused on her. "*Hello . . .* Susan *. . . working late?"*

Ignoring the user-friendly bitch, Susan strode into the *Parlor.* If she thought the *outside* had seemed odd without Citizens milling about, it was *nothing* compared to the eerie silence of the main lobby. Susan had never glimpsed this place without at least a dozen Citizens waiting impatiently for their next dream sessions. Drawing a breath, she strode up the short steps into the lobby proper . . .

. . . and nearly ran into another employee.

The salesman—*Derek* was his name—seemed just as surprised to see her. He also appeared *stoned* out of his mind. He sprouted a greasy grin, and they both said, "Hey!" at the same time. He then considered her semi-familiar face. "You are, uh . . . ?"

Recovering quickly, Susan returned his smile and replied, "I, uh, I just came by to catch up on some late-night work."

Derek chuckled knowingly. "Marvelous. There's no need to *lie* about it, though."

"I'm not lying," Susan replied flatly.

Derek openly laughed now. "Come ooonn!"

Susan glanced to the left—no help there . . .

"We *all* treat ourselves to the *Parlor* after-hours—it's one of the *perks*!"

Susan glanced to the right—no help there either . . .

"Here at the *Dream Parlor*, you can be *every*thing you want—"

Susan finally hauled off and punched Derek squarely in the face with all the might her petite body could muster. The salesman dropped like a rock, sprawling onto the lobby floor without so much as a facial tick.

Despite the wave of nausea the act induced, Susan found she felt *better* rather than worse.

Well . . . one way or another, I'm committed now . . .

Not knowing what else to do but leave Derek where he lay, Susan moved on . . .

* * *

In the corner of the basement laboratory, the hatch leading down to the drainage system creaked open. With considerable difficulty, a sweaty, exhausted Eli wedged a hand through the gap, then proceeded to push the heavy lid open with his *head*.

Once he was far enough in to employ his shoulders, the going got relatively easier. Careful to push the lid back as far as it would go—he had a brief, uncomfortable vision of the damned thing falling back down on his head with a skull-cracking *bang*—Eli twisted and squirmed until he pulled his devitalized body from the shaft. Leaning heavily against the wall beside it, he proceeded to close the lid—and further revealed how tired he was by letting it drop much too loudly. He flinched against the raucous metal *clang*, then slowly straightened and took a curious look around this little chamber he'd discovered.

He wasn't alone. Before his eyes had swept the entire space, the sound of slowly clapping hands brought him around in a sharp spin.

In the opposite corner stood Doctor James Corbit, who had

clearly watched his awkward entrance in silence, choosing only now to reveal himself with his mocking applause. Between the two men sat some metal-and-wire encrusted monstrosity that bore some resemblance to the dreamslabs throughout the rest of the *Parlor*.

"Very clever." Corbit commented as he took a few steps forward. "Very . . . *dramatic*."

Eli said nothing, contenting himself to stare daggers at the murdering bastard.

Pointing casually at Eli's glowing IDC, Corbit noted, "You'd better cover your chip, Rudolph. Until you plug in, you're broadcasting live, and if the Organizers storm this place, it could be bad for business." Scooping up a peculiar contraption from a work table, Corbit held it high for Eli's inspection. "This should diffuse your signal. Put it on."

Corbit tossed the object across the dreamslab to Eli, who instinctively caught it. A brief scrutiny revealed that it was some sort of metal gauntlet, and Eli decided that he had nothing to lose by complying with the Doctor's wishes on this point. As he slipped it past his IDC, he probed in a toneless voice, "Tell me what your business *is*."

Corbit didn't miss a beat. "Boy likes hardball—haven't played that game in *years*. Lay down."

Eli glanced over at the rudimentary dreamslab, then looked pointedly away.

"Its *bark* is worse than its *bite*," Corbit assured him. "If you want your answers . . . "

"I'm *curious*, not *crazy*."

"Fine," Corbit shrugged, holding out his hand. "Then give me the glove and wait outside on the front porch for an Organizer."

Staring hard at Corbit, Eli kept the glove and slowly ambled around to Corbit's side of the room.

Although he was playing it cool on the outside, trying to perhaps suggest that he was in no way surprised to find Corbit waiting for him, Eli's mind was actually running at top speed. What was he supposed to do *now*?

The *hope* had been that he could find his way out of wherever he ended up and make his way to a dream room. The *assumption* was that he would find the source of the dumped bodies, and perhaps even gain access to a dreamslab by whatever means possible. *Susan* should be on her way to Corbit's office by now, with the expectation of monitoring his progress, to try and help him past any system failsafes he might encounter as he attempted to inject the virus—what would she do when she found no current dream activity in the mainframe? Eli had no way of letting her know about this little hitch. If Corbit wanted him on the dreamslab for some reason, maybe he should just go along with it—this might be his only choice! That way, there was always their *backup* plan . . .

"You're a brave little warrior, coming here like this," Corbit remarked.

"I'm *addicted*," Eli replied sarcastically.

Corbit grunted. "*Bullshit*." As Eli climbed onto the dreamslab, Corbit turned away and began firing up his equipment. "You're behind the security breaches of the outer-compumatrix. You know all about the Establishment's plans for my *Parlor*. And I gather from your unconventional entrance . . . you found my *dirty laundry*."

Corbit paused for just a moment, then continued as he crossed

As Eli climbed onto the dreamslab, Corbit turned away and began firing up his equipment.

the room and powered up another apparatus. "So *now* you're determined to stop 'the evil Doctor Corbit'—*so* determined that you're willing to risk a trip to the Execution Channel . . . " Corbit looked over at Eli, who sat silently on the slab, staring straight ahead and offering no reaction of any kind. Corbit could tolerate a few things in life—being *ignored* was not one of them. Three long strides brought him to Eli's side, and he placed a firm grip on the back of the boy's neck. "Or maybe a *public beating*, like your *old man*, huh?"

Eli turned his head and looked into Corbit's near face. Breathing heavily, he spat through tight lips, "You don't know me." He shrugged Corbit's hand away from his neck with partial success. "You have *no idea* why I'm here."

"Frankly, I don't give *dick* why you're here . . . " Corbit told him seriously, before adding a cheerful, "I'm just glad you *came*. You see, *this* is where it all began, right here in this very basement." Suddenly thoughtful, Corbit folded his arms and paced casually over to lean against the nearest wall. "Let me tell you a true story. Once upon a time, I was sitting in my office . . . "

* * *

The turret elevator opened, and Susan stepped hesitantly into Corbit's office.

After a cursory look around the spacious study-like room, she made her way to the Big Man's mirrored desk. The winged-backed chair faced away, and when she sat down and it automatically swivelled into place, she had to bite her lip against a yelp.

The desk controls were familiar enough—although overly-decorated, the track-ball and gel interface on either side of the control panel were evident. One primary element was missing: The *retina scope*. How was she supposed to access cyber-limbo without a retina scope?

Thinking back, she recalled the one time she had been in the room before. Corbit hadn't been present, but the Senior Technician showed her the office on the off-hand chance she were ever summoned before the Master. Didn't the desktop have some sort of holographic display? She wasn't sure how that would help her access the computer network, but by now she had nothing to lose.

Making sure Eli's scrambler was firmly connected to her IDC, she placed her left hand on the track-ball, and slid her right into the oversized gel interface.

The response was instant. The trusses along either side of the room began humming, and the large golden spheres atop each crackled with electricity. A rippling wave of power actually crept into view, and a form began to take shape. Not on the *desktop*, but hovering in the center of the *room*. Susan had never seen anything like it.

Within seconds, a massive representation of Corbit's face scowled at her, spanning perhaps two meters from top to bottom. The face was somewhat transparent, but the *brain* behind the eyes was far less so.

God, what an ego *the man must have!*

"Hey, Doc. Working late?" When the hologram spoke, its voice was

A massive representation of Corbit's face scowled at her. The face was somewhat transparent, but the *brain* behind the eyes was far less so.

much more . . . *alive* than the usual cyber-limbo dopplegangers. This one must be an artificial intelligence—she realized it would be wise to keep that in mind.

"Yes," she answered. "I'd like to access any current dream activity in the mainframe, please."

The AI's brow furrowed. "*You sound* strange, *Doc. Are you sick?*"

"I'm fine," she assured it. "Access current activity."

The AI said nothing, but continued to scowl at her.

Trying to maintain her equilibrium, Susan decided to switch tactics. "Let's try this," she said as she reached across with a trembling hand and inverted two of the scrambler's switches. "Access any personal *logs*, specifically those relating to Citizen One-One-Eight-One-One." If she couldn't get into the system right away, perhaps she could learn something of why Corbit was interested in Elijah Barrett—Eli might or might not have reached a dreamslab by now, but if he had, he would just have to hold his own for a while.

The AI blinked, then its demeanor lightened just a bit. "*Absolutely, Doc*," it acceded. "*Accessing logs now . . .* "

* * *

"*Smart move*," Corbit assured him, "because once the IDC was perfected, it wasn't that difficult to find the key signals to affect the brain." Corbit grinned. "You mix the right *endorphin treats*, and the old noddle will sit up, speak, or play dead."

Stepping away from his spot against the wall, Corbit slowly began pacing around the dreamslab upon which Eli sat.

"What I've been looking for," he clarified, "is a way to *reverse* the flow—to get the *mind* to find its way back into the *machine*. Now, I've managed to *push* a few NCs over the hump, but getting them *in* proved a lot simpler than getting them back *out*." He pointed a finger at Eli. "Then *you* come along . . . and I see my ticket to *Paradise*."

"Why do you want to 'reverse the flow?' " Eli asked evenly.

Corbit stopped, clearly irritated at the interruption. "None of your business," he snapped. "Does it make a difference?"

Eli snorted. "People have *died* because of you. Yeah, I think it makes a difference."

Corbit was unmoved. "People will *continue* to die until I have what I want." Stepping over to the main control panel, he again leaned back casually and faced Eli. "You could *help* me . . . but it's my guess you've come here to *bushwhack* the mainframe in some clever way. Think of this as an extra hurtle."

Eli wasn't buying Corbit's oversimplification of the situation. "You *want* me to trash your computer?" he asked skeptically.

"No," Corbit answered. He reached around and flipped another switch. "I want you to *pop the cherry*, so when *I* make penetration, it won't shock the system . . . or *me*."

The lights directly over the dreamslab increased in intensity and began pulsing. Eli recognized them as early versions of those upstairs. The computer softly announced, "*Link to mainframe established. Awaiting IDC interface.*"

This was all wrong. When he first sat down, he was hoping to trick Corbit into giving him access to the mainframe under the guise of cooperation. But Corbit seemed too eager to go along with Eli's little plan—who knew what preparations he'd made in anticipation of Eli's "attack?" Proceeding with this charade no longer seemed like such a good idea.

"I don't trust you, Corbit," Eli muttered as he swung his legs over the side of the techno bed.

"Gee, I wonder why," was Corbit's caustic response. He stepped closer to Eli, who paused in his position on the edge of the dreamslab. "It doesn't matter—you have no other *viable* option . . . and neither does your buddy, *Jacob*."

Eli's stomach dropped down to his feet.

"Yeah, he lost his Citizenship, you know," Corbit continued as he returned to his casual pacing. "It seems he used his work station to break into *my* computer. What a pity . . . poor boy. Hunted fugitive and all. It's just a matter of time before he ends up on the Execution Channel. That's assuming, of course, that his *Parlor* addiction doesn't kill him first. Now the *moral* of the story, Eli, is that your reputation is only as *good* as the company you *keep*."

Eli was rolling through waves of nausea that had nothing to do with any *Parlor* conditioning. Once Jacob had gotten away from the Organizer, and then *Eli* had become the target of the hunt, he'd just assumed . . . no, he hadn't "assumed" anything, because he'd been so caught up in his tagging and his plans and Sara's death that he hadn't thought about *Jacob* at all. He'd done it again—first Nora, now Jacob.

Corbit was suddenly leaning next to him, almost whispering into his ear. "I think you owe your buddy an apology." Corbit then straightened and deliberately turned his back on Eli. "And I think it's *your* responsibility to take out the man who *reported* the security breach, don't you?"

All of Eli's pain and misery suddenly funneled into near-blinding rage, all of it focused at one James Corbit. Eli glared up at the older man's turned back, then threw himself at the son of a bitch . . .

But the son of a bitch was ready for just such an attack. Moving with surprising strength and agility, Corbit spun on his heel, knocking Eli's outstretched arms aside and seizing him by the back of the neck. With a primal roar, he threw Eli back down onto the dreamslab face first, using his own weight to add to the impact and then to pin the shocked and winded Eli in place.

Corbit's controlled posture slipped to the wayside. He vented years of pent-up frustration into Eli's ear, spittle spraying Eli's neck as he hissed through clenched teeth. "*Quick review*, son: I want *out* of this hell-hole, I want *Nirvana*, and I need *you* to open the door so that *I* can walk in and set up shop! I want to spend the rest of my life *joyriding* on other people's *dreams*, and I want *control* of it! *No one* will ever take anything away from me *ever* again! And when I'm on the inside, I'll have'em *all* by the *balls*! I'll be *God*—the *Duke—A-Number-One*!"

With a sharp shove, Corbit pushed himself off and away from Eli. He panted and rubbed his arm where he'd blocked Eli's assault, but it was his own flowing *irk* that had him far more winded than the physical exertion. Eli rolled over onto his back as Corbit's tirade continued.

"Now, if you're *half* the cuss your old man was, you may be willing to sacrifice your *own* life to one-up me. I *promise* you: *Jacob* will only be the *beginning*!" His voice dropped as he spoke with pronounced emphasis. "I'll *hang* every Citizen or Non-Citizen that you ever so much as *stood* next to, and I'll make it my mission in *life*." His face twisted with pure malice, he spat, "Do we have an *understanding*?"

Eli responded by removing the gauntlet, and Corbit nodded in satisfaction.

Before slipping his hand into the gel interface, however, Eli told him, "When you finally get the courage to step into *my* dream . . . I'll be *waiting* for you." Eli afforded himself one more glimpse at his glowing IDC, and then he thrust his hand into place.

The last thing he heard as he began his rapid decent into induced REM sleep was Corbit's amused warning: "Oh, by the way, there's no guarantee that you'll *stay* in your *prepared dream* . . . "

NIGHTMARE

The transition was unlike any before it.

Even when he'd entered the last dream—the one where Susan conjured up the imagery of the dead bodies and the mutilated girl with her—he'd still experienced the same sense of wonder through his entry into his dream state. That passage had been abrupt, yes, but it wasn't until he arrived to find himself in a different locale that he had truly known something was amiss.

This transition was harsh, too, but it was more *than that. The "old rush," as Jacob had called it, was completely gone. The dreams had always boasted themselves as* lucid, *but this was different. When he'd planned to enter the dream and insert the virus through whatever means necessary, he had also prepared to* steel *himself against the allure of the* Parlor's *wiles.*

It turned out not to be necessary. The crossing was swift and oppressive and totally unappealing.

A falling jolt found him lying on his back amidst the same woods as last time. A glimpse at himself revealed the modern clothes he'd worn on the outside—the only difference upon his person was the presence of his familiar, dreamworld VanDyke. When he rose to his elbows, he dis-

covered his equally familiar medieval garb lying on the ground beside him, waiting to be donned. With the time or inclination, he might have analyzed the implications of this situation in comparison to his previous mental states—was it because he had entered the dream with a changed level of self-consciousness?—but for now, he had neither to spare.

"Susan?" he whispered tentatively into the air around him. Was she in position yet? How closely would she be able to monitor his movements from the outside, and would direct communication be possible? Or might she have fallen to their backup *plan—to find another dreamslab and actually* join *him on the inside? If so, would Corbit be able to* detect *her if he weren't looking?*

So many uncertainties . . .

He tried again. "Susan?"

Nothing. And he wasn't sure whether that was good or bad.

Affording himself a brief sigh, he reached for his appropriate armor . . .

* * *

"Eager beaver," Corbit commented as he watched Eli's progress through the waveforms of his scope. No sign yet of the boy's infamous second waveform pattern, but still . . .

The computer reported its findings, "*Enhanced REM achieved. IDC link: Stable. Bio-feedback: Optimal. Monitoring subject progress . . .* "

Corbit dictated into his logs, "The subject reached enhanced REM faster than *any* before him. At this accelerated rate of decent, it'll be interesting to see what the mainframe kicks out to prevent him from scoring a touchdown."

Preparing to launch the networking protocols that should fire Eli's pattern straight toward the heart of the mainframe—an event the boy had nearly managed on his *own* during his last dream session—Corbit glanced over his shoulder at the sleeping form.

"Watch your *step*, boy . . . here it *comes* . . . "

* * *

Without warning, the ground collapsed beneath Eli's feet. He caught himself quickly enough, but the unpleasant drop left him shaken. His feet kicking in open space beneath him, Eli struggled to pull himself from the diminutive but dangerous pit.

So far, things weren't going at all as planned. Setting aside the fact that he hadn't expected to run into Corbit in the Parlor's basement in the middle of the night, Eli's designs had also counted on finding that portal-like structure pretty much where he left it. His guess was that it represented a link to the mainframe itself, but it was nowhere in sight.

He slipped, nearly falling all the way back into the hole before he finally dragged himself onto solid ground. Crawling over to a nearby tree, he collapsed at its base for a moment's respite while he again called out, "Susan . . . ? Come on, Susan . . . "

When he was greeted only with silence, he pushed his cloak away from his legs and clambered to his feet . . .

. . . and ducked just in time to avoid the axe that sought to separate his head from his body.

Whatever the thing was, it was big. Sporting a horned, skull-faced helmet and leather-armor approximate to the period of Eli's own attire, it wrenched the imbedded broadaxe free from the tree it struck in place of Eli's neck.

Eli's mind was a whirlwind of shock and adrenaline—he'd never encountered anything like this in his Parlor dreams before—but he managed to dance away from the creature's swinging assault long enough to draw his sword. If Corbit wanted to kill him, why didn't he just pull the plug on Eli's real body in some fashion? What in the world was that madman up to?!

The creature swept its axe across and down, catching Eli's sword just right and stabbing both blades into the ground. Releasing his weapon, Eli seized the helmet by one of its horns and drove his fist into the open lower-half of its faceplate. He hoped to connect firmly with its *chin, but instead his hand sank* all the way *into its face—or the void where its face* should *have been.*

Scalding steam erupted all around Eli's trapped hand, and he screamed . . .

* * *

"*. . . when previous subjects interfaced with the net,*" the AI Corbit explained to Susan, "*the mainframe interpreted them as an* invading virus *and defended itself, which resulted in their* deaths."

Shaken with far more knowledge than she'd had before, Susan asked, "How did the dreamers die?"

"*The dreamers translated the computer's resistance as a* nightmare—*their dreams were torn apart. When they didn't awaken, their nightmares grew steadily* worse, *until it finally ended in brain death . . . or* suicide."

Susan's heart was in her throat. This was all wrong—Eli didn't know about *any* of this when he'd devised this *stupid* plan of his! If only she'd scouted this information *before* he—but, he was tagged now, so they couldn't really—they—he—!

Swallowing, she tried to get a hold of herself. She had to contact Eli, to warn him and get him out of there before Corbit's machines ripped his mind to pieces!

"Access current dream path for One-One-Eight-One-One immediately!" she ordered. When the AI merely stared at her, she snapped, "Access *immediately*!"

"*What's your mother's maiden name?*"

Startled, Susan choked, "What?"

"*Your mother's maiden name,*" the giant face repeated, "*what is it?*"

Trembling, Susan withdrew her hand from the gel interface . . .

. . . and looked on in shock when the hologram remained right where it was and an alarm sounded.

"*What is your mother's* maiden name?" the AI demanded menacingly.

Susan looked back and forth between the gel and the face. How could the thing still be *running*?

The face increased in size, and the golden spheres atop the trusses began crackling with more than just holographic energy. "*Her* maiden name—*what—is—it?!*"

Desperate, Susan stood, grasped the gel interface housing, and pulled and twisted until it ripped from the desktop in a shower of sparks and smoke . . .

* * *

Smoke billowing around its head, the masked creature straightened to its full height, but not before Eli stole a dazed glance at the empty space within the horned helmet.

Eli's hand was scorched. Even as the creature reclaimed its axe, it took a great deal of concentration simply to grasp his sword once more to protect himself.

Again the creature came with a flurry of metal, leather, and animalistic rancor. Eli could not find time to think—it was react,

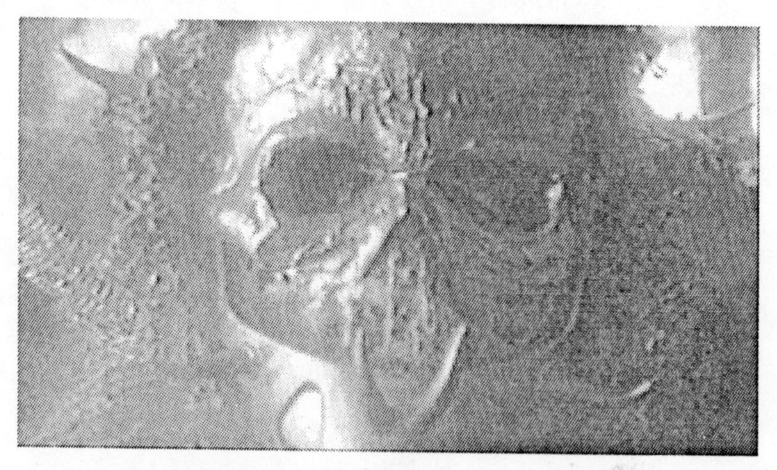

The masked creature straightened to its full height, but not before Eli stole a dazed glance at the empty space within the horned helmet.

or die. He tried to tell himself that this was only a dream, but the wind of the axe passing his face and the jarring of his wrist as their mutual blades connected—and the burning sting of his hand—suggested it wouldn't be a great idea to take a stand on the issue.

His feet shuffled through the grass and dirt as he steadily retreated, searching for some avenue of escape or counter-attack but finding none.

This . . . is wasting my time . . . I need to plant the virus . . . find Susan . . . plant the virus . . .

The axe swept, he nearly stumbled, his sword was deflected, the beast snarled viciously, he ducked, he dodged . . . until his right foot found no more purchase.

Teetering dangerously, Eli glanced back at the hole through which he had fallen earlier. What appeared to be sunlight *was shining* up *through the aperture now, but he didn't have time to think, he had to keep moving before—*

The axe swept in fast, past his guard and toward his face. His blockade suddenly became his only hope, and Eli stepped backward, voluntarily falling through the opening . . . falling through the opening . . .

falling . . .

*

falling . . .

falling through the opening . . .

Even as Eli laid his eyes upon it, the body was falling through the opening.

Opening? The body? What the hell—?!

The rope around his neck was tugged harshly, and Eli was pulled the last few steps to the top of the gallows. The black-garbed executioner, silent beneath his bandana-covered face, shoved him into place.

What—what's happened—where—?!

Eli felt as though he were one step behind in a desperate race for his life. He remembered a horned, masked ogre of some sort, an axe, a hole in the ground . . . and then he was here. *But* where *was "here?"*

The sun blazed fiercely hot from above, but only barely hotter than the dry wind. Eli found that if he tilted his head forward, the glare was shaded from his eyes, because he was now wearing a hat—probably a cowboy *hat, if his new environment were any indication. The executioner beside him was of an* Old Western *theme himself, as was the hooded body that had just fallen through the gallows trapdoor . . . and the surrounding town . . . and the hooded audience lined up before the wooden structure, either waiting their own turn or looking on through their burlap masks to witness Eli's hanging, he could not say.*

Just like . . .

The rough rope was tightened around Eli's throat further, and the executioner tossed the free end over the crossbar before securing it near the back.

An image flashed through his mind: The cover of a book . . .

Just like *Windsong* . . . the Western setting from *Windsong* . . .

And all of it was proceeding as though this *were his dream from the beginning. It was too much, happening too fast! His hands were tied in front of him, the body hung lifelessly beside him, the unmoving audience watched silently before him . . .*

He hadn't even devised an escape from the horned creature—how was he supposed to escape a hanging*?!*

Feeling defeat like a yoke weighing him down—or like the thick rope cutting into his throat—Eli lowered his head . . .

* * *

Corbit lifted his head, staring down at the wavering subject before him.

This couldn't be happening—not again! Eli had seemed so promising, so capable . . . but in spite of it all, the mainframe had him on the ropes. His waveform—although still that of a "spiker" if ever Corbit had seen one—was fluctuating dangerously. And, as yet, there had been no sign of that unique, bizarre *second* waveform that Corbit had witnessed before, most notably when Eli had nearly interfaced with the mainframe during his last dream.

How could the boy have gotten so *close* on his own, only to *flounder* under Corbit's guidance?

That second waveform—*whatever* it was—where was it *now*?!

"Fight it, boy," he urged. "Ride's not over yet. Show me how you do it . . . " Desperate, Corbit actually reached out a soothing hand and stroked Eli's sweaty forehead. "Show me the way in . . . "

* * *

With dramatic flare, the burlap hood was removed from the hanged body's head, revealing the fresh corpse as Jacob Moore. Eli looked down at the image of his friend . . . and was moved in a way far different from what the executioner must have intended.

The sight filled him with anger.

So what if the dream had shifted into some Western sham, or any other *environment? Corbit had mentioned that possibility at the last minute, hadn't he? Did that make Eli's goal any less vital? A dream was a dream, and he would not submit to a hanging any more than he had the horned creature's attempted beheading!*

As the executioner threw the lever to the trap door beneath his feet, Eli quickly raised his arms over his head. His wrists were tied together, yes, but he was still able to seize the rope in a double-handed grasp. The trap door gave way, and the jolt wrenched his shoulders, his gloved hands, and—yes—his throat painfully . . . but his neck was not *broken, and he was* not *giving up!*

The executioner's face was covered, but he still managed to appear stunned *as Eli kicked and twisted in a choking effort to find purchase with his legs. After a stilted moment, the black-garbed assassin reached down and pressed against the top of Eli's head, adding his own bulky weight to the pressure against Eli's throat.*

Eli's eyes rolled upward as the air was cut off completely.

Don't give up, don't give up, don't give up . . .

A flash of metal caught itself in his fluttering vision. A gun . . . the executioner wore a modern Organizer's firearm *on his hip!*

The executioner watched as Eli kicked and twisted in a choking effort to find purchase with his legs.

Releasing his grip, Eli reached for the weapon. Before the executioner could react, the gun was in Eli's hands and its crystalline barrel was pressed against the taut rope. The retort echoed through the quaint Western town as the rope exploded, and Eli dropped through the trapdoor to land clumsily on the packed dirt below.

Gasping for breath, the more rational parts of Eli's mind couldn't believe he was still alive! He clutched the Organizer gun tightly, throwing wary glances up through the trap door but too winded to take much action beyond wheezing and coughing. It wasn't until he heard the creaking of rope from the other *trapdoor that he brought the weapon fully to bear.*

The sound issued from the lowering of Jacob's body. Jacob . . . who swivelled around to look directly at Eli as he whispered in an echoing, other-worldly voice, "Don't rock the boat."

The sight of Jacob's puffy, bluish face got to Eli far more than he was prepared for, and he found himself nearly panicked as he frantically rolled out from under the gallows. He was well aware that he was exposing himself quite openly to the executioner, who could very well have a second firearm, and he rolled up onto one knee, his pilfered gun at ready.

Nothing. The executioner was gone.

Letting himself breathe deeply once more, Eli glanced cautiously over his shoulder toward the hooded "townspeople." They stood silently, perfectly still . . . except to turn their covered heads just enough to stare back at him.

As when Jacob's identity was revealed, the nightmare's gesture did not have its intended effect. Abruptly, the still figures no longer seemed like townspeople to him—they represented much more than that. To Eli, they were suddenly the faceless masses of people who had carelessly allowed themselves to fall into this bland, controlled world that his father had fought so fiercely to prevent!

"Wake up," he muttered, rising to his feet—the figures took no action as he advanced upon them. His wrists were still bound, but he managed to grip his weapon firmly in his right hand as he reached out with his left. "Wake up," he commanded as he pulled the burlap hood off of a woman's head. She stared straight ahead, her face blank, and that non-reaction fueled his rampage further. "Wake up! You people aren't dead*!" He moved on to the next person, a man, and removed the hood. Still nothing. "Wake up! What's the matter with you people?!* Wake up*!" Another hood, then another. He found himself screaming in the man's expressionless face. "I'm trying to help* you, *now help* me*!* Wake up*!!"*

Eli moved through the crowd at random, removing hoods and demanding that they awaken. Another person, another hood . . . none of them reacted. He knew that he was allowing himself to once again stray from the mission at hand, but at the moment he was beyond caring! Feeding NCs, erasing names from the Execution Channel . . . why was he *always protecting the world? Couldn't* any *of them help* themselves *anymore?*

He advanced upon a lone woman near the back. "I said wake up*—!"*

The frenzied, blood-streaked face of Dana Levy laughed at him in hideous, inhumanly hysterical bellows. He stumbled backward, falling smartly onto his ass before he could catch himself. Still laughing, Dana slowly advanced upon him.

"Susan!" he called out, suddenly no longer interested in rousing the general public. "Susan, I need your help! Sus—!"

He slowly became aware that all *of the dehooded people were shuffling toward him, each muttering Susan's name. Desperately, he scooted backward across the hot, hard dirt.*

"Susan, Susan," *they mocked, their echoing voices a resounding cacophony of deathly moans and wails that quickly became a* chant. "Susan—Susan—Susan . . . "

"Susan!" Eli cried. "Susan! Suussaaaaaannnnnn!"

* * *

Panting frantically, Susan raced through the hallways of the *Dream Parlor.*

She knew that she had to reach a dreamslab—*any* dreamslab—as quickly as possible, to warn Eli of the unsuspected dangers of attempting to insert the virus into the mainframe. She was *also* aware that, if she were too late and the mainframe was already reacting to his presence, then she might be committing *suicide* by entering the dream herself.

She didn't care.

Throwing aside the decorative curtain at the entrance of Room 222, Susan dashed inside. Taking a quick moment to activate the primary systems, she strode across the room to the dreamslab, tossing her work smock to the ground along the way . . .

* * *

Tossing the ropes from his wrists and neck to the ground, Eli recollected the gun and stood, shifting his hat as the sun blazed on. Susan had not come to the rescue, but he'd found himself motivated enough to elude the shuffling zombies back in the town square. Unfortunately, he was beginning to suspect that they had allowed *him to escape, as he now found himself wandering through rocky, arid terrain, with no shelter—or portal—in sight.*

Sighing, Eli gazed out at the wasteland around him and tried to formulate some sort of plan.

Corbit's warning that his dream might change did not explain why *it had changed. Was it an indication that his mind was losing* cohesion? *He supposed it only made sense that his subconscious had held on to an environment parallel to Sara's* Windsong *book. After all, he and Susan fashioned their first meetings after its influence, and its world quickly became their habit—up to and including its sway on the design of the portal itself.*

He would have to watch himself—if it would do any good—or he might find himself in the third and most dangerous *setting from little Sara's book: The prehistoric jungle, where the hero fought against the—*

"Mister Eli . . . "

Eli glanced over his shoulder toward the sound of the voice. "Sara?" he whispered.

He saw nothing but a towering rock face . . . but he was certain that he'd heard . . .

Don't fall for it, Eli. Whatever Corbit's up to, he's twisting this dreamland into some sort of *deathtrap*. Your subconscious mind is becoming *his* weapon. Just ignore it.

"Mister Eli . . . "

He took one step forward . . . and then another . . .

Ignore it!

But how could he? He knew *this was just a dream, but . . . to have a chance, however illusionary, to say* goodbye, *to tell her that he* loved *her, that he was so* sorry *. . .*

Before he'd even made a cognizant decision to follow the voice, Eli was already several meters up the steep, rocky tower.

It was rough going, and his cowboy boots slipped on several occasions. He felt incredibly torn over the admitted futility of this venture, but before his doubts could turn him back . . .

"Mister Eli . . . where are you?"

Sara!

What was the harm *in heading this way, anyway? He didn't know* where *the portal was—maybe it was just over the next ridge! He moved onward.*

"Mister Eli . . . I thought you was *smart* . . . "

He didn't want to think too hard on that sentiment, but it was omnidirectional enough to bring him to a halt. Had her voice come from the left, or the right? Or from above? He scanned the higher rocks . . .

He jerked to attention when he spotted the executioner, standing some fifty meters above him . . . and with his back *turned no less! For once, Eli felt like he'd actually been handed the advantage! He raised his gun, took careful aim, and fired!*

The executioner whirled, holding before him the most terrible of protection.

Nnooo!

It was far too late. Before he even finished his anguished thought, the swift projectile closed the distance and exploded squarely in Sara's young gut. Sara made no move—made no sound*—as she tumbled forward.*

Eli dropped his firearm even as Sara plummeted to the rock scant meters before him. There was no cry of pain, no disbelief, no blame *. . . she merely lay there, lifeless and silent.*

But then, she doesn't really *need* to cry blame, now does she?

No, she didn't. This *might all be a dream, but none of it was far from* reality, *was it? Sara died because she'd had the misfortune of knowing Eli Barrett, had taken the very bullet that had been intended for him. This dream merely displayed what he'd known since before he conveniently washed her blood from his hands—Corbit might have killed Nora, and his* Parlor *might have even killed Dana . . . but* Eli *killed Sara, and that was the undeniable, inescapable* truth.

Falling to his knees, Eli removed his leather gloves, then carefully grasped the Organizer gun. Steadily, determinedly, he lifted the gun and pressed its barrel to his temple. His finger tightened on the trigger . . .

. . . and some external force suddenly tugged the weapon away *from his head. Frustrated, Eli struggled against his invisible, unwanted savior . . .*

* * *

More desperate than he'd ever been in his life, Corbit struggled to keep Eli's hand away from his temple. "No, no, no, don't do this . . . "

It had been so close—he'd turned from his instruments just in time to see Eli's pantomimed movement, and to guess what it *meant* . . . but he knew his was a *futile* gesture. If Eli were tricked into *killing himself,* as so many before him had been when pushed toward the mainframe, how long could Corbit stop him?

"D*amn it,* Eli, you can't *do* this to me!"

Then, unexpectedly, Eli *stopped.* As Corbit slowly released his grip on the boy's wrist, he witnessed a confused, and somewhat *relieved,* expression wash over Eli's face.

"What's going on, boy?" he asked his sleeping subject. Staggering back to his instruments, Corbit peered into his scope.

There it *was*!

As Corbit watched, the second waveform crept into view—although this time it seemed to be taking longer to fall into sync with Eli's primary pattern. And even here, with all of his personal instruments, Corbit *still* couldn't determine how it was happening!

"How are you *doing* that?" Corbit muttered in frustration.

* * *

"Eeeellliiii . . . ?"

Letting his arm fall away of its own accord, Eli dropped the gun and sighed in heartfelt relief. "Susan," he breathed. Her voice sounded far, far away, but it was her—*he* knew *it was!*

"Eeelllllliiiijjjahhh . . . ?"

"Susan . . . "

Her voice was like cool water in his feverish face! Dear God, he'd been about to . . . but he wouldn't think about that for now. This dream was taxing *him far more than he'd been willing to admit. It was as if he'd never quite caught up when the setting shifted—he'd been running more on instinct than thought since he'd appeared on the gallows. Thank God for Susan . . .*

The question was: Had she somehow reached him from the outside, *or had she actually* joined *him in the dreamworld? She'd taken so long . . . but then, he'd never met up with her, had he? She couldn't even know where he* was!

"Susan!" he called. "I'm in the basement!*" Slowly, he clambered to his feet. "I'm in* the basement!*"*

* * *

"*Two* waveforms," Corbit snapped into his hand-mike as he paced back and forth beside the dreamslab. "Clever little *bastard* is doing it again. It doesn't make any *sense*! Without neuro-synthetics, it's *impossible* for *one* person to do what Eli is doing . . . "

Corbit was fully prepared to ramble on, to pace in frustration as Eli performed his inexplicable magic, when it slowly sank in that the boy was talking in his sleep.

"Sus'n," Eli mumbled through sluggish lips. "Sus'n . . . mm in th' bazemen . . . th' bazemen . . . Sus'n . . . Sus'n . . . "

Corbit froze . . . and a new possibility slowly began to form in his disbelieving mind . . .

* * *

"Susan?" Eli called as he struggled up the side of the rocky cliff. He'd quickly realized that her voice sounded the strongest from above, but once he'd began his climb, her cries had fallen unnervingly silent.

"Come on, Susan . . . " he gasped as he crawled upward, ". . . talk to me . . . say my name, Susan . . . say my name . . . "

Hand over hand, his feet slipping behind him, Eli forced himself onward. As he'd thought when he'd followed the ghost of Sara's voice: Where else did he have to go?

Finally, he approached a plateau. Gripping the side, he pulled himself upward as he again called out, "Susan, say my name—!"

The executioner's masked face was suddenly centimeters from his own as it roared in a hideous voice, "EEELLLLLIIIIIII!"

More startled than scared, Eli pulled away . . .

. . . and lost his grip. Tumbling backward, he rolled head-over-heel as he plunged toward the rock face below . . .

* * *

At the end of a nondescript hallway in the *Dream Parlor*, a familiar stone-on-wood "DP" symbol rotated 90 degrees, revealing a clandestine doorway as Corbit crashed through from the basement below. Leaving the secret entrance standing open in his haste, Corbit thundered down the corridor . . .

* * *

Thunder rumbled through the prehistoric jungle. Lifting his head with a surprised jolt, Eli studied his new surroundings . . . at least, he studied as well as he could *in his present state.*

Shuffling to his feet, the bearded, long-haired, and hide-clad Eli peered into the foggy gloom around him. He had some sense of having been somewhere . . . else . . . *before, but he couldn't recall where that was. Likewise, this place seemed vaguely familiar in some strange way, but he didn't know why. And hadn't he been following something? Trying to reach someone? It was so hard to think . . .*

"Eeellllliii . . . ?" *a feminine voice called from deeper in the forest.*

Eli looked around. That was him, *right?* Eeellllliii . . . *that was* his *name, wasn't it? And that voice . . . that voice belonged to . . . to . . .*

"Sus'n," he grunted. Yes, he knew that *was right—it belonged to* Sus'n.

"Eli?" *she called again, sounding closer than before.* "Elijah, I'm here . . . "

"Sus'n," Eli grunted again, shuffling forward uncertainly.

"Elijah, where are you? Elijah . . . follow my voice . . . "

Gaining confidence, Eli sprinted through the steamy jungle into the mist . . .

* * *

Corbit strode swiftly into the *Parlor's* main lobby. He afforded the briefest, barely-curious glance at the still-unconscious Derek as he moved to the reception desk. Slapping his hand onto the track ball, he punched a few commands into the small keyboard.

The display screen lit up, confirming his suspicions: There was an unauthorized dreamer in Room 222.

Literally shaking with rage, Corbit slammed his fist onto the desktop. "*Damn!*"

* * *

Rounding a massive tree, Eli approached the clearing. Creeping through the thicket, he spotted a woman—Sus'n?—dressed in soft flowing clothing, standing before . . . before . . . something. Something large, hollow in the center. He felt he should know what to call the thing with the hollow center—a shifting center that rippled like the wind, there and yet not there, but . . . por-al? Por-tal*?*

Eli crept forward, grunting the woman's name. "Sus . . . Sus'n?"

She did not turn around.

Eli reached out, touching her hair, sniffing the air. Something didn't smell right. Gripping her shoulder, he pulled her around to face him—

It wasn't Sus'n! It wasn't a woman *at all anymore! It was a monster! A large, fur-clad man with a dinosaur skull for a head! It raised its arms and roared a challenge at Eli!*

Eli raised his own arms and yelled right back at it! He was not afraid of this man-monster who wore a skull for a mask! He was—

He was an unfortunately easy target, but with his limited reasoning, he didn't learn this until the man-monster head-butted him right to the ground.

But he was Eli*! He would not submit to the man-monster!*

Shaking his head, he seized a large, nearby rock in his calloused hands and rose to meet the challenger once more. The man-monster bore down upon him, and he swung the rock around, smashing it

It was a large, fur-clad man with a dinosaur skull for a head! It raised its arms and roared a challenge at Eli!

across the thing's face once, then again. The man-monster was staggered, but it retaliated—only his thick hide saved Eli from being gored in the side as a massive horn-bone knocked him back.

The man-monster shook its head and roared another challenge, but this time Eli waited, waited for it to come to him. It shook its head again, then charged, its horns ready to tear, its bone-plate ready to crush . . .

At the last moment, Eli side-stepped, slamming his rock not into the thing's head but into its gut. When the man-monster doubled over, Eli lifted the rock high and then brought it smashing down against the back of its neck.

The man-monster fell forward onto its stomach, spasmed for a second, then collapsed.

Triumphant, Eli glared down at the creature, oblivious to the pulsing changes in the por-tal behind him. Setting the rock to one side, he rolled the man-monster onto its back, then removed the large skull-mask so that he could see . . .

He froze when he saw the face staring silently up at him. It wasn't what he'd expected—it was . . . familiar. *He knew this face . . . it was . . . was . . .*

Eli . . .

That's right. It was Eli.

He had been mistaken all along. He had thought that he *was Eli, but that was wrong.* He *was not Eli*—Eli *was* evil. *Eli hurt the people around him, Eli let people die. Eli spit in the face of his father, Eli did things that were small when he promised to do things that were big. Eli fed people, then took their food away. Eli made friends, then betrayed them. Eli killed No-ra. Eli killed Ja-cob. Eli killed Da-na. Eli killed Sa-ra.*

And if Eli wasn't stopped . . . Eli would kill Sus'n.

He knew now. He knew what he must do.

Eli was evil. *He must* stop *Eli—he must* kill *Eli.*

Determined to end the evil here and now, he reclaimed his rock and lifted it high over his head.

"Elijah, stop*!"*

Sus'n's voice—that was the only reason he hesitated. She was . . . speaking to him*? Maybe . . . if the evil one was* Eli, *maybe* he *was* Elijah? *Maybe . . . but he knew what he must do, he must—*

"Elijah, listen *to me."*

She appeared from behind the thick tree. And this time she looked right, *not in the soft, flowing clothing, but in . . . tighter clothing, m . . .* mo-dern *clothing. This was the* real *Sus'n. And she called him* Elijah*! He could* trust *this Sus'n . . . or so he thought.*

He slowly lowered the rock as he listened to her . . . but he did not *put it down.*

Sus'n approached him carefully as she spoke, ignoring the evil one completely. Soothing him with her voice, she told him, "This nightmare is created by the mainframe defense programs—it's what killed *the others. If you* die *in this dream . . . then you* die.*"*

What was she saying? Main-frame de—de-fense . . . ? He didn't understand all her words, but he could sense *what she was trying to tell him—she didn't want him to kill Eli!*

But . . . that wasn't right! Eli was evil*! Eli* hurt *people*! *Why was she trying to stop him?!*

Elijah, *a familiar voice—father's voice—whispered in his mind,* listen to her. Listen to *her* voice . . .

No! They wanted to confuse him, to stop him from doing what must be done!

Elijah, *father whispered,* this is the danger . . . the danger of destroying *yourself . . .*

No! He was not destroying himself—he was destroying the evil! *The* Eli! *He must . . . he must . . .*

Images and voices flashed through his mind . . .

A large, rotund man wearing a little hat on his head, smiling at him . . .

"you've really got to work on your approach"

A woman, dirty but pretty, holding a baby, H—Ha-na . . . Hannah . . .

"don't you believe in Guardian Angels"

A younger man, with glasses—but it was someone else's *voice who spoke when this image came, a* hated *voice . . .*

"that's assuming of course that his *Parlor* addiction doesn't kill him first"

Parlor *addiction . . .*

More images, alien thoughts, most of which he couldn't understand . . .

Vi-rus . . . neu-ral net . . . main-frame . . . vi-rus . . . eye-dee-see . . . eye-dee-see . . . IDC sig-nals . . .

Vi-rus . . . virus . . . virus . . .

"work on your approach"

"Guardian Angels"

"*Parlor* addiction . . . kill him first . . . "

Frustrated, feeling as though his mind were about to burst, he raised the rock once more, howling his frustration . . .

"No!" Sus'n cried, trying to stop him.

The rock was coming down . . .

Elijah

. . . coming down to smash . . .

Elijah!

. . . to smash into the ground beside Eli's head.

It was over . . . and the mainframe *apparently knew it. In a mild pulse of light, the fur-clad Eli and his skull-mask faded from existence.*

When Susan stood, it was a modern-dressed and very tired *Elijah Barrett who stood next to her. He wondered if she would ever* appreciate *how close it had been—if she had called him "Eli" instead of "Elijah" . . .*

"Can you still generate the virus?" she asked.

Panting, Eli nodded. "Let's do what we came here to do . . . before Corbit *finds out."*

Together, they turned to face the portal—their entrance into the mainframe . . .

* * *

Corbit bolted down the hall, catching the doorframe to swing himself into Room 222. *There* she was, the *bitch*! If he had the time, he'd show her what happened to those who crossed James Corbit . . .

. . . but he *didn't* have the time. Striding across the small room, he seized the woman—"Susan"—harshly by her ankles . . .

* * *

Without warning, the ground came alive! With a crackling rustle of leaves—or the warning of a rattlesnake—vines slithered up her boots, wrapping tightly around Susan's calves. All she could do was gasp as her legs were yanked out from under her.

Eli turned and dove for her, but it was too late! Screaming, she was dragged bodily under the massive tree, her cries echoing away as she disappeared into the ether . . .

* * *

Susan's cries echoed down the hallway as she collided with the wall opposite the dream room doorway. Her chin struck the hard surface beneath the decorative fabric forcefully enough to chip two of her teeth against one other, and it was all she could do to keep from sliding to the floor as she moaned.

Satisfied for the meantime—he would deal with her *later*—Corbit stepped back and pressed his IDC against the scanlock. A failsafe for those rare patrons who turned sleepwalker before the kill-switch could be activated, a thick metal door slammed down from above, effectively sealing the room from either side.

Corbit then moved swiftly into the control booth. Now that he knew what the hell Eli's "second waveform" had been, mimicking the same effect would be child's play—he *cursed* himself for not having figured it out before! Hadn't he always *intended* to use the mainframe to adapt dream-links? He didn't know how *those* two managed to pull it off without specific manipulation of the net . . . but he had other matters to attend to right now.

"*Establishing path to Dream One-One-Eight-One-One,*" the computer announced.

Practically throwing himself onto the dreamslab, Corbit shoved his hand into the gel interface . . .

* * *

"Susan . . . "

Eli dreaded the implications of her abrupt, violent departure. What was happening on the outside? Had Corbit found her? He must have. Should he proceed—if he even could; *look how long it had taken to find the portal without her!—or should he try to* wake up, *to find her and help her . . .*

Behind him, the portal began pulsing again, this time more fiercely and accompanied by a higher-pitched wail. The wind picked up through this mock-jungle, and there was a flash high in the sky. As Eli watched, the flash turned into a fiery comet, a comet that was heading straight for—

The fireball struck him full in the chest, knocking him to the ground even as it crushed the wind from his lungs. The fire didn't truly burn, *however, and a moment later he found out why.* Corbit *appeared from the heart of the "comet," and he advanced upon Eli without hesitation.*

"You slippery little prick!*" he raged as he kicked Eli in the cheek.*

Eli rolled away, feeling the blood flow into his mouth.

Corbit loomed over him, allowing him to slowly regain his feet. "I put my head on the chopping block to keep you off the Execution Channel," the Doctor spat, and Eli wasn't certain whether the disgust in his voice was aimed outward or inward.

"Where's Susan?" Eli muttered as he wiped blood from his lip.

Corbit chuckled, and the malevolence dripped from his words. "Limbo land—I sucked her brain dry.*"*

Gritting his teeth, Eli leaped forward and slammed his fist into Corbit's face . . .

* * *

Disoriented, Susan stumbled through the corridors of the *Dream Parlor*. She'd been working here for a while, and yet now she couldn't seem to find her way.

The "basement." Eli told me he was in the "basement."

It had taken her a while to catch up to Eli in the dreamworld—especially when the environment suddenly changed!—but she *had* been there, and she *had* heard him calling. She'd never known there *was* a basement to this place . . . but she had to find it. Eli was *exhausted* from his run-in with the mainframe—he was in no shape to take on that egomaniac!

Trying to clear her head, she pushed herself onward . . .

* * *

Corbit shoved Eli to the ground, his hand clutched tightly around the younger man's throat. He pressed his weight down onto Eli, shoving his knee into the boy's gut while he was at it.

"You still . . . " Eli managed to choke, ". . . need me . . . to get . . . into your mainframe . . . "

"Not anymore I don't," Corbit growled. To think that he'd actually believed this pathetic son-of-a-bitch was some kind of wonder child! "I figured out your little trick! You are useless to me!" He pulled Eli's head up just to slam him back down even harder. "Worthless!"

* * *

Susan staggered into a junction and spotted a turret elevator. Diving into it almost before its doors could open, she gasped, "Basement . . . "

"*I'm sorry,*" the annoying voice prattled, "*there is no 'basement' access in my program.*"

Susan cried out in frustration and slammed her hands into its sides. What if Eli had been *delusional* when he'd told her he was in the basement?!

The doors opened once more. Glancing briefly back the way she'd come, Susan moved on . . .

* * *

Eli gripped at Corbit's trench coat, but it appeared that the fight had gone out of him. Corbit punched him squarely in the nose once, then again. Eli lost his grip and fell to the ground.

Corbit stood up straight, panting and shaking his head. "What a disappointment *you must be to your old man," he marveled in abhorrence before turning to face the portal.*

Panting even harder, Eli rose to his hands and knees. He saw Corbit approaching the portal—what was it the Doctor said he wanted? To spend the rest of his life "joyriding on other people's dreams?" To have them all "by the balls?"

Corbit was enraptured as he contemplated the portal. To him, it was beautiful*! So simple, so symbolic . . . so* accurate*! In a moment, he would finish the bastard off, force himself to awaken . . . and then set out making his* plans.

No one knew about the basement laboratory. He could set himself up with intravenous sustenance, probably a catheter, too. Oh, he supposed he should awaken himself every once in a while to check on his body's status . . . but how long would he even need *his body? Now that he knew how Eli had accessed the mainframe so safely—by dream-linking to that skinny little tramp—he could use neuro-synthetics to impersonate a second set of his* own *waveform pattern! He could step right into the mainframe and then, if his theories were correct, he might even be able to move his consciousness* inside *the mainframe and throughout the neural net itself!*

Corbit was gaping at the portal, actually stroking *its perimeter while gazing into its flashing, pulsing center, when Eli tackled him from behind. The older man lost his balance . . .*

When James Edward Corbit finally traversed the portal into the heart of the mainframe, Elijah Barrett journeyed right alongside him . . .

THE MAINFRAME

Flashing . . . pulsing . . . similar to the journey into his Parlor *dreams, but . . .*

Violent . . . awesome . . .

Somewhere along the way he was separated from Corbit. He wasn't sure when or how—he wasn't even sure how long the transition had taken.

He could see, but only in fits and spurts, as if the world around him thrived in the center of a strobe light. He could hear, but none of it was pleasant. The voices emanating from the portal had been a mere taste *of the horrible disharmony that reverberated through this place.*

This place . . . the mainframe.

Eli tried to remind himself that—as with the portal itself—everything he perceived here was mere interpretation, not unlike cyber-limbo in a way. His consciousness was currently interfacing with a computer—an incredibly advanced *computer, but still a computer nonetheless. The strobe was very likely the existing electricity pulsing from hard drive to hard drive, gel pack to gel pack. And the* voices . . . *he could only guess that they represented all the Citizens using all the* Parlors *around the world right now.*

As his eyes slowly adjusted to the throbbing visibility, he realized that he could see what appeared to be people as well. This . . . place . . . was filled with a shimmery, translucent, tissue-like substance. It reminded him of a cross between melted plastic and a spider's web. The humanoid shapes, the people, were wrapped and sprawled and intertwined throughout the filmy material. He tried not to touch it—he didn't like how warm, how alive it felt—but it was hard to navigate without pushing his way through it.

One thing was for sure—he hadn't expected anything like this. When he conceived of implanting the virus, he'd thought . . . well, that he would just stick his hand through the center of the portal, or something. He hadn't really known—as Susan suspected, he'd been making this up as he went along.

He was clearly going to have to rethink the notion of the virus . . . but he'd worry about that after he located Corbit . . .

Meanwhile, much closer than Eli suspected, the Doctor was relishing the experience. Unlike Eli, Corbit had dedicated a great deal of thought and imagination into how the mainframe would seem from the inside. While he'd never pictured anything quite like this, he found it far less alien than Elijah Barrett. Inhaling the ozone fragrance that his mind perceived as air, Corbit laughed out loud.

Eli heard the laughter—it chilled him. The man was sick!

"You did it, boy!" Corbit's voice drifted, its resonance far more than a mere echo as the words repeated themselves in their entirety several times before dying away. "You got me into the mainframe!"

". . . the mainframe . . . the mainframe . . . the mainframe . . . " drifted the reverberation.

In his haste to pursue what he thought was the source of the jeering voice, Eli nearly collided with a row of bodies. He forced himself to take it slower, and his ears strained for any further indication of Corbit's location . . .

Through a curtain of the gossamer strips, Corbit spied a brighter light source—this one steady rather than strobing, and much closer to an incandescent. He pushed a few strands out of his way . . .

There it was. It looked organic, like a husk of innards. A thick *trunk of the surrounding milieu converged near its center and stretched up higher than Corbit could see. It was lit as much from within as from without.*

Corbit smiled broadly—how fitting! He knew what it represented, and he wasn't surprised by the form it had taken for him.

"This is it!" he called out to the boy whom he knew still lurked about. His words repeated themselves—he liked *that somehow. "A* dreamslab. *It's* beautiful*! My* link *to the* world*!"*

"... to the world ... to the world ... " *agreed his own voice.*

Pushing his way through, Corbit moved toward his rightful throne ...

... and was caught off-guard when Eli suddenly leaped onto him, jamming his hand into Corbit's face and digging at his eyes.

Corbit grunted and immediately fought back. The two of them whirled about, each one determined to tear the other's face off, throat out, or body apart—whatever *it took to achieve their respective goals.*

* * *

Susan hesitated, trying to regain her bearings. She needed a back-up plan, and fast! She clearly was not going to find this "basement" Eli had indicated—perhaps there was some way she could return to the dream room and force the door, or find a different dream room and then ...

Something caught her attention—the sound of machinery and ... *gasping* ... ? Looking over her left shoulder, she peered down the short junction. For a moment she thought her eyes were playing tricks on her.

Is ... is that wall *ajar?*

One of the stone-on-wood "DP" symbols adorned it ... but that symbol was cocked out of alignment. And there was darkness from beyond ...

The gasping grew louder.

Susan strode toward the anomalous opening, her pace quickening with each step ...

* * *

The masks of fury that Corbit and Eli wore were all but indistinguishable. Each with their cause, each with the determination to do whatever it took. All things being equal, they might have brawled to an utter stalemate.

But all things were not *equal.*

As Susan had feared, Eli could not escape the fact that he'd been through hell and back in his battle with the mainframe's defenses. In the end, with her help, he had overcome the guilt *that the anti-virus protocols had tried to use against him, but that victory had left him physically, mentally, and emotionally* drained.

He realized at the last moment that Corbit was using a semi-Judo maneuver to turn and trip him . . . he simply could not react quickly enough to do *anything about it.*

At Corbit's mercy, Eli stumbled headlong into a wide "sheet" of the slick membrane. He coiled to one side, then the other . . . he couldn't get any air! Corbit gripped the back of Eli's head firmly, pressing him into the sheet. Try as he might, Eli couldn't twist free!

Black spots that had nothing to do with the mainframe's strobe collected before his eyes, and he began to weaken . . .

* * *

The gasping escalated to a frightening pitch just as Susan reached the bottom of the stairs. She stepped into the doorway to the basement laboratory, and her eyes widened.

"Elijah!" she cried, racing into the room.

Eli sounded as though he were *suffocating*, although she could see nothing blocking his air passage. Had he swallowed his tongue?!

The computer rattled off warnings to the absent Doctor, ". . . *lethal psychosomatic reaction—subject will* not *survive. Warning . . .* "

"Elijah!" Susan sobbed, panicking. She touched his forehead, desperate to take *some* action—*any* action! The only idea that occurred to her was very much grasping at straws, but what else could she do?! "I'm here!" she told him as she made her way around to the accessible side of the dreamslab. "I'm coming!" She stretched across his writhing chest . . .

. . . and slid her IDC hand into the gel interface right on top of his!

"I'm coming!" she managed to say once more before her hand jolted with an electric discharge and her eyes rolled up in her head . . .

* * *

A fiery discharge jolted Corbit's entire being! He gasped and staggered back, away from Eli. Had that explosive shock actually come out of the boy's body*?!*

Suddenly reinvigorated, Eli calmly turned to face the Doctor.

Corbit's jaw dropped—the boy's eyes *were* glowing*!*

"Hey, Corbit," Eli said casually. "Is it true that if you die in your dreams . . . *you* die*?"*

For once in his life, Corbit was speechless. The azure light emanating from Eli's eyes grew so intense the Doctor had to avert his own gaze. Eli spread his arms, and that same, azure energy flashed around his body until it consolidated into a sphere before his chest . . .

. . . a sphere that launched forward and struck Corbit head-on!

The Doctor cried out in agony as the concussive force of the blast threw him bodily across the membranous expanse. He sailed through the "air," flailing and spasming, until he ripped right through the trunk sprouting upward from the organic dreamslab.

If Eli found their entrance *into the mainframe "violent," he was fortunate he would never know what Corbit experienced as he was ejected the other direction. As Corbit himself told Eli before, he had forced a few NCs to interface with the mainframe, but getting them* in *had proven a lot simpler than getting them back* out *. . .*

* * *

In Room 222, James Corbit convulsed until he fell completely off the dreamslab. He lay on the floor, gasping like a fish out of water, his eyes staring blankly off into space . . .

* * *

When the light that had enveloped Elijah Barrett finally dimmed, he was no longer alone. Susan was with him, she had saved *him, and he gazed into her eyes with a love like he'd never known. She returned that love, that warm smile, and regardless of their bizarre surroundings, they might have embraced then and there had they not slowly, reluctantly, become aware of the changes in the multitudes around them.*

The plethora of voices that had constantly hissed and whispered throughout the membrane shifted in their tenor. They were no longer muttering through whatever dream-fantasies they experienced from their individual Parlor *outlets around the globe. Their tones darkened, twisted, until every single one of them was crying out—moaning, groaning, shaking, reaching out, and lamenting in every sort of anguish Eli could imagine!*

They held close to one another as they peered around themselves, aghast but at a complete loss. It wasn't until Eli caught sight of the thrashing, trembling dreamslab in the now-waning light that understanding slowly began to dawn on him.

Susan followed his gaze. "It's damaged," she breathed.

"It's dying,*" Eli corrected her as he slowly crept forward. Whatever his objective mind tried to say about perceptions and psychological interpretations, there was* nothing *"mechanical" about the pain he witnessed here. The passage Corbit's expulsion had cleaved throbbed like a terrible wound through a significant portion of the dreamslab's massive stalk. Hadn't Corbit said that this would serve as his link to the world? If that were true . . .*

"There's no time to make the virus."

Susan joined him. "Then . . . everyone will die *. . . "*

No. No, he couldn't let that happen. Eli knew what had to be done. Deeply dismayed, he realized, "I have to stay *. . . "*

Susan looked at him, shaking her head unconsciously. What was he talking about? How could he stay *in this* hell*?!*

Eli was unnerved, but he was convinced. He *would have to take Corbit's* place*—maintaining his consciousness within the mainframe, using* himself *to bridge the damaged rift, at least until he could manually wean the world from its* Parlor *addiction. And Corbit's charts had indicated that would take* months *. . . what would happen to his physical body in that time?*

Turning toward Susan, aching *for comfort, he whispered, "Hold me . . . please . . . "*

Teary eyed, Susan gently took his head in her hands and pulled his face into the crook of her shoulder . . .

*

And, on what could be deemed "another plane of existence," in the setting of a small, basement workshop, a young boy laid his head in the crook of his father's shoulder. The boy sighed deeply, taking in the comfort that he knew could not last, and his eyes drifted toward the cross that hung from his father's neck.

Mencer stroked the boy's hair, gently rocking him, until he finally stated, "It's time, Son . . . "

*

Eli laid back upon the organic dreamslab, repulsed by the fact that it was amazingly comfortable as it conformed to the shape of his body.

Susan watched from the perimeter, witnessing every moment but unable to draw any closer to this God-forsaken act.

Looking up into the only incandescent light, Eli slipped his right hand into the organic sac positioned approximate to the familiar gel interface housing. There was no IDC on his dream hand, but the chip was hardly necessary. His mind *was far closer to the mainframe now than the IDC's sinister nervous system tap had ever accomplished.*

The instant he penetrated the sac, the surrounding voices began to quiet. It suckled his hand, and Eli felt his awareness shifting to another level, one he had never suspected could exist . . .

*

The boy left his father's arms and moved to the stairs. The light from the open basement door was far, far more intense than any sunlight had ever been, but that did not stop the boy. He climbed the stairs, step by step, as he merged with the light, and embraced his destiny . . .

* * *

In Corbit's secret basement laboratory, Susan slipped her hand from the gel interface and slid off of Eli's body. He lay there, so still, so . . . *lifeless* . . .

. . . except for the rapid movement of his eyes beneath his closed lids.

I love you, she wanted to say, but somehow it seemed almost blasphemous, now that he would not be able to hear her. Slowly, she backed away from the dreamslab until she collided with the equipment against the far wall, her heart sinking every step of the way.

Heedless of *whom* its audience was comprised, the computer announced its latest findings: "*Subject's life-signs: Stabilized. Note:* Unprecedented *fusion with mainframe core. Range of influence:* Global. *Long-term effects of fusion* . . . unknown . . . "

Unknown . . .

A REAL PIECE OF WORK

"Private Entry . . . "

It took a moment for the computer to accept and adjust to the slurred, thick-tongued quality of his voice now. When it was satisfied that it was listening to the proper individual, he continued.

"April Fifth . . . "

*

The basement door was still ajar, just the way he'd left it, but he couldn't hear any sounds from his various machines. The bio-link to the mainframe was a relatively hushed process, but as he ran most of these systems independent from the rest of the *Parlor*, he'd wired his own generators long ago—generators that had been *on* when he bolted from his lab late last night . . .

When he struggled to the very bottom of the stairs, he also realized that the *lights* were out as well. His vision was shot to hell, but he could still tell the difference between darkness and illumination. Reaching clumsily around the door frame, he flipped the master switch, and even then only *half* of the normal lights responded.

Regardless of the decline in his eyesight, he still looked around the room in shock, unable to accept the evidence before him. His milky, lax left eye remained unfocused, but his blood-shot right widened in disbelief.

It was gone. His entire dreamslab was *gone.*

Shuffling over to his workstation, dragging his left foot along behind him the whole way, he leaned back and considered the *implications* presented before him.

He'd been unconscious for hours. The morning shift had already come on—it was sheer luck that his dignity was saved from being discovered on the dream room floor. The technicians he'd passed on his way back here were far too astounded by his appearance to offer him any assistance, so he was fairly certain none of them had gotten close enough to smell the urine on him. It wasn't until he'd found his covert entrance to the hidden stairwell *closed* that he began to suspect what *might* have transpired while he was in la-la land.

He had built this special dreamslab with theta frequency emitters, so that it could be transported anywhere and still maintain its link to the mainframe. He'd designed these advantages with his *own* mobility in mind, and it had understandably never crossed his mind that someone might *steal* the damned thing! That skinny bitch could never have moved it on her own—Eli must have had a *lot* of friends, friends who could have come and gone through here with hours of privacy . . .

For a few seconds, he entertained the thought of starting over. Now that he knew *how* Eli had performed his magic, he could rebuild a *new* special dreamslab. He could . . .

He glanced down at his numb left hand, then over to his twitching right . . . and his moment of denial passed . . .

*

"Been a week now since . . . my prize bird took a shit on my head. He's already causing a stink that . . . makes the sewer smell like roses. It appears that parts of the compumatrix, private *parts . . . have suddenly*

been exposed *to the* Powers That Be. *There's a lot of questions . . . questions about Kirk . . . questions about my personal activities. Personal activities that will* not *make the Ice Bitch a very happy camper . . .*

"The techies can't explain it. They say that the files exposed themselves *for no apparent reason. They're baffled . . . but* I'm *not . . .*

"He's a real piece *of* work *. . . that Eli . . . "*

*

Tony Paolino, Senior Technician of the original *Dream Parlor,* entered the office reluctantly. He recalled a time not so long ago when he had dreaded this place because of the cantankerous man in charge, or the company he sometimes kept.

Things had changed.

Tony found him sitting at his desk, as expected. After all, the man wasn't entirely *mobile* these days.

"Doctor . . . ?" he said softly.

He awoke with a jolt. His milky eye danced its random dance, but the other fixated on Tony with a pitiful glare. He looked away almost immediately, as though Tony were *still* not important enough for his time. His right hand twitched.

Swallowing his sigh, Tony reported, "There's a team of *Organizers* here to see you, sir."

Tony had his attention once more.

"They say it's official business, sir. They're at the front desk."

Somehow, he managed to look even *more* ill than before. He looked away from Tony to gaze out the windows of the French doors. Tony hesitated, then decided that his sad duty was complete and left the man with his thoughts . . .

*

"Big Brother just came by to chat. They want to talk about my boy *. . . whether they* know *it or not. Quite frankly . . . I haven't felt like this since my first IRS audit . . . "*

*

Slowly, he shuffled down the corridor of his magnificent *Dream Parlor* with as much dignity as he could muster. He folded his hands behind his back and held his head high until he reached the dream room. Room 222, by no coincidence . . .

*

"Oh, well. It doesn't matter what I say—the snowball's in motion. People on this God-forsaken planet are finally gonna get to think for themselves *again. I wish I could be around when the shit hits the fan . . . "*

*

In the control booth, forcing his traitorous right hand to follow a few last commands, he flipped every switch and turned every dial to their highest marks. A red light began flashing.

The computer protested, "*Warning: Current levels exceed regulations. Unacceptable risk to Dreamer. Recommend controlled shutdown immediately.*"

He ignored it. With a great deal of effort, he worked his way onto the dreamslab, making himself as comfortable as possible . . .

*

"They wouldn't like what I'd have to say, and people who upset Big Brother tend to find themselves on the Execution Channel . . . "

*

He opened the lock box he'd once used to threaten the great Elijah Barrett. When he began setting the kill-switch for a ten-second delay, the computer responded immediately.

"*Warning: Rapid shutdown is* not *recommended. Current levels will—*"

The presage fell short when he pressed his IDC against the override. After all, the computer assumed that *he* of all people *must* know what he's doing.

He did.

Stretching out his arm, he slipped his hand into the gel interface. Looking up into the now overly-bright light, he awaited his fate.

*

"I've always enjoyed being famous, but I never really wanted to be on TV . . . "

*

James Edward Corbit heard the tone indicating complete neural overload . . .

. . . and then he heard nothing at all.

It's been eight months since Elijah left me . . . left us *. . . to preserve the mainframe and wean the people from their addiction.*

Susan stood on the beach, a short distance away from the others. She could hear different conversations, all of them mixed with healthy laughter—she overheard Eli's friend, *Jacob Moore*, laughing particularly loud as he labored over the campfire—and the children squealed with delight as they played in the sand. The sun would set soon, and she basked in its fading light.

Some time passed before we started seeing changes. People grew restless. The Dream Parlor *attendance began to drop. Recent civil demonstrations and new followers give me* hope *. . . but sometimes it's so difficult to have faith that Eli is still* alive.

Eli lay upon Corbit's special dreamslab, situated in the storm drain cavern so that as much sunlight could reach him through the ceiling grates as possible. It was Derby and Elizabeth's turn to watch over him, a duty neither of them minded in the least.

The people whom Eli sacrificed so much for risk everything to keep his work alive, and to protect him. Day and night, Eli's friends—his family—*guard the tunnels at every entrance . . .*

Derby massaged and exercised Eli's lean muscles as Elizabeth washed him with a cloth. It bothered the big man to see him looking so frail, but he knew that intravenous feeding wasn't exactly known for its heartiness. Still, neither of them commented on how Eli looked more ashen than ever this evening.

Stepping away for a moment, Derby checked to make sure that the old generator was still functioning properly. If they ever lost power, the dreamslab batteries could only run for so long—they'd learned *that* lesson with almost fatal results when they'd moved the whole damned contraption into the cavern all those months ago.

Elizabeth noticed a change in Eli's face. She slowed her strokes of the cloth and pressed her fingers against the side of his neck, quickly followed by her ear against his gaunt chest . . .

When Elizabeth placed her hesitant hand upon Derby's burly shoulder, he peered up at her questioningly, but her expression alone was enough to bring his attention swiftly around to the dreamslab . . .

Nothing can take him from us now . . .

*

Pulling her shawl a little more tightly around her, Susan waited for the sunset. Movement over the nearby ridge caught her attention, and she glanced down the beach to determine its origin—she remained calm for the moment, but in a time when an Organizer raid could come at any moment, one could never be too careful.

She made out the silhouettes of Derby and one other person. Elizabeth? Probably—the two of them had grown quite close in the past months. Hannah certainly took to the big man in no time at all, which was rather . . .

Susan's stomach fluttered. Weren't Derby and Elizabeth supposed to be watching over Elijah? Why would they leave their post early?

Trying not to answer her own question, she steeled herself against the news she'd feared would inevitably come. She would need to be strong for the people if Eli had . . .

She squinted into the sun's glare. She'd *thought* she had seen *one* person with Derby, but now she wasn't certain. She could only make out two heads, but she spied *three* pairs of legs. Was it the shadows?

No . . . he was carrying someone! Derby had his arm around someone!

Susan broke into a run . . .

The four met some fifty meters from the camp. The beaming Derby and Elizabeth stayed just long enough to ensure that the weakened Eli could stand on his own, then moved on to give them their privacy. Eli and Susan merely stared at each other for a moment, then he melted into her arms . . .

* * *

Eli sat on the ridge, idly toying with the cross around his neck. It had taken a great deal of effort to convince Susan that he wanted this moment alone—they'd been separated for so long already—but she'd finally given in to his wishes. She was back at the camp now, consulting with Derby and Elizabeth on the best way to break the glorious news to their fifty or so followers present on the beach.

It would take Eli a while to . . . *acclimate* back to reality—perhaps as long as it had taken to wean the last *Parlor* addicts. As inert as he must have *appeared* over the last months, he had been *far* from inactive. His unbelievable experiences while merged with the mainframe had changed him—even he couldn't know how much. Only time would tell.

But enough delay. His divorce from the mainframe provided more than his return to the living—it offered the perfect opportunity for an impeccable, symbolic gesture. When he joined the group around the fire for the chilly night, he would bring something with him.

Slipping Corbit's gauntlet from his hand, he gazed down upon his still-glowing IDC. When Corbit mentioned that plugging in would cut off its transmission, he doubted the Mad Doctor had known how *long* that connection would last. Still, he was out now, and any Organizer who passed close enough would come running.

That was just the straw that broke the camel's back, of course—this had been coming for a *long* time.

Dropping the gauntlet, he picked up the small knife he'd gotten from Derby. Taking a preparatory breath, he reached out and slipped the tip of the knife between the edge of his IDC and the adjoining flesh.

Gritting his teeth—and wishing he'd placed some sort of bit between them—Eli worked the knife all the way under the chip until the blade appeared on the opposite side. He then carefully sliced forward until it cleared the housing tube.

Dropping the knife, he plucked the loose end of the chip with his left hand and pulled steadily upward. He allowed himself the luxury of a deep-throated groan as the IDC came free, dragging the internal wires along with it. The wires emerged from his flesh—four centimeters long . . . then six . . . eight . . . ten . . . He would have cursed the makers of the chip had he not known it would lead to a cry that would echo up and down the beach all the way to . . .

With mild, final resistance, the wires let go of his flesh. As he gasped openly with relief, Eli watched the red light on his Identification Chip dim . . .

. . . and then snuff out altogether.

It took a system of absolute power to corrupt—and it took a man of absolute conviction to restore. Elijah Barrett had the courage to dream. He believed in something good, *something* more *than himself . . . and his faith set him* free.

It set us all *free . . .*

Did you enjoy

Dream Parlor

the novel?

Be sure to see

"Dream Parlor"

the movie!

Check out **www.dreamparlor.com**!

We'll let you know when and where you can see this independent feature film from Timeless Entertainment! Film festivals, public screenings, movie theaters, and more!

For more information about Timeless Entertainment, send an e-mail to tefilm@pacbell.net.

SNEAK PREVIEW

of Christopher Andrews' next novel

PARANORMALS

FIVE YEARS AGO

EMMETT

Emmett Morris was at home the Night of the White Flash.

As a twenty-seven year veteran of the United States Post Office, Emmett sure appreciated his routine. Never having the public relations skills necessary for a position as a clerk—and pulling in every favor he earned to stay forever out of the back rooms and warehouses—Emmett enjoyed his pick-up and delivery beat just fine, thank you very much. The few individuals who took the time to greet him were usually the nice sort (unlike the perpetual bitchers who flooded the lobby every weekday and Saturday mornings, too), and he rarely had trouble with neighborhood dogs. Bad weather generally didn't bother him either; for every day of showers, there was another of crisp sunshine. The quiet routine provided him with plenty of time for reflection and amateur poetry writing, though if he had a dollar for every line he'd lost when he didn't take the time to write it down because he was just *sure* he would remember it later, he could retire to the Bahamas. Unlike so many in his age group who found themselves longing for some other career—usually *anything* besides what they had chosen to do with their lives—Emmett Morris had no complaints.

Well . . . maybe *one* complaint: *Bone spurs.*

In the last few years, Emmett had developed bone spurs, essentially little *spikes,* on the heel of his left foot. He'd tried changing his shoes and adding special pads to the interiors, but any relief provided by these measures was nominal. His family doctor had informed him that these things weren't uncommon with individuals who spent a great deal of time on their feet. They had treated the condition twice now with injections of cortisone, but each time the little bastards slowly crept back out, and the doctor was hesitant to recommend a third cortisone shot because of the long term effects it could have on the bones of his whole foot. It was like having little bits of *gravel* stuck in his shoe, and the worst part was his doctor's warning that it was possible—maybe even *likely*—that he would eventually get them on his right heel, too. A couple of tablets of Buffrin with breakfast and lunch held the nastiest ache at bay as he performed his rounds, but by the time those last letters left his hands, he felt like he was walking on *glass.*

So, combining both his doctor's advice and his own assumptions, Emmett had taken to keeping off of his feet whenever possible . . . pretty much from the minute he got home until the minute he went to bed, calls of nature notwithstanding.

It didn't take very long for this to first annoy, then irritate, then wholly *piss off* his wife.

Judy was almost ten years younger than Emmett, and though she never had cause for complaint before, she "sure as hell" wasn't ready to spend her every evening lounging around at home. She had a day job, too—the nice little *sitting* job of a secretary—and when she came home, the first thing she wanted to do was go *out.*

At first Emmett had tried to compromise. Her favorite activities weren't that demanding: Dinner, a movie, visits to the shopping mall, whatever. But as the bone spurs sharpened their way into his flesh, Emmett found it easier to resist her whining. Unfortunately, soon enough, the whining turned into all-out *bitching.*

Emmett was a fair enough man, but he also had no desire to

listen to the same tone of voice at home that he so steadfastly managed to *avoid* by keeping away of the Post Office front desk.

So Emmett encouraged Judy to go out *without* him. And she did, rarely coming home before ten o'clock, and returning well after midnight on more than one occasion.

It wasn't until about a year ago that Judy stopped wanting to have sex with him. Emmett assumed that it was her way of getting back at him for making her go out alone so often. Truth be known, as he approached the big Five-Oh, he found that his potency wasn't what it used to be anyway, so if it was revenge she was after, he hoped she never realized that it wasn't bothering him that much.

So Judy Morris pretended to be frigid as a punishment to her lazy husband. That was what Emmett Morris decided.

And that was what he continued to believe until the Night of the White Flash.

Emmett was one of the few people to actually *see* the Flash. Many people caught it out of the corner of their eye, of course, and many more noticed the pulse-like brightening that never quite dimmed back to its original levels. But Emmett was actually looking up into the sky at the time.

As he often did during warm summer nights, Emmett was sitting out on the front porch in his rocker. The battered notebook that he used to doodle out his novice lines of alliteration was in his lap, but his muse was somewhat quiet this evening, so he had turned off the porch light and taken to star gazing—frustration from writer's block aside, he didn't mind the lack of attention the darkness offered from the local insects. He was rocking gently to and fro, careful as always to use the toes of his good foot, never allowing the traitorous left heel to so much as touch the wooden deck. Michael Bolton's "How Am I Supposed To Live Without You" whistled through his pursed lips. He, of course, would have *preferred* if Judy had been here with him—in one of her *good* moods for a change—but otherwise he was about as content as could be.

The White Flash originated just to the left of the Little Dipper. The display was actually less *dramatic* than accounts to later generations would suggest, but it was still a sight to see. Michael Bolton's tune dried up between Emmett's lips as his eyes widened. It was like something out of a science-fiction movie, like the Death Star blowing up at the end of "Star Wars" . . . no, wait, that wasn't it. It was like that *other* sci-fi series, "Star Trek." In one of the films, the opening credits had climaxed with the explosion of a Klingon moon. There had been a flash, and then a shockwave of pure energy shooting outward like a ripple in a pond. *That's* what this was like. Just to the left of the Little Dipper, a *pulse* of brilliant light, then a wave of energy shooting out three-hundred-sixty-degrees. The wave spread from the point of origin to the edge of the horizon in less than five seconds.

A lot of people panicked that night, but for some reason Emmett did not. He was captivated by the sight of what the White Flash left behind: What before had been a relatively clear section of sky was now a new, *very* prominent star. Or at least, Emmett *thought* it was a star at first. Upon closer scrutiny, he realized that it was in fact *several* stars. *Seven*, if he was counting correctly. They were clumped together in the tightest constellation Emmett Morris had ever seen—people around the world would soon be referring to them as the Seven Stars.

Emmett sat there for several long minutes, staring intently at these Seven Stars. He paid no attention to the sirens that began wailing in the distance. Somewhere fairly close by, a woman screamed, but he paid no more attention to this than he did the sirens. He simply gazed up at this fascinating new constellation, his breath tight in his excited chest.

Then he saw something *else.*

It's not that it obscured his vision—he could still see just fine. It was almost like a double image, some sort of *overlay* that he had again seen in the movies. His *eyes* still saw the sky and the Seven Stars; his *mind* saw a motel room.

In this motel room, a man lay upon a bed. He grunted and flexed and panted and humped. Emmett did not know this muscular, dark, thirty-something man.

Also in this motel room, a woman knelt upon the man. She also grunted and flexed and panted and humped. Emmett *did* know this woman, knew her very well.

Emmett watched in numb, nauseating, growing horror as his wife rode the younger man and rode him *hard*. She pulled his hands to her breasts and urged him on, showering him with lewd compliments that she had *never* offered to the man she had vowed to honor and cherish for the rest of her life.

Allowing a whimpering sob to escape him, Emmett shut and covered his eyes; he only succeeded in blinding himself to the celestial display—the vision of the motel room remained.

Judy was having an affair.

Emmett forgot all about the White Flash, the Seven Stars. He forgot about his bone spurs as he reopened his eyes and clamored to his feet. The double image of visual and mental caused him to stumble and bump into things as he found his way back into the house.

Emmett ascended the stairs, hoisting himself hand-over-hand along the railing, and he nearly fell over backwards at the top as he saw . . . no, not "saw," *witnessed* . . . as he *witnessed* Judy move off of the younger man and onto all fours, encouraging her partner into a position that she had always told her husband she did not care for because it was too awkward.

Finding his way into the bedroom, some small part of Emmett that was chiefly self-respect and preservation realized what the majority of the shocked and shattered Emmett was planning to do. That small portion began pleading with the rest of himself. She wasn't worth it, not *this*. Didn't he want to know what had happened in the sky tonight? Wasn't he *enthralled* by this new ability, regardless of what it had unfortunately selected to show him first? Didn't he want to explore the possibilities, try out what promised to be an all-new and different life? *Didn't he*?

It didn't matter. None of it did. Maybe he didn't feel like going out with her anymore, and maybe he didn't lust for her like he once did, but the inescapable *fact* was that Emmett Morris loved his wife dearly, and she was *rutting* with another man in a motel room even as he . . . *witnessed* from home.

Emmett pulled the .45 caliber pistol from the shoebox on the top shelf of the closet. He confirmed that it was loaded, pulled back the hammer, and placed the barrel between his teeth.

For God's sake, pleaded the little voice one last time, *aren't you* worth *more than* this*?!*

In the motel room, Judy Morris screamed with orgasm.

In their bedroom, Emmett Morris pulled the trigger, and the vision, mercifully, ceased.

THE CHILD

The child—whose name would have been *Tran Nguyen*—was inside her mother's womb on the Night of the White Flash.

The child was entering her third trimester of existence, and the rudimentary higher brain functions that could be construed as *thoughts*—a relative term, granted, for an entity with virtually no intellectual understanding of her own self, let alone existence beyond her five budding senses—were slow in formation. The child's mother was violently addicted to heroin, and she had not allowed anything so *incidental* as a *pregnancy* curb her habit. The child had been conceived in error, but her mother had not wanted to risk her still deceptively clean legal record in order to subject herself to the required tests for an abortion. She had considered trying some self-induced home version, until the thought had occurred to her that a good deal of money might be made off of *selling* the baby, money that would keep her well supplied with *hits* for the foreseeable future.

So the child, regardless of entering her third trimester or third *decade* of life, would never develop the mental capacity to equal a dull-witted lower primate, much less a homosapian.

Straight intelligence was one thing. *Emotions* and *sensations* were something else.

The child might not have *understood* her *surroundings* or herself, or the sounds that perpetually filtered through her mother's flesh and muscle and embriotic fluid. She did *feel*, however, and a vast majority of the time, she felt uncomfortably *hot*.

Through the miraculous tragedy of chemical interactions, the mother's narcotic habits left herself and the child with an incessant *fever*. The mother's body temperature rarely, if ever, dropped below one-hundred, and spent a fair percentage of its time hugging just over one-hundred-one. The mother paid no heed to the flushed constant—so long as she had her Product, she paid heed to very little.

The *child*, on the other hand, with her limited capacity of sensation, found the excessive warmth quite unpleasant. The periods of increased temperature had threatened to stop her developing heart more than once, but what was a fetus to do?

So the child merely suffered the existence of physical discomfort, never comprehending that there was any other *kind* of existence to be had.

And that was all she *could* comprehend until the Night of the White Flash.

The child's mother currently resided in Garden Grove, California, so the Seven Stars appeared a little further to the east, and the White Flash took a bit longer to cross over the horizon than it did for Emmett Morris' parts of the country. The child's mother was oblivious to this, of course, and would have given it only the briefest attention if she had bothered to notice. She was sealed up in her tiny studio apartment, enjoying her latest *hit* and wondering if a woman roughly seven months pregnant could still manage to sell her body for a few more dollars. The White Flash did not affect *her* as it was a growing handful around the world.

It did, however, affect the child.

As Emmett Morris suddenly witnessed what he would never have asked to witness, the child had a revelation on her own, limited level of comprehension.

It suddenly "occurred" to the child that perhaps she did not *have* to be so hot all the time. This was the worst it had been in a while and her heart was fluttering in response, but maybe there was something . . . *else*. How could a brain-damaged, unborn child understand the possibility of another, as yet unknown condition of life? She did not. She simply *felt*, and acted on those feelings.

Invisible waves of power flowed outward from the child's underdeveloped mind, and almost instantly the surrounding heat began to abate. The child knew a *relief* unlike anything she had ever experienced. And when she found something that she enjoyed and gave her pleasure, as children of any age are prone, she wanted *more.* She reached out with her new power, more fiercely this time.

The child's mother was suddenly overcome with a terrible chill. The elevated warmth she had known almost constantly since she was twelve suddenly left her, and if she hadn't known better, she would have sworn the temperature in the apartment had suddenly dropped ten degrees. She stumbled to her feet and stole a glance at the thermostat, but it insisted that nothing of the sort was transpiring. The child's mother cursed loudly, throwing around accusations of cheap equipment to no one and nothing in particular, and clutched at herself, shivering. Her teeth chattered, and her belly felt as though a bucket of ice had been poured into her bowels. She wandered back to her familiar paraphernalia, and managed to deliver herself a tremendous *hit*. If the chill wouldn't go away by itself, she would simply *numb* it away.

The child felt a sudden wave of heat threaten to overwhelm her once more. With a child's rage, she fought back.

The child—whose name would have been *Tran Nguyen*—would never know that the cost of her immediate gratification would cause her mother to die of internal hypothermia in the middle of summer, and that said death would swiftly end her own life as well. And even if she *could* have known these things and understood them, based on her life experiences thus far, it is doubtful that she would have cared.

PATRICIA

Patricia Brown was walking her dogs on the Night of the White Flash.

Life-long lovers of animals themselves, Patricia's parents had successfully urged her to follow her natural inclinations and pursue veterinary medicine as a career. Her parents loved every four-legged creature under the sun, but while Patricia enjoyed helping *any* animal in need, she had always been partial to *dogs*.

Big dogs, medium, small, toy dogs—Patricia loved them all. One of the reasons her parents' guidance had proven so frictionless was due to an event before Patricia's eighth birthday. One night, a young Collie had been struck crossing the main road near her home; the driver had not bothered to stop the car and see how the animal had fared. Patricia found the animal the next morning, its hind legs broken, its tail hanging loose and limp. The pain-stricken, terrified animal had bitten her twice as she transported it home. Her parents were still asleep, and rather than take the time to rouse them, she had called the closest animal hospital herself.

The Collie had lived, and *thrived*. The dog had no collar, and none of the neighbors recognized it. The vet suggested that someone might have brought the unwanted animal from the city to get rid of it. In the end, Patricia had been allowed to keep the Collie, and her bond to canines was forged for life.

While her internship could have been more pleasant—she had taken an offer in Louisiana, only to discover that the white owners there didn't particularly like a *black woman* caring for their little darlings, be they dogs, cats, or parakeets—this past year had found her as the third partner of a successful animal hospital . . . and proud owner of *six* dogs, a personal record-breaker for Patricia.

On this particular evening, she was walking three of her beloved kiddies—her black Lab, "Winston," her Pug, "Brutus," and her Boston Terrier, "Cookie." Despite his greater size, Winston was, as always, the easiest to manage on these ventures. Brutus and Cookie managed to tangle themselves, Winston, and her together in the leashes so frequently that it tested even *her* monumental patience from time to time. Amber, Chelsey, and Pop-Eye had already had their daily walks—she avoided walking all six at once for obvious reasons—and now she needed to get these three done. But the night was warm, if a bit windy, and she was in a good mood, so she and Winston let the wild pair have their fun. Patricia loved her dogs, often times understanding their wants and needs better than those of other people, and she felt that she was as close to them as any human being could be.

She only felt this way, of course, until the Night of the White Flash.

The park where Patricia walked her dogs had a long-standing reputation for being quite safe. Local parents could even allow their children to play after dark without excessive cause for concern. Patricia had developed a passing acquaintanceship with a few of the other dog lovers who walked their prides and joys at this park. Brutus and Cookie pulled her back and forth and sometimes in opposite directions, marking territory and "checking messages," as Patricia called it. Winston quietly did his necessary business, then joined Patricia in sighing at the smaller and younger ones, occasionally throwing her a sympathetic look that seemed to say *They're so silly, aren't they?* Patricia offered no arguments.

Patricia was chastising Cookie for another wrap-Mom-up-with-the-leash job when the Seven Stars burst into sight. The pulse of light from above confused her enough that by the time she looked straight up, the White Flash had almost reached the horizon. Brutus barked, while Cookie remained oblivious. Winston merely stared up with her.

"What in the world was *that*, Winston?"

Anthony Deutsche, the man lurking in the bushes and shadows a few yards ahead of Patricia, glanced up with little interest. He had seen the pulse of light wash over the land, but his skyward view was blocked almost entirely by the lush foliage of a tree, so his curiosity died quickly and his attention returned to his intended victim. He was perturbed that Patricia wasn't carrying a purse, but she *was* wearing a fanny-pack, so he figured there might be hope yet.

Patricia stared after the wave of the White Flash, but there was no encore performance of this phenomenon. The Seven Stars shone brightly above, but Patricia had never been much of a star-gazer and did not make the connection. In the distance, she heard a siren wail, and Brutus felt the urge to join in.

"Come on, kids," she said, "let's head home."

Winston stood ready to go, but Brutus continued to howl at the alarm, and Cookie searched for fresh territory to mark.

"Come *on*, fellas, okay? Mom wants to go home now. Brutus, knock that off!"

Suddenly, Cookie stopped sniffing at the ground and instead stared ahead, straight into the shadows where Anthony Deutsche stood in silence. An unimpressive growl rumbled through the Boston Terrier's little throat.

bad man

Patricia looked around, startled. She could have sworn that she heard someone speak, but she appeared to be alone.

bad man

The voice, or the *echo* of a voice, floated to her again from some unknown source. "What?" she said aloud. "Who's there?"

Anthony stiffened. Had he given himself away somehow?

bad man Winston over here bad man Brutus over here

Patricia was confused and frightened now. The words weren't really *words*—except for the echoes of the Lab and Pug's names, which came through clear as a bell. They were more like *impressions.* Less than words, more than feelings.

Brutus stopped howling and glanced in the same direction as Cookie. Winston stepped forward, his attention following the Boston's as well.

where?

bushes

sure he's bad?

bad man

bad man

Cookie right Winston smell him too man bad man

Patricia's educated mind struggled to reject what she thought she was hearing. She was so caught up in the wonder and impossibility of it all that she didn't really pay attention to *what* her dogs appeared to be saying to one another.

"Winston?"

The Lab looked up at her. *Bad man Mom bad man . . .* Then the words/thoughts paused, and Winston assumed the most human-looking expression of bafflement Patricia had ever seen. If her mind had not been such a whirlwind, she would have laughed. *Mom you hear Winston Mom?*

"Yes," Patricia blurted through a strained chuckle, seriously entertaining the distinct possibility that only a crazy woman would answer a question she thought was directly posed by her pet. "Yes, I hear you, Winston, and I think that Mom needs a drink."

no time for fuzzy stuff, Winston scolded her, *bad man in the bushes Mom bad man you need to go*

Winston!

Winston!

When Patricia appeared to start talking to her dog, Anthony decided that enough was enough. What was she, the "Daughter of

Sam?" It didn't matter—a loony would be that much easier to handle anyway. He stepped from the shadows, waving his knife back and forth so that the blade would glisten in the scattered park lights.

"Gimme your pack," he threatened curtly, stepping close.

Patricia stared at him numbly. The startling events were making it difficult for her to shift gears—at first, she even thought he was referring to her *dogs*. "Wha—?" was all she managed to say.

Brutus and Cookie barked at Anthony. Winston growled.

"Don't push me, bitch," he snapped. "Hand over the pack or I'll cut you, and your little dog Toto, too." When Patricia still failed to move, Anthony reached down with impressive speed and plucked Cookie up by her collar. She yelped, both in the real world and in Patricia's mind. "I'm not fooling around, bitch. Hand it over." He held the blade deliberately against the Boston's throat.

The man could have intimidated Patricia all night, and in her current state of mind, she would probably have just sat there like an idiot. But when he made the mistake of threatening one of her *kids*, her disposition turned icy cold.

"Fine," she said. Dropping the leashes and reaching back to unclasp the pack, she said, "Put her down first."

"You're not in the position, lady," Anthony leered. He flicked the blade and Cookie yelped as he cut her. Not too deep, not yet, but enough to draw blood. Brutus and Winston growled in unison. "Better keep the Lab back, too. Now hand it over."

bad man hurt Cookie get him Winston get him can't he has shiny sharp metal might hurt Mom

"How do I know you won't hurt her anyway?" Patricia demanded.

"Oh, for Christ's sake, that's *it!*" Anthony threw the Boston down hard and kicked the Pug harder as he moved on her. The blade came at Patricia's throat now . . .

. . . but not before Winston's jaws locked onto his wrist.

Giving the devil his due credit, Anthony did not cry out or

panic as others might have. He merely grunted and, without missing a beat, started pounding the Lab in the face with his free hand.

ow ow ow ow

Patricia could sense Winston's discomfort, but the husky dog refused to let go. Patricia leaped at the man, too, clawing at his face.

"Shit!"

Anthony shoved her away, knocking her to the ground. He hit Winston again, and a squeak of pain made its way from behind the man's trapped arm.

And *that* was enough of *that*!

Cookie, Brutus, she called in the same fashion she had heard, and with the same instincts employed by Emmett and the Would-Be-Tran, *his feet! Get his* feet*!*

The smaller dogs rushed to obey their Mom. They each went for an ankle.

Cookie, your mouth's too small. Get his shoelaces, his shoelaces*!*

Cookie was familiar enough with chewing on Patricia's shoes to know exactly what she meant.

Bite him hard, Brutus. Hard*!*

Anthony had stopped beating Winston now, and was trying desperately not to lose his balance.

Winston, hold on!

yes Mom

Scrambling to her feet and charging forward, Patricia slammed into Anthony as hard as she could—and Patricia was far from a petite lady herself. Anthony went down on his back, the breath exploding from his lungs as a rock broke one of his hind ribs. Winston lost his grip on the man's wrist in the tumble, but his teeth raked deep valleys in the bad man's flesh, and the knife dropped away.

Cookie, Brutus, get his hands. Bite down on his fingers, bite hard. Winston, get his throat, but don't bite down. Not yet.

yes Mom yes Mom yes

The dogs did as told, and Anthony was shortly helpless, trying to do nothing but draw a breath as Patricia knelt over him, her knees in his gut. His eyes bugged and gawked at the Black Lab perched at his throat, his mind incapable of grasping or accepting what was happening here.

"All right, mister," Patricia did not bother to hide her satisfaction, "let's see what you've got. Winston, if he moves, kill him." She reached under him and felt his back pockets. Sure enough, she came back with the mugger's own wallet. "Gosh, aren't we cocky, you stupid asshole."

Patricia opened the wallet, going straight for the driver's license.

"Well, *Anthony Deutsche*, looks like you're up shit creek without a paddle now."

She climbed off him, making sure to really grind her knees while doing so. She stepped back.

"All right, kids, back off," she ordered as she stooped and delicately picked up the man's knife. *But growl at him,* she added mentally, *growl at him* loud. *Really give him a good show, especially you, Winston.*

The dogs retreated a few feet and inundated Anthony with the noise of their fierceness.

Anthony slowly rose to his feet, dividing his attention between fearful glances at the militant dogs and dagger looks aimed at Patricia.

"I'm not prepared to escort you halfway across town, mister, but you'll be hearing from the police soon enough." She waved the knife and wallet at him. "Now turn and walk away. Stick to the path so that I can see you in the lights all the way out of the park. And if you try anything clever, I'll have Winston here rip your *balls* off and share them with Brutus and Cookie as a treat. Comprende?"

Anthony nodded glumly and limped away, keeping to the path as instructed.

"Good work, kids."

Bad man we bit the bad man and helped Mom we get treats when we get home?

Patricia laughed and answered Brutus and Cookie, "Sure, kids, you get treats. Double helping."

Even though she was now speaking with her mouth instead of

her mind, it was evident that they understood her better than ever before. Brutus and Cookie jumped up and down in excitement, Cookie throwing a bark or two after the bad man.

Winston looked up at Patricia with eyes that now seemed uncannily wise to her. *how Mom?* he asked. *how can you hear us?*

I don't know, Winston, she answered, *but I* do *know one thing . . . I'm about to become the best damn* veterinarian *this world has ever seen.*

She smiled and, removing their unnecessary leashes, led the kids home.

YESTERDAY

TO ALL FACULTY AND STAFF:

The following is a report presented to me by Jeffrey Lawrence, one of my 5th grade students. Jeffrey recently returned to class after missing two weeks, courtesy of the chicken pox, and had fallen considerably behind. Rather than force the young man to attempt two weeks' worth of backed up homework, I offered him the option of instead completing an extra credit assignment. My suggestion had been a book report, but I left the proposition intentionally vague, hoping to see if he would come up with something on his own.

He did.

Upon reading his essay—an effort that took him a mere two days to complete and return to me—I felt that perhaps we would all benefit from reading it. It offers us an insight into how our youth perceives these frightening times in which we now live, times that *we* could not have imagined (or, perhaps, could *only* have imagined) at Jeffrey's age.

It is my further suggestion that we consider setting aside a day as soon as possible to discuss the Paranormals with our student body as a whole, and that perhaps *together* we can find a light at the end of this increasingly dark tunnel.

Ruth Plummer

THE PARANORMALS
BY JEFFREY LAWRENCE
5TH GRADE—MISS PLUMMER

Almost five years ago, the Seven Stars appeared in the sky. The White Flash that followed their appearance scared a lot of people, but the White Flash did a lot more than people first realized.

Scientists still have not figured out exactly what the White Flash was. Some say it was a kind of radiation that we have never seen before that caused mutations. Some people think that maybe God or the Devil did it, but the Scientists won't listen to that explanation. They also can't figure out if the Seven Stars just came into existence or if they were always there and the Earth just could not see them until now. The people who work for S.E.T.I. (that's for Search For Extra-Terrestrial Intelligence) have also started picking up strange sounds on their big radios, but so far no one can agree on what they are or what they mean.

More important, though, is what has happened here on Earth. Some people were changed by the White Flash, something the Scientists call the "Paranormal Effect."

Not very many people have been changed by the Paranormal Effect. According to a report on "60 Minutes" last week, the Scientists say that less than 1/10th of 1% of the people of Earth were changed, and less than 1% of those have any changes that we can see or that are any big deal (my Dad heard about a man at his company who could change the color of things. This is not something the Scientists would call a "Class One," but I think the man got fired from his job anyway, and that is sad).

Some people were changed right away, and these people had mostly mind powers. Some people hid their changes, so it took a while before the Scientists could start studying the powers.

After a year went by, other people started changing, and some of the powers started getting more physical. Some people are really strong, others can run fast or fly or shoot laser beams and stuff from their eyes. After a couple of years, other people even got changed in the way they look (there was a sad story on the Internet about a man who grew bat wings and got burned by his church because they thought the Devil turned him into a gargoyle). The Scientists can't figure out why some people change and others don't. Old people, young people, black and white and Asian people, tall people or short people all change. Some babies even change before they are born. The only family members who sometimes change together are twins, and Scientists think this is because of something called "DNA," (that's Deoxyribonucleic Acid) and that's really close together in twins. We don't know if Paranormal parents can give their powers to their kids yet, but the Scientists think it could happen.

People were changed by the Paranormal Effect all over the world, but most seem to be in North and Central and South America. The Scientists think this is because it was nighttime here when the White Flash happened.

After a bunch of bad guys started using their powers for crime, the United States started a group called the "P.C.A." (that's for Paranormal Control Agency). They took agents from the F.B.I. and the C.I.A. and the Secret Service and gave them the job of stopping the bad guys. They call the bad guys "Rogues." Later they started a P.C.A. Academy, and this is the first year people will work for the P.C.A. who graduated from the Academy.

I think it is sad that so many people changed by the Paranormal Effect want to be Rogues. My big brother has always read comic books and he read comic books to me when I was a little kid. I think it's sad that no Paranormals want to be super-heroes. Why don't they want to be like Superman or Spider-Man or the X-Men? In the comic books the bad guys always lose, but how can they lose in the real world if there are no super heroes to fight them? There are some Paranormals who work with the P.C.A. against the Rogues, and that's a good thing, but it would be cool if somebody wanted to be a real live super-hero. If I ever get changed by the Paranormal Effect, that's what I'm going to do.

A lot of people are scared by the Paranormals and hate them just because they got changed, and I think this is sad, too. In Miss Plummer's class, we learn about stuff like Civil Rights and how prejudice is bad, so I think people should remember these things when they think about the Paranormals. The Paranormals are just people like you and me who got changed and they did not ask for it to happen to them. The Rogues are uncool and should be punished, but regular people who turn Paranormal should not be punished if they aren't Rogue.

Paranormals are just like you and me, only different, and if people with different colored skin and who have different religions should be treated equal, then a man who can change the color of things should be treated equal, too.

My name is Jeffrey Lawrence, and if another kid in my class turned Paranormal, I would still be his friend, and I hope that if I turned Paranormal, other kids would still be my friends, too.

And if a Paranormal decided to be a super-hero, I think that would be COOL!!!

PARANORMALS

COMING SOON!

90000>
9 780738 827902

Printed in the United States
3210